BREAKTHROUGH

A THRILLER

JUDY KROLL

Published by ARBORESCENS BOOKS

First paperback edition

Cover design by Tim Barber

ISBN 979-8-218-69512-5

ONE

COLD AIR STREAMED RELENTLESSLY from an overactive vent above me in the cavernous lobby of the El Cortez Hotel. The historic structure in downtown Los Angeles had not been designed with modern air conditioning in mind, and the chilly air defied the warm color of its original tile, the plush furnishings, and the palm trees towering outside. My shoulders grew tense as I hunched over my phone, trying to reach someone—anyone—back at the office.

"Should have worn pants," I mumbled as I pulled my blazer tighter.

My older brother, Dr. Charles Emory, and I had rented a meeting room at the hotel to pitch our medical device company, Angiras, to the heads of twenty venture capital firms that invested in biotech start-ups. Two years before, Charles had cobbled together enough money to launch our firm, but we needed a much larger influx of cash to keep the doors open.

Apart from shivering, I was also tense with worry. I'd stepped out of the meeting because our lead engineer, Alex Ruindes, who was vital to our presentation, hadn't shown up and wasn't responding to texts. Even my calls to Kimberly, his boss, went straight to voicemail. So I gave up and went back inside, where

Charles was describing our research program. As he spoke, a projector cast images on the small screen behind him. I stood near the door at the side of the room, trying to read the investors' body language in between desperate glances at my phone. When Alex did eventually show up, I'd need to brief him quickly before we introduced him to the group. The plan was for him to present the technical details of our product, which I would then follow with the financial projections. As the CFO of Angiras, I would face close scrutiny from the would-be investors as they evaluated the risk-reward benefits of funding us. If all went well—and it was crucial it did—in a few days we'd have commitments from at least one of these savvy backers.

"Medical device research is usually done the old-fashioned way." Charles smiled at the group. "Experienced engineers work collaboratively through stages of development from concept to prototype. And it's done in a traditional work environment—nine to five, more or less—with design software, brainstorming, and creative thinking. At Angiras, we've added a revolutionary component. We're using lucid dreaming to tap the *subconscious* creativity of our research engineers."

One of the investors, a lean elderly gentleman in a three-piece suit, gripped a well-used leather notebook. "Dr. Emory, what is lucid dreaming?"

"We all dream most nights," Charles replied. "If you've ever had the experience of being conscious that you're dreaming, that is a lucid dream. And with training, you can take control of a lucid dream, decide how the experience will progress —whether to fly above the trees, pilot an alien spacecraft, have a conversation with a long-gone relative, or"—here he paused—"find new ways to innovate."

Murmurs floated through the group. Charles took a sip of water and glanced at me, raising an eyebrow ever so slightly to inquire about Alex. I shrugged.

He turned back to the VCs. "Let me share with you a few examples of creativity born of the dream state. Then I'll explain how we're using lucid dreaming to develop a novel medical device. One day in 1964, Paul McCartney awoke with the entire melody of 'Yesterday' in his head. The music was so complete he was sure he must have heard the song from some other artist. He hadn't. In 1845, Elias Howe, a machinist, dreamt of being chased by cannibals, and the holes in the shafts of the spears they carried gave him the idea for sewing machine needles, leading to a patent and subsequent birth of the modern garment industry. Finally, Mary Shelley, at the age of eighteen, penned *Frankenstein* after a particularly vivid dream. These are only a few of the masterworks that have originated during the sleep state. Think about what might have happened if McCartney, Howe, or Shelley had mastered the power of directing their dreams, becoming lucid in the dream state to facilitate even more creativity.

"At Angiras, we train our engineers on techniques for attaining a lucid dream state, and for directing their dreams toward problem-solving in product development. Each afternoon, our engineers take a nap in a comfortable, controlled environment in our offices. They are monitored for breathing patterns and eye movements, which indicate dreaming is occurring. After they awake, they immediately record any dream that involves the work they're doing."

"Well…" Another investor spoke up, a tan blond who must have played linebacker in college. "That gives new meaning to the phrase 'sleeping on the job.'"

We all laughed.

"After a few months using this technique," Charles continued, "Alex, our lead engineer who you'll meet shortly, dreamt of a miniscule tube, similar to a syringe, which dispensed tiny amounts of medication deeply into a lung. His dream led to a prototype we call Alvee. And when attached to a bronchoscope, Alvee is capable of dispensing medication with pinpoint accuracy into the lung tissue of a patient suffering from respiratory disease." Images of Alvee appeared on the screen. "This direct delivery of medication is revolutionary, because it avoids many of the pitfalls of current oral medications."

The only female financier in the room began jiggling her leg. Had we piqued her interest? Or was she bored?

"Lucid dreaming has helped resolve several technical obstacles as we've moved toward completion of Alvee," Charles wrapped up. "And we're putting our faith, and hopefully some of your money, in the dream program to finalize the device."

I looked again at my phone. Nothing. We'd have to proceed without Alex. A long lock escaped the pins I'd used to secure my hair on top of my head. I yearned to get out of the heels and dress I'd endured all day, but I was up next.

"Let me ask you." The elderly man scratched his chin with his pen. "Why is putting the medication directly into the lung better than current treatments?"

"Some patients experience difficulties from taking drugs orally. Steroids, for example, have many undesirable side effects. The current therapy for pulmonary fibrosis includes antifibrotic medications, which slow down the scarring of lung tissue. That's good. But they can cause nausea, vomiting, weight loss, and sometimes more serious conditions. Delivery directly into the tissue provides therapeutic benefit without the downsides."

"You assume this dreaming program will get this product, Alvee, to market faster. What evidence do you have it'll speed things up?" the woman asked, her leg in high gear.

Charles nodded. "Most novel medical devices take an average of ten years to develop and receive FDA approval for use. We're nearing completion of Alvee after only two years. We have a functional prototype with one development step left: The tube apparatus that dispenses the medication does not currently empty completely. It's at about eighty percent, up from where we started at only ten percent seven months ago."

"Okay, and what are we talking about here? How many patients are there?" The older man leaned forward.

"That's all in your packets, which we emailed you. But

briefly, Alvee has application for any disease of the lung where traditional medications are ineffective or nonexistent, or where the medication has significant side effects and dispensing it directly into tissue is optimal. Cystic fibrosis, pulmonary fibrosis, and primary ciliary dyskinesia, or PCD, are a few of the lung diseases this product will target. There are over three hundred thousand people in the US alone who suffer from pulmonary fibrosis, including our younger brother, Daniel."

The jumpy leg abruptly stopped. "So this is a very personal mission you're on, you and your sister?"

"Yes, and our whole family. But let me be clear. Neddy, our board, and I believe the dream program's potential goes far beyond Alvee. It's a whole new way to innovate. We're asking for your vision to think beyond the initial product. The dream program alone is enough to warrant investment."

"Do you have a patent on the dream program? How do you protect it from copycats?" the elderly man asked.

"We don't have a patent on dreaming, no one does. But the products and processes that come out of the dreams can be patented. With that said, mastering lucid dreaming is a rare and difficult feat. Out of hundreds of applicants, we've only success-fully trained five engineers to be reliable, regular lucid dreamers."

The Linebacker looked around the room. "Everyone ready to move on?"

"Wait, I want to know a little more about your background, Dr. Emory. Did you specialize in the physiology of dreaming?"

"It's all in the bio he included in the email." The Linebacker didn't bother to hide his disdain for the older man.

I grabbed a hard copy of the business plan we'd sent them three weeks before. "Here you go, sir. Our bios are included."

He smiled at me and lowered his voice. "I don't really like computers. Too hard to find what you're looking for."

"I don't blame you," I whispered back.

"No problem, I'm happy to catch you up," Charles said, "and it won't take long," he laughed, "because I spent my entire professional career in one type of medical development or another. After my cardiovascular residency, I was recruited to work in cardiovascular clinical development for Johnson & Johnson. I led a team running clinical trials for three new anticoagulants. That was a tremendous opportunity for a young physician. From there I went to Bayer, then to a smaller biotech firm where the learning curve was even steeper. Perhaps the best thing I took away was how to operate on a shoestring budget. And when they were bought out—ironically by Bayer—I took a package, found some investors, and started my own pharmaceutical firm, Paramount. We had a promising drug for hypertension, but then it failed its second trial. At about the same time, our brother, Daniel, was beginning to suffer greater impact from his illness, so the time seemed right to switch from developing medicines to novel drug delivery, and we launched Angiras."

"Thank you, both. I won't hold things up anymore. Please, proceed."

Charles nodded at me. I took a deep breath and walked to the podium.

My knees shook as I methodically presented each detail of the financial projections I had calculated over the previous six weeks. I included several slides, graphs, and three sales forecast scenarios. I shared our organizational chart, modest as it was. I wanted them to know we were lean and wouldn't be using their capital frivolously. As I moved into our equity situation, I saw Charles step out, presumably to check on Alex.

"We started the company with capital from four individuals, including Charles; our father, Edgar Emory; Max Sheldon, the CEO of Sheldon Pacific Entertainment; and Dr. Phil Harris, former executive vice president at Mayan Pharmaceuticals. In addition, we received substantial grants from the American Lung Association and the NIH. As far as equity, Charles holds the largest position at sixty-five percent; the remaining thirty-five is split evenly among the other individual investors."

Charles and I had been hopeful of generating interest among several of these executives, but so far only three were asking questions.

"The NIH gave you a grant?" the woman asked.

"Yes, in part because Daniel is very young to be suffering from pulmonary fibrosis. He's just twenty-four. The disease usually affects people between fifty and seventy, so his situation is extraordinarily unusual, and without a breakthrough, his prognosis is bleak." I swallowed hard. "The NIH was quite interested in the development of a treatment option that could improve outcomes for all patients, but especially the youngest."

"I see. And just to be clear, you don't have an equity stake then, Neddy," she asked.

"Not currently."

"So, the family collectively holds about seventy-seven percent." Her fingers flew over her laptop.

"Which will get diluted once you get new investors," the Linebacker said. "So why did you leave your previous job at AT&T?"

"Sorry?"

"You left a cushy corporate job to help run a tiny start-up with less than a fifty-fifty chance of getting off the ground. I'm just wondering why."

I'd been prepared to field questions about my background, but I hadn't anticipated such a derisive challenge. My first instinct was to defend my decision by minimizing the differences between what I'd done in the past and what I was doing at Angiras. Big or small, it was all managing money. Then I thought of Daniel, now nearly bedridden and out of treatment options. Unless we were successful, he would face increasing breathlessness, pain, nausea, possibly delirium and depression—horrible physical and mental anguish only death would relieve. And our parents: Mom struggling to care for him and stay optimistic,

Dad watching our every move at work for signs of progress. My nervousness began to give way to grief. I grabbed both sides of the podium to steady myself and keep my composure. Then I looked the Linebacker straight in the eye.

"It's my brother's life. Who wouldn't want to be a part of that?" I turned back to the others. The woman caught my eye and gave me a thumbs-up.

"Okay, so what else do you have for us?" the Linebacker asked, changing the subject. "Are we going to hear from your engineer?"

"Unfortunately, Alex had a family emergency and can't join us today," Charles said as he stepped back into the room. "But we'll make him available to you individually just as soon as possible. Among our engineers, he's the one who has the most frequent lucid dreams. And he's the main architect of Alvee. I know you'll all want to connect with him."

The group began to break up.

"I'll have my admin contact each of you to arrange a meeting," Charles assured them.

"I don't think I need that," the Linebacker said, as he stood and headed for the door. "Thank you for a very interesting afternoon."

Charles and I exchanged glances. We'd lost him.

The others chatted with us for a few minutes, then left one by one until only the elderly gentleman remained.

"I'm Frank Brazil," he began. "Neddy, thank you for your kindness earlier." He patted the business plan. "I like your ideas. And your product. I've funded medical devices in the past, and I would be very interested in speaking with Alex. Engineering expertise is vital to the success of these endeavors. Just one final question for you two: What in the world does 'Angiras' mean?"

Charles smiled. "Angiras is a Hindu sage, a teacher of divine knowledge and a mediator between men and gods."

Brazil smiled back and nodded. "'Mediator between men and gods,' eh? Kind of like a doctor."

"He seems interested," I said to Charles as we packed up our briefcases.

"He's old-school but seems very shrewd. Don't let his lack of tech savvy fool you."

"It's a good sign that he wants to meet Alex. By the way, did you find out what happened to him? What was the family issue?"

"No clue. I just punted."

On our way out, we stopped at the front desk to pay the bill.

"Was everything satisfactory today?" the desk clerk recited without bothering to make eye contact.

"Yes," I responded just as automatically.

Charles tapped me on the shoulder and headed toward the restroom.

I turned back to the clerk. "Actually, the air conditioning was too high. Uncomfortably high."

While Charles was using the men's room I called my parents.

"Dad, what's up? How's Daniel today?"

"The fever finally broke, but he's more tired than usual. Mom gave him his meds and he's been napping most of the afternoon. One step forward and another—never mind. How did the pitch go?"

"Decent turnout, most of them just listened but there is definite interest from one guy, a very seasoned investor who asked a lot of great questions. We'll follow up with everyone."

"That's it? We need more than one fish on the hook."

Another call, from Kimberly, was coming in. I silenced it, feeling annoyed both at her tardiness and at my father's attempts —grounded in his love and worry for Daniel's health—to micro-manage our business. "I know." I changed the subject. "By the

way, Dad, the El Cortez is beautiful. They kept a lot of the original details when they remodeled. It's stunning."

"That's nice. Your grandfather was ten years old when they
built that. He always loved that place." He yawned. "Okay. Let
me know what the plan is for the next round of pitches. And ask
Charles to call me later. "

"I will, and I'll call Daniel tomorrow. Love you, Dad."

"Thanks, Neddy."

A text arrived from Kimberly:

Call right away!

She answered on the first ring. "Neddy, something horrible
has happened. Alex went berserk this afternoon when his wife
came to pick him up. He's been arrested."

"What?" I spun around to look for Charles.

"He assaulted his wife just as she arrived to pick him up. A
couple of employees had to pull him off her out in the parking
lot." Kimberly's voice cracked.

"Oh my God, was she injured?"

"She's bruised, her lip was split open. It was awful. We called
the paramedics and they came right away. Once they heard what
happened, they called the police."

"Oh my God. Shit, does he have a history of this?"

"No one knows. After the sleep session today, he was disoriented. He didn't seem to recognize where he was. It passed after
a few minutes, but—"

"Never mind. Is his wife going to be okay?"

"The EMTs took her to the hospital as a precaution. I sent
Tim with her. He's going to text me when he knows more."

"Okay, Kimberly, let me know as soon as you hear anything.
Charles is here—we'll call you back when he's out of the men's
room."

"Shit!" I cursed out loud again. A bellhop walked by and
stared.

TWO

BY THE TIME we arrived at the office it was nearly six thirty. Kimberly met us at the entrance and gave us an update as we walked toward the elevator: Alex was in county jail, charges pending. His wife, Erin, had been released from the hospital and was expected to make a full recovery, though she was badly bruised and shaken.

"What now?" Kimberly asked when we reached Charles's office on the third floor. "We're down two engineers."

"Two?" I asked.

"Stevie—she's been out sick all week. And now Alex."

"First, let's be clear," Charles said. "None of this has to do with us, with the business. Just because it took place onsite, we shouldn't overreact. We need to talk to the other engineers. Make sure there's no panic," he said. "Hopefully we've only lost Alex for a few days."

"A few days?" I said. "He attacked his wife right outside the building. Beyond the trauma that's caused our staff, we can't accept him back until he completes some kind of probationary program—anger management, a psych evaluation, something. We won't just be letting him back in."

Charles paced. "I know, I know. I'm not— Kimberly, are the other engineers still here?"

"They weren't getting much done, so I sent them home."

"Okay. Kimberly, please set up a department meeting for eight thirty tomorrow morning. Let's focus on reassuring them that we're taking this seriously and their comfort and safety are our top concerns. And let's all remember: This horrible act has nothing to do with the company."

"Well," Kimberly interjected, "Alex did have a weird episode this afternoon just as he woke up from his sleep session."

"What do you mean?" Charles motioned for her to sit.

"Alex was disoriented, shaking, mumbling. And he didn't know where he was. It took about five minutes for him to calm down and recognize the rest of the team."

"That's very odd," I said. "Has that ever happened before?"

"Not to my knowledge." Kimberly sighed. "But it makes me wonder if whatever made him snap in the parking lot has anything to do with that weird episode."

"No." Charles stood up and walked toward her. "That sounds more like the remnants of a nightmare, probably a very vivid nightmare so that when he woke, he was still in the throes of the dream."

"Are nightmares caused by lucid dreaming?" I asked.

"No." Charles was adamant. "Look, Neddy, let's let Kimberly get out of here. She's had a very long day. You and I can hash out tomorrow's approach to ensure we take care of everyone and don't lose another day of work on Alvee."

That night I slept fitfully. At one point I dreamt about my ex-husband, Jeremy. We were sailing on a yacht, the wind whipping past, the ocean swelling and pitching. Under the foam, the water was a deep shade of blue I'd never seen before. I sang a childhood rhyming tune when Jeremy fell over the side, flailing as he hit the water. He called to me, desperate for help. I yelled at him to swim, that he'd be okay if he just kept swimming. Feeling no fear for him, I didn't understand his panic. I felt pressure against my leg, and suddenly, an alarm blared. As I slogged out of sleep, I realized the alarm was my own. Leaning on me was the warm, furry lump of my pug, Waldo.

Charles and I had agreed to speak early that morning, after he'd had the night to sort through all the details of yesterday's events. I showered, pulled on wool slacks and a warm sweater, and took the dog out, my mind still muddled and uncooperative. Normally, I liked to walk at a leisurely pace, enjoying the Southern California morning air and the scent of granite, dew, and oak, which exists nowhere except in that vast basin. But this morning was downright cold, and the streetlights were off. I made a quick circle of the block surrounding the complex, not wanting to linger in the inky darkness. As I stepped onto my own walkway, my neighbor opened her front door.

"I thought I heard you moving about." She clutched her robe tight around the neck.

"Oh, Mrs. Gladstone, I hope I didn't wake you up. I have an important phone call early this morning."

"Oh dear. Is Daniel okay?"

"Yes, thank you. It's not a family thing. I'm so sorry."

"Don't worry, dear. I'm always up early anyway. I don't often hear you at this hour, so I thought I'd check."

Waldo pulled at the leash.

"Good morning, Waldo, you sweet boy." She bent down to pet the dog. Mrs. Gladstone was a good neighbor—a bit nosy, but with the watchfulness came a certain level of security. She kept an eye on my place and walked Waldo for me whenever I was unexpectedly delayed. They'd grown quite fond of each other.

My phone rang. I waved to her and went into my unit.

Charles and I agreed on a strategy for the morning meeting with the engineering team: We would ensure everyone was comfortable and felt safe continuing work while insisting on their discretion. It was a fine line to walk.

We then turned to our immediate time crunch.

"I'd suggest hiring some temp engineers, but with money so tight—" I began.

"The learning curve is too steep." Charles took a deep breath. "I'll have to rejoin the engineers in the lab for a bit."

"Charles, no. You almost killed yourself the last time you tried to run the company and get the dream program off the ground."

"We have operational help now. We're more settled in. And I don't see any other choice. It takes months to train lucid techniques, and we can't lose any more time. It'll be fine, Neddy. I'll start once I get back from the biotech conference next week."

"That conference is *next* week? Crap!"

"I know. I'm one of the keynote speakers, otherwise I would cancel. *And* everybody in the business will be there. I can feel out some prospective partners. Someone's going to be interested in what we're doing and maybe invest, or even consider a licensing deal. I'm afraid we can't rely on the VC guys who showed up yesterday."

"I blew it with that big jerk, didn't I? I shouldn't have been so—"

"Stop it. He *was* a jerk and you handled him perfectly."

"Oh God. The timing for you to be away couldn't be worse."

"I can't skip it, Neddy. You keep things together here. And once we get a cash influx, things will be easier. Don't worry."

"Worrying is my specialty."

"Have you read the book on meditation I gave you?"

"Not yet. But thankfully, you meditate enough for the both of us."

He laughed. "I'll see you at the office."

At seven a.m. I swiped my security card and entered the empty lobby of our company headquarters. Our board chair and cofounder, Max Sheldon, owned the building and provided a significant discount on rent. After two years of occupancy, the three-story modern steel and glass structure still smelled new.

Once inside my office on the second floor, I walked past my desk and headed for the comfortable, oversized plush chair I'd brought with me when I started work at the company. I'd spent many hours there problem-solving, and it was my favorite place to think. The day ahead promised to be brutal, so I took advantage of the quiet. As the sun peeked over the horizon, my reflection in the window sharpened. I'd lost twenty-five pounds in the last two years, ditched cigarettes, and extracted myself from a bad marriage. At thirty-seven I had a great job, felt better physically than I had in a very long time, and lived independently. The woman staring back at me appeared healthy and pulled-together.

She hid her insecurity well.

The text from Charles read:

Stuck in traffic.

"It's already eight twenty. Damn," I muttered. Kimberly had been waiting outside my office. She and I would have to start the meeting without him.

"How are you feeling this morning?" I asked as we turned and walked down the corridor toward the engineering office.

"Oh, I'm okay. Didn't sleep much."

"Yeah, me neither. I'll do the talking until Charles arrives. We spoke this morning and agreed on a communication strategy."

She stared at me for a long moment before we entered the double doors leading to the cluttered office of the product engineering team. Jeff Choy, Tim Morgan, and Ryan Belkey looked up from their workstations as we entered. The TV on the wall blared a classic rock video.

"Good morning. Can we switch off the music so we can get started?" I noticed their curious glances. "Charles asked me to get things moving. He's on his way."

As everyone settled in, I took in the large office, nicknamed the Hovel, which resembled more of a dorm room than an innovation center. State-of-the-art engineering laptops and high-resolution printers sat next to mismatched chairs, tattered desks, and an indoor basketball setup. Charles and Kimberly, despite their respective fastidious natures, had agreed it wasn't worthwhile to fuss over the engineers' housekeeping habits. Or their wardrobe choices.

"Thanks for taking a few minutes with us. I wanted to make sure you are all aware Alex will not be coming to work for some time—we're not sure how long." I wanted to convey both empathy and professionalism but not discuss Alex's personal life. The three men nodded without much expression. "Family issues have come up, serious enough to keep him away for a while. I know you all are close, but please try to refrain from discussing Alex with other employees."

"I hear ya," Ryan said.

"Look, we get what's going on." Jeff crossed his arms. "He flipped out and beat the shit out of his wife. You don't have to sugarcoat it."

"Why don't you tell us how you really feel, Jeffy." Ryan's joke landed flat. Jeff glared at his coworker and shook his head.

My face grew hot, but I stayed on topic. "The point is, we have to treat this with discretion. Do you all understand? He and his family have a right to privacy. So no discussing this among yourselves, no speculating, and *please*, no discussions with employees outside this department. Understood?"

Ryan and Jeff nodded again.

Charles entered, sat cross-legged on the floor, and waved toward me, indicating I should continue.

Tim, who had been silent up to this point, stood up and walked toward the window. "Yeah. The thing is, Alex was… struggling at work for a while." Tim glanced at Charles and then Kimberly.

"What do you mean?" I said. Was this old or new news?

"Sometimes Alex had nightmares. During the dream sessions. Or maybe not nightmares."

"No, definitely nightmares." Ryan drummed his fingers on his knee.

"He generated a great number of ideas," Charles said. "Especially in the last few months."

"Yeah, way more than the rest of us." Tim crossed his arms and looked at Charles. "I can't help wondering if we missed something though. Some warning sign."

"No, no, no." Charles jumped up from the floor. "Don't blame yourself for not being able to foretell the future. No one could have predicted this. Or prevented it." He shook his head. "Look, I can only speculate about what made Alex behave this way. Maybe a history of violence. Or PTSD, or some other problem. The point is, we must move forward. We must continue developing Alvee. So tell us if you need anything. Anything at all."

The inflection in his voice said the meeting was over, and it surprised me. Usually empathetic and always effusive, he tried to rush through a disquieting moment for the team. He looked around the room and turned to leave.

"I keep wondering if the dreaming has some bad side effects." Tim's voice was so quiet I nearly missed his comment.

"Unequivocally not." Charles had almost reached the door.

He spun and walked toward Tim, then stopped and lowered his voice. "We evaluated lucid dreaming judiciously. All the experts assured us it's safe. Lucid dreamers don't do things in the waking state they wouldn't normally do." He turned to the rest of the group before continuing. "This has been a shock for all of us. Alex is our colleague, our friend. And it's heartbreaking, what's happened." Charles walked to Tim and put a hand on his shoulder. "But it didn't start here."

Tim thanked Charles, then sat down.

"Have the rest of you experienced anything odd?" I asked. The group turned to Charles. I followed their gaze and saw his jaw tighten.

"No," Ryan said. Tim shook his head, then opened his mouth to speak, but Charles cut him off.

"I understand your concerns. Affirmative. Alex had some nightmares during the dream sessions, he wasn't himself, and now he's done something unthinkable." Charles bowed his head and tented his hands. After a moment, he continued in a low voice. "Let's all keep Alex and his family in our hearts. If you believe in prayer, pray for him. If you believe in karma, resist the negative thoughts you might be overwhelmed with, and wish for him love, generosity, and abundance. Alex needs healing."

This was the Charles I knew—sensitive, compassionate, warm. Knowing exactly what to say. Ryan closed his eyes solemnly, as did Tim. Jeff stared at the floor, then sat back against the sofa. If he still held contempt for Alex, it was no longer obvious.

"As for possible side effects of the dream program," Charles said, "let's make sure you can truly 'sleep well' knowing it's safe." The team groaned at the pun. "How about this: Starting today we'll have all of this investigated—all of it. We'll follow up with Alex and his wife, take another look at the data on lucid dreaming—a comprehensive evaluation of everything we're doing. Think of it as an audit."

"That's solid." Ryan looked at the others.

Jeff shrugged. "I don't think it's necessary, but sure."

"Tim?"

"An audit is a good idea. Who's going to complete it? Some consultant?"

"We can hire a consultant. And I'm willing to do so, if you prefer," Charles said. "But finding one will take at least a week and a half, which is precious time. So, I think Neddy is a good choice. She knows the business, she's analytical and tenacious. Boy, is she tenacious! And she can start right away." Charles turned to me. "You'll have access to whatever you need."

I was shocked. The engineers reported to Kimberly, who in turn reported to Charles, and I wasn't usually involved with their team. Worse, I had no background in medical research or the obscure science of lucid dreaming. Worse still, the thought of approaching Alex or his wife made me nauseous.

"Neddy's not as close to this. She'll be more…objective. She'll look at everything from a fresh perspective."

"I think that's a good idea." Kimberly glanced at me. "Really good. I suggest Neddy observe a sleep session as part of the audit process."

Charles smiled at Kimberly, then turned to the rest of the group. "And until Neddy's satisfied this regrettable episode is an isolated incident, none of you should feel obligated to use the sleep lab," Charles assured them. "Work with the ideas you've already generated."

"And on a positive note," Kimberly added, "Stevie called this morning. She'll be back at work in a few days."

After the meeting, Charles motioned for me to follow him. We took the stairs to the third floor, walked down the corridor, and arrived at his office. "Close the door."

He crossed the room and entered the small Jack and Jill kitchen that connected his office with the sleep lab. I waited while he brewed coffee, staring out the windows of his large workspace. The surrounding garden and grounds had been cultivated to complement the interior space with its tranquil, cool color palette. A long, polished walnut conference table was the sole lateral work surface, flanked by a credenza; both sat near the main door we'd just come through. Several side chairs of varying design sensibilities sat at the other end of the space, near a low glass coffee table where hibiscus soy candles glowed, adding a floral note to the smoky aroma of the coffee. Adjacent to the seating area, a sunken alcove was set up with a yoga mat facing a four-foot-long, narrow wrought-iron table with a thick marble top. A statue of the Hindu god Shiva centered the piece as an altar.

Charles handed me coffee, then walked toward the mat, gesturing to a nearby chair, where I took a seat. Once he reached the mat, he sat, took a deep breath, and closed his eyes. I waited until he moved from this meditative moment into a standing yoga pose and his eyes reopened.

"Let's talk about this…situation." Charles took several deep breaths in and out. "I want to make sure we're not getting distracted by circumstances out of our control. This horrible thing Alex has done—I don't want it slowing things down. You need to manage this."

"But why me? Why not Kimberly?"

"She's too close to it. We need an objective, analytical viewpoint."

I sighed. "I wish you'd asked me before you announced it."

"Why? You're the perfect choice."

"I know so little about the whole program. And it will distract me from the finances."

"Great opportunity to learn."

"And what did you mean by 'follow up with Alex and his wife?' I hardly know Alex."

He waved a hand. "You only need to do that if you find any

evidence of lucid dreaming causing violent behavior, *which it does not.* So that part's already off your plate."

I was relieved for myself, though his suggestion was not exactly what he'd promised the team.

"I want Alex and Stevie back in here quickly and for us to get the program back online. So please be as efficient as possible. Start with being circumspect in how you talk with the team."

"Circumspect?"

Charles exhaled and began moving through a sequence of yoga poses. "Be careful about leading questions, like asking if they've had any 'odd experiences' with the sleep lab, or however you phrased it. In situations like this, people can start to conjure things. So much emotional energy about their friend's predicament."

"I didn't think of that."

Charles moved onto hands and knees, taking deep breaths and exhaling audibly. He lowered his forearms to the floor, clasped his hands together, and placed his head to the mat. With hips high, he maneuvered his body into a headstand. "During periods of turmoil, people are susceptible to one another's apprehensions. And opinions."

"It seemed a logical question, but I see what you mean." I studied my upside-down brother, long legs swaying as he maintained balance, his face a peculiar countenance with the lips and eyes in converse locations, nostrils gaping skyward, and gravity tugging at the skin. For a moment I was reminded of aliens in a science fiction movie I'd watched with Daniel the previous week, a dated, low-budget affair including Martians who resembled humans, but with a twisted visage and features in all the wrong places. I stifled a smile at the similarity. Daniel was extremely intelligent and well read. But he had a soft spot for cheesy science fiction movies.

"Make sure they don't get distracted. Or become unproductive." Charles lowered himself to the floor and remained still for a minute. "They'll run out of ideas soon if they don't get back into the lab, and that will delay development. So keep your questions focused on process, and observable actions. Don't let them speculate."

"Anything else?" I tried to keep the sarcasm out of my voice, but I was tired and hungry, realizing I hadn't eaten breakfast.

"No. I'll stay out of your way, I promise. And remember, this is for Daniel."

THREE

THE NEXT MORNING, Friday, Charles flew out to the conference, and I started researching lucid dreaming, reading article after article, searching for clues or evidence that the practice might trigger nightmares or unusual behavior. I contacted a researcher in North Carolina, Dr. Kate Jorgensen, who'd studied the practice for over twenty years. She assured me the intentional manipulation of dreams was safe and surprised me, quoting research proving such control can treat several maladies, including sleep disorders, phobias, pain, and nightmares.

"Wait, lucid dreaming is used to *treat* nightmares?" I asked. "Does it ever cause nightmares?"

"No," Dr. Jorgensen responded. "A nightmare can occur in any dream. But a lucid dreamer has an advantage: He or she can learn to neutralize the nightmare, using thoughts to disrupt the narrative and take the experience in another direction. Dreams are highly thought-responsive. If you're lucid in a nightmare, you can think of something or someone helpful appearing, and it *will* show up, dissipating the fear. Of course, the person needs to be aware they have that kind of control and choose to use it."

I shared the work we were doing but did not include the disturbing events of the past two days. Kind and reassuring, Dr.

Jorgensen followed up by sending me a link to the book she'd authored on the subject.

By late afternoon, I had a decent understanding of the science and had prepared for Monday's interviews with the engineers who participated in the sleep lab research. We'd just confirmed Stevie would be returning to work on Monday, and I was anxious to talk to her. The faster I got through this audit the better.

I checked in with Lupe, Charles's assistant. Smart and self-sufficient, she rattled off a series of minor operational issues that had sprung up during the day, which she'd handled.

"Fantastic, Lupe. Thanks."

"Oh, and I forwarded a message meant for you from First Valley Bank. It landed in Charles's voicemail. Dial by Name strikes again."

"An occupational hazard of shared surnames," I laughed. The company's automated voicemail directory for our landline frequently misfired, sending messages meant for Charles to my mailbox and vice versa.

At last, I turned to my regular job, hyper-focused on accuracy. Cash flow remained a top priority, and the board scrutinized every dime. I grabbed some popcorn and a soda from the snack bar adjacent to the elevator bank, walked to my office, and settled into my chair near the window, balancing my laptop and pulling a shawl around my shoulders.

Nothing in the numbers appeared out of place until I turned to the payables and came across something I didn't recognize. Eight hundred dollars paid by handwritten check—that was odd. I phoned our accounting manager and asked for a copy of the check, which he forwarded to me. Then I searched for and found sporadic payments over the last year to the same individual, someone named Ron Dorsey. Curious, I did a quick search on the Internet and found several Ron Dorseys in the Los Angeles area, including a disc jockey, a chemist, and a therapist.

Only the disc jockey had a robust online profile, and I knew he wasn't our man.

I made a note to ask Charles about Dorsey. The checks didn't represent a lot of money, but we were watching every dime.

———

On Monday morning I met with each of the engineers. My plan was to speak with them first, since they were the active participants in the lucid dreaming program, and wrap up with Melody, the lab assistant.

Stevie Mortenson came in first. Tall, thin, and fair with jet-black hair, her brown eyes met mine as she took a chair across from my desk.

"How's Alex?" she asked. Though younger than I, perhaps late twenties, Stevie was poised and gave the impression of a woman wiser than her years.

"We haven't spoken to him," I said. "How are you feeling?"

"I'm good now. I woke up with temporary paralysis last week. It's related to my epilepsy."

"I'm glad you're recovered and back with us."

"Yeah, thanks. So, Tim tells me you're investigating the dream program. What's that all about?"

"There was some—a small—concern, after Alex's incident late last week, and we want to make sure we've thoroughly vetted all our processes, and everyone is safe and comfortable continuing."

"Have you ever been in the lab during a sleep session?" she asked.

"Not yet. I'll be scheduling an observation soon though."

Stevie explained the process: The engineers went into the lab after lunch for about two hours. Each was assigned a comfortable cot and had blankets and eye pillows at their disposal.

"Charles often gives us something specific about Alvee to

focus on. The goal is to have a lucid dream about the design issue of the moment so maybe a solution is found."

"How often do you all dream about the same issue?"

"Not very. But even if only one person comes up with an idea, it's worth it."

"Go on."

"Melody attaches monitors that measure blood pressure, heart rate, and ocular movement. She used to be a nurse's aide, so she's on top of all that."

I recalled Dr. Jorgensen telling me eye movements were key indicators of the dream state.

"Recently, we've also been given tea to drink before we settle down. I don't know what flavor—it's kind of funky tasting—but Melody said it's supposed to help with lucidity. Alex said it worked really well, but we all hated the taste."

I made a note to investigate it.

"Anyway, sometimes Charles chants while we drift off, sometimes he'll do a guided meditation. There's usually some soft music playing—it's nice because it's the kind of music you can either ignore or focus on and drift off. And of course, we focus on the lucidity techniques."

"Can you describe these techniques?" I asked.

"It takes practice, but we've learned to focus on what we experience right before sleep sets in. You know when you're first drifting off? You see images, hear sounds or parts of conversations—things your mind conjures up. We try to remain aware and focus on them. And when we can stay focused, those sensations change into moving scenes, dreams with action, like a movie. That's when we can begin to direct the dream."

Her description synced with what Dr. Jorgensen had described to me. "How often do you have lucid dreams, Stevie?"

"I dream almost every day. Not all are lucid dreams. But there have been a few instances, for example, when I asked my dreaming mind—that's what Charles calls our lucid sleep—when I asked: 'Show me the scope and the tube, and how to fix it.' Or 'show me how it works.' And sometimes I get an idea I can use. It's exciting when I do."

"How often do you get a useful idea?" I asked. "Something you can follow up on?"

"In the beginning, when we first started, not often. A lot of the time—a *lot* of the time—the dreams went off in strange directions, like most dreams. But more recently, I've been waking up with an idea for an assay more often than not. I guess we've all become better at—"

"Assay?"

"Test—sorry—a test we haven't tried before. And the waking-up process, by the way, is crucial. Because the idea, the thought, the thing to try—it's fleeting. You have to grab a notebook or a laptop right away and make sure you write down whatever you can remember."

"I've heard that before."

"Melody knows when we're starting to wake up and she makes sure to be right there with our dream logs."

"What happens next?"

"We're done in the lab itself. I usually grab some of the breath freshener Melody keeps on hand for us, go wash my face, and I'm back at the computer in our office. I feel energized by the routine."

"And in general, do you feel comfortable continuing in the lab?"

"Yes, I find the lab very helpful. Alex generated some great ideas. The whole idea of planting the medicine deep in the lungs came out of a dream Alex had. Why? You're not thinking of stopping it, are you? I mean, I know Tim thinks there might be a connection between Alex's behavior and the stuff we're doing, but I've never experienced any nightmares. In fact, I like to rest in the middle of the day. My husband says I'm less cranky at night."

"We want you to be a hundred percent comfortable with any work you do here. That's our responsibility as an employer."

"I'm thrilled to be doing this. It's a whole new way to innovate."

The other discussions proceeded quickly. Tim voiced the same concerns he'd mentioned before, wondering whether the nightmares Alex experienced were symptoms of some undetected side effect of the dreaming program. I shared what I'd learned from Dr. Jorgensen and encouraged him to reach out to her if he had further questions. He seemed satisfied.

Ryan expressed concern for Alex and Erin. "I'm prayin' every day for them," he said. He reported no concerns with the sleep lab and felt whatever had happened with Alex was unrelated to the program.

Jeff, while also seeing the dream program as helpful, showed less sympathy toward Alex.

"He's an asshole."

"We're not focusing on Alex. We're making sure our methods are solid."

"He's still an asshole."

"What's with Jeff?" I asked Kimberly once the interviews were over. "Has he always been hostile toward Alex?"

"Jeff is an excellent engineer, but he's been angry about his divorce for a long time. He tends to look at the world in a black and white way—he doesn't do well with ambiguity. I think Jeff might also be a little jealous of Alex's success in the lab."

"Then we'll always know where he stands, won't we." I yawned, reading through the notes I'd scribbled. "All the engineers support the dream program. Before we started this process, I'd wondered about that."

"And they're being paid well for it," Kimberly said. "Most of them don't have degrees, so working here is a big deal for them."

I came to the end of my interview notes. "The only consistent complaint, if you can call it that, is the tea. They all described an unpleasant taste. Jeff was particularly harsh in his comments about it."

"Mugwort tea. Yes, they've never cared for it," Kimberly confirmed.

"Kimberly, as manager of the engineering team, you get a vote too. Are you concerned about the program?"

We were sitting in her office, a small but airy space adjacent to the engineer's suite. She took a long time to answer. "No one else has had nightmares or mood swings, so there's no logical reason to be concerned, I guess. It's hard for me to accept that my friend Alex could do something so awful. But at my last company, I was an IT manager, and I found out all kinds of things about the people who worked for me when I performed an audit on their company laptops. So maybe I shouldn't be so surprised."

I walked to my office. I still needed to talk to Melody, but first I had one more bit of online research to do. I quickly found several references to mugwort tea as a sleep aid and an enhancement to lucid dreaming. A few articles claimed the tea was "psychoactive" and could therefore affect mood, another advised against "heavy use" but didn't define that term, and all cautioned against use by pregnant women. The taste was alternately described as bitter, bark-like, and tart. Numerous ads popped up, offering different brands of the stuff; it appeared to be widely sold and consumed. Poking around for a few more minutes, I searched for and found several alternative teas that didn't taste bitter but had a more benign profile. I figured I'd try the mugwort myself before making any recommendation. I picked up my phone, dialing Melody's extension. The call went to voicemail.

"Melody, it's Neddy. I finished talking with the engineers and want to stop by and chat for a few minutes. As you know, I'm auditing the sleep program and have a few questions for you. Also, I'd like to try some of the mugwort tea the team uses. Can you please call me back?"

Then I dialed Charles.

He answered on the first ring but was tied up. "I'll be home day after tomorrow. Everything okay there?"

"Yeah, lots to update you on, but it's all good."

"Tea" I typed into my calendar, and highlighted it. I'd ask about it when he returned.

"Thanks for keeping an eye on things. We'll talk tomorrow."

I walked up to the third floor and down the corridor to the sleep lab, hoping to catch Melody. I didn't know much about her, except she was quirky—a bit of a loner who wore only orange—but she'd been a loyal assistant to Charles since they'd worked together at Paramount. He relied on her to ensure smooth operation of the sleep lab.

The lab was a large interior space encircled by the third-floor main corridor. Three wide windows lined a portion of one section, allowing passersby in the corridor to see into the lab. During sleep sessions, blinds were lowered so the team had privacy. There were two workstations nestled into cubicles and metal cabinets near the windows. Across the room on the far wall were the cots and monitoring equipment. Access to the lab was through an interior door off the main corridor and down a short hallway. Upon entering the hallway, one first walked past Melody's office on the left, then past the small Jack and Jill kitchen on the right—which also connected to Charles's office— and finally to the lab itself.

I stood in the hallway in front of Melody's office. The light was on and the door ajar. I knocked as I entered, not realizing Melody was behind the door locking up a storage cabinet. She wore an orange-and-black-checked jacket over an orange T-shirt. Her pumpkin-shaped handbag was slung over one shoulder.

"Oh, looks like you're ready to leave," I said, after I'd apologized for nearly knocking her over. "You're the final person I need to interview to close the audit."

"Oh, hmmm, yeah. I have to leave in a few minutes." Eyes down, her voice was just above a whisper.

I stepped back into the hallway to give her some space. "I

won't take long—I've spoken with everyone else on the team—but I don't want to interrupt your evening. Can you spare fifteen minutes?"

"Okay."

We sat in the cramped space, the desk adorned with personal photos, mugs, and mementos—everything in shades of orange. I asked about her responsibilities in the lab.

"I'm always here when the engineers come in for the sleep session. I attach the monitors and watch the vitals from my computer, either here or at one of the workstations. When they wake up, I give them a tablet or pad of paper to record their dreams on. That's about it."

"The engineers mentioned tea. Do you prepare it?"

"No. Charles makes the tea. I store it here"—she motioned to the storage cabinet—"but he makes it in the kitchen."

"Can I get some from you? I want to taste it."

"Sure. You might not like it though. No one does." She stood and dug into her handbag, pulled out a set of keys, unlocked the cabinet, and produced three bags of mugwort tea from a box tucked in among pads, pens, and ink cartridges.

"Thank you." I tried again to make eye contact. "Have you noticed any unusual readings from the monitors?"

"No."

"You were here the afternoon Alex woke up disoriented, correct?"

"Yeah."

"What did you notice?"

"Nothing similar ever happened before. The whole thing was weird. The rest of the team members were fine, so I thought maybe Alex had the flu or something."

"Okay. I have what I need. Thank you, Melody, for staying a few minutes."

"Sure."

She stood, looking at the floor while I squeezed by her and out the door.

I went downstairs to the second-floor snack bar and filled a cup with hot water. I took a whiff of the mugwort tea bag before submerging it, then put a plastic lid on the cup and walked to my office. I packed up my laptop, forwarded my phone to my cell, grabbed my purse and the cup, and headed to my car. I wanted to pick up Waldo from home before I went to visit Daniel and my parents.

Before I turned on the engine, I took the lid off the cup and inhaled, expecting an unpleasant aroma. Then I took a sip. The tea, while earthier than I prefer, was pleasant enough. I tasted it again and wondered what all the fuss was about.

FOUR

AS SOON AS I let Waldo off the leash, he bolted down the hall toward Daniel's room. I followed as happy barking filled the house. A wonderful combination of spices and braised meat drifted in from the kitchen.

"There's my boy!" I heard the distinctive animation in Daniel's voice, a cadence reserved only for my little dog.

"You all in there?" I called, rounding the corner toward the back bedroom, where Daniel slept most nights. "What are you cooking? It smells divine."

"In here, Neddy," my mother called.

Daniel sat in his recliner, an old La-Z-Boy my dad had used for years before handing it down. He'd tried several chairs of more recent vintage, as well as a hospital bed we rented for a month, but Dad's well-used leather favorite provided the most comfortable position, given Daniel's compromised breathing. I leaned down to hug him, angling around Waldo standing on the wide arm of the chair, desperately trying to lick Daniel. Of the three of us, Daniel had been blessed with the most striking features, including olive skin and deep brown eyes ringed with flecks of hazel. That day, his dark hair needed cutting, and he was paler than the last time I'd seen him. Those beautiful eyes, though clear, seemed sunken.

"You look good," I said. In truth Daniel had not appeared healthy for quite a long time.

"I'm going to check on dinner." My mother stood. "Spanish stew with chorizo."

"You feel well enough to chow down with us?" I asked Daniel.

"Yeah, I think I can sit up for a while with you guys." He stroked the dog's back as Waldo settled onto his lap.

"Have you talked to Charles today?"

"Yeah, he called this morning. Said he's still in Honolulu at the conference. Must be nice being the boss." Daniel grinned.

"I wouldn't know. I keep my nose to the grindstone."

"What's a 'grindstone'? Where do you come up with this stuff, Neddy." We both laughed. Jeremy's family, especially his mom, had been notorious for idioms. I hadn't realized I'd picked up the habit. "It's a real old saying. I guess it means, keep toiling over and over. Something to do with pushing a grinding stone—you know, for wheat or grain—in the days before motors."

Daniel looked at me as if I'd sprouted two extra heads. "That's you for sure. You never give up. Waldo, why is your mother so goofy?" A coughing fit erupted, forcing Daniel to reach for his oxygen mask, closing his eyes as the cool, humid air settled the hack. When able to speak again, he gave me a look that I knew meant bad news.

"We got the latest blood work results today. Not so good." He smiled at me apologetically.

"What did Dr. Samson say?" I stroked his arm and glanced at my dad.

"Same as always—'it's to be expected.'" Daniel exhaled deeply before continuing. "Doc-talk for 'you're not getting better.'"

"Danny, that's *not* what Dr. Samson said," Dad scolded.

I fought to keep my gaze even.

Daniel pulled Waldo close and snuggled into the dog's fat neck. "What does that quack-a-doodle doctor know anyway, huh, Wally-Baby? Hey, Neddy, did you hear the one about the doctor who asked his patient if he wanted the good news or the bad news?"

"That joke's as old as the hills, Daniel."

He cocked his head and raised an eyebrow at the turn of phrase. "Two so far, and you've been here, what, ten minutes?"

I marveled at his good spirits despite the test results. "Okay, okay. But the joke's still ancient."

"No, it's not. It's different, listen: The doctor asks his patient, 'Which do you want first, the good news or the bad news?' The patient says, 'Give me the good news.' The doctor says, 'Congratulations. You're about to have a disease named after you.'" Waldo turned and licked Daniel's cheek, as if he approved of the punchline.

We all laughed at the dog as Mom called us to dinner.

I helped Daniel maneuver his walker to a spot at the end of the table, closest to his room, then positioned a pillow behind his back for support. "Good?"

"Yeah, this is fine, thanks. Mom, you outdid yourself," he said as she put a plate in front of him. He took a small bite of the stew and chewed slowly.

"Too spicy?" Mom asked. Daniel shook his head no. Dad and I filled our plates and dove in.

"Oh, this is delicious. So good."

"Mmm." Dad nodded. "Thank you, Myra. Neddy, everything okay at work?"

"Everything's moving along, but I'll be glad when Charles gets back. There's a lot of moving parts. I don't mind being second in command, but I hate when I have to lead it all."

Daniel coughed repeatedly and I glanced at him, waiting for the fit to subside. Finally, he wiped his mouth, sipped some water and began eating again.

"Charles plans to go back into the lab for a couple of weeks."

"Why?" Daniel asked.

"Alex is out for an indefinite leave."

"What's going on?"

"A family issue." I didn't dare elaborate; telling the whole story would feed their anxiety about our progress.

"Hire more engineers," Mom said.

"Maybe." Dad and I exchanged a look. I hated to lie, but we'd agreed not to talk about our dwindling finances in front of Daniel. Just then, he erupted into another coughing fit, which sent us scattering for his oxygen and more water. By the time his cough settled, the meal was over, and Dad and I had dodged the bullet about hiring.

After dinner, I helped Mom clean up. Dad took Daniel down the hall to get ready for bed and give him his night-time meds. When we heard Dad switch on the TV in the family room, we knew Daniel was settled in for the night.

"How *is* the research going?" Mom asked.

"About the same as last week. Charles knows more of the details, but the team is totally focused on it."

"Can't they go any faster?"

"They're doing their best, Mom. I know it's small comfort." I hugged her. The TV blared the opening jingle to a show I didn't recognize. She patted my back, then pulled away from me.

"When will Charles be back? Your father always feels better when he's around."

"We *all* feel better when he's around."

"He takes such good care of us. I hope he's taking care of himself."

"I think he does. The yoga, meditation, gym membership—it's all great for stress relief."

"I guess," she said as she yawned, "it helps keeps the anxiety at bay."

"He'll be home day after tomorrow. And I'm going to ask

him to talk to Dr. Samson again to make sure there's nothing else we could be doing."

"Neddy, I don't want to annoy Dr. Samson by asking too many questions."

"I don't care if it annoys him or not. Charles is an excellent doctor, they speak the same medical language, and we should be doing everything possible, turning over every stone."

"I know. But it's not the way I'm used to dealing with doctors. In my day, you did everything the doctor told you, and nothing more. I wouldn't have dared question the way you kids do."

"It's a new day, Mom. People have to advocate for themselves and their loved ones. And sometimes that includes questioning what the doctor tells you."

She sighed. "Let's go sit with your father."

"You ever watch this?" Dad asked as we sat down.

"No. By the time I get home I'm beat."

He stared at the game show, hosted by a popular comedian who insulted the contestants mercilessly, to the hilarity of the studio audience. As the show progressed, I half listened to Dad's running commentary on every round of the inane competition while my mother sat, staring at the television without expression.

I caught her eye. "What *is* this?" I whispered.

Mom rolled her eyes and waved away the question. Years ago, my mother told me she'd learned early in the marriage how to manage Dad. "I used to argue with him about every little thing," she'd said. "Then one day I figured out if I let the little things go, I'd have more say over the bigger things, the stuff that really mattered." Letting him distract himself with mediocre television programming was another benign coping strategy Mom had worked out.

The drone of the show made me sleepy, so I stood up to leave, stopping in Daniel's bedroom to collect Waldo, who snored at the end of bed. Daniel often joked that the dog's noisy breathing, caused by the breed's iconic short snout, made his own tortured respiration sound like a lullaby.

Dad poked his head in. "Why don't you leave the dog here tonight? He'll cheer Danny up tomorrow."

"Okay. But please don't overfeed him."

Dad walked me to the car, closing the front door behind us. "Neddy, where are you guys on the project?"

"Status quo. The engineers are stuck on the same problem: getting the tube to release all the medication."

"Why is this taking so long? It's the middle of March already."

The pain and fear were aging my father.

"I can't stand watching Danny suffer. And it's killing your mother."

"Charles says it's not taking as long as most projects." This was of no comfort to either of us. "Dad, Charles will find a way. He's so creative and thinks of nothing but Daniel, night and day. And the engineering team is dedicated to this."

"I hope so. Good night, honey."

I sat in my car, worried sick about Daniel. I yanked my cell phone from my purse, intending to update Charles on Daniel's lab results, but I noticed a voicemail alert—a call forwarded from my office line—and decided to listen to that first. A woman's voice, tinny and high-pitched, gradually grew louder.

"Hello, uh, Dr. Emory, this is Erin Ruindes, Alex's wife. I'd like to talk to someone at Angiras about my husband." The message continued, "I'm sure you're aware, uh, of the... situation. I want— I have some questions. I left a message with your secretary yesterday, but I didn't hear back. Sorry to be a pest, but can you please call me?"

Another message meant for Charles. I sighed with fatigue. "Why don't people listen to the greeting?" I mumbled. And why hadn't Charles responded to her first call? "Because, Neddy, he's swamped at the conference," I admonished myself. Pushing down my exhaustion, I dialed.

When I reached Erin, her story poured out in a rush of half sentences, punctuated by halting sobs and apologies. I eventually pieced together the gist of it: Alex had been agitated for weeks, was not sleeping well, and complained of headaches. "I begged him to call his doctor."

"He didn't talk to his doctor?" I took notes by hand, scrunched in the driver's seat.

"No."

"Did Alex say what he thought was wrong?"

"He just…brooded. All the time. Men—they don't talk about their feelings."

She said this as if it were an epiphany rather than a cliché.

"Once, I asked him about the work. I wondered if the weird dreaming thing caused his cicadian rhythm—or whatever it's called—to be off. Giving him insomnia and such." She sniffed.

"You mean because he slept part of the day, at work?"

"Yeah. Right. I mean, that's not the time of day people normally sleep."

"I see. Did you ask Alex about it?"

"Yeah, of course. I mean, I asked about everything that might be making him cranky, but he brushed it all off. He thought the dreaming helped him in his job and he liked it."

I wrote fast, in my own version of shorthand. I scrawled the word "nightmares" and drew a slash through it—Erin hadn't mentioned those. If Alex had had nightmares at home, she either wasn't aware or didn't think much of it.

"That afternoon when I went to pick him up, he just wigged out. He screamed about me not supporting him, not loving him anymore. I-I…walked toward him and—"

For nearly a minute, she sobbed into the phone. I listened, fighting the urge to end the call. I wanted only to be home, curled up in my bed.

"I'll call you back," she gasped, and the call ended.

The next day, I leaned against my car in the parking lot of the Midway Diner, waiting to meet Erin Ruindes. The restaurant's neon sign, shaped like a chef's hat, flashed unevenly, reflecting green and red shards off the building's dirty windows. The parking lot was gutted with potholes and faded striping.

An hour after I'd spoken to her the previous night, I sent Erin a text suggesting we meet for lunch. Although I hadn't planned on including the Ruindes family in my audit, the conversation she'd started was now a loose end. As much as I dreaded meeting her, I hated loose ends even more. I'd suggested we meet at a café near her home, but she'd picked this place, much farther away. She was late, finally arriving in a faded, noisy sedan with body damage. She stepped out of the car and waved tentatively.

Erin was a woman of average height but very thin, the kind of woman I looked at and thought: eating disorder. But her purple cheek and swollen eye stole my attention, and that of the restaurant occupants. Even the oversized sunglasses failed to conceal her injuries. Once seated, she spoke in rapid-fire bursts, frank and to the point.

"Alex was never violent before. You get that, right?" Erin wore a plain white T-shirt and very tight jeans. Her hands, over-loaded with cheap-looking rings and jangling bracelets, never stopped shaking.

"I understand." I did understand. But I didn't believe her.

"He went crazy. Which doesn't make any sense. I think the stress of the work—it all just…exploded."

Not wanting to hear the details of the assault, I shifted the conversation. "Erin, how are you now? I hope you have people to support you."

"The police sent a social worker to talk to me. She was kind of lame, but yeah. My sister is helping me. And Alex already has Dr. Rogers— oh, I forgot to call him about the meds," she mumbled, grabbing her phone and typing a reminder.

Meds. I waited, thinking about what this might mean.

"He took them religiously, you know." Erin nodded several times, as if to reassure not only me but herself. "Maybe they need to be adjusted. *Gotta* call the doctor." She put the phone down and shook her head.

I fought the urge to ask what prescriptions Alex used. "Do you know what's happening with Alex's case?"

"His attorney said Alex doesn't remember hitting me. He doesn't remember any of it. He's totally confused." I saw she believed the attorney.

"Oh, that's…unusual." The waitress arrived.

"I'll have the burger, but with no onions and no bun. And fries, unless they're breaded."

"No, we just serve plain fries." The waitress looked a little too long at Erin, took my order, and then we were alone again.

"And if I don't press charges, which I'm totally not going to, then he'll probably be cited and given some kind of anger management class. I guess they have to do something." She removed her sunglasses and rubbed her fingers up and over the cheekbone, exploring the anguished flesh. My own face stung at each compression, and I had to look away.

"I don't get it," she continued. "Alex is the most easygoing guy. I'm the one who flies off the handle. He's always thought of me first." Her voice quavered. "Which restaurant I prefer, what brand of toothpaste should he pick up. Alex loves dogs, but we decided to get a cat because I wanted one." She looked away and shook her head. "And he's been a fantastic father. A Scout leader. I mean, never, ever did he act like this."

I listened to her without nodding, still not believing it.

"The worst thing is"—Erin's expression melted as the tears began to flow—"I can't see him. The police told me I'm a… imperial witness or something. Do you know what that means?"

"I believe it's material witness. It means—"

"Whatever." Her face turned resolute again. "The police and the prosecutor want to nail him, but I'm sooo not pressing charges. Look." She lowered her voice. "I don't want Alex to lose his job over this. It's embarrassing, but it's a one-time thing. He and I can handle this. Please don't fire him." She brushed away a tear in a quick, automatic motion, wincing when her hand compressed her cheek.

I swallowed and tried to look past the injuries, past the denial I knew she lived in, past the urge to grab her by the shoulders and set her straight. I'd been her, once. I knew how much Erin wanted to believe Alex was not a violent person. I'd nurtured the same naïve beliefs about Jeremy for fifteen long years. Whenever he drank too much, Jeremy found a way to blame me for his failings—his troubles holding a job, his friends pulling away from him, our financial struggles. According to him, I wasn't supportive enough. I didn't believe in him or his money-making schemes. I wanted to spend too much time with my friends. The beatings were always followed, once things calmed down, by the most wretched guilt, pleadings for forgiveness, and promises he'd never again lay a hand on me. When he broke my jaw, I left.

If Erin were a friend, my advice would have been: "Get your own attorney. Find a good therapist. Get a restraining order. Get a divorce." I felt selfish and irresponsible for not saying these things and more. But Erin was not my friend. She was the wife of one of our most talented engineers and we needed him back.

"We've always valued Alex. He's been a key contributor to the development of the scope. And of course he has never exhibited any problematic behavior while at work." Technically this was not a lie—Ryan had said Alex suffered from nightmares and he'd been disoriented the afternoon before he assaulted Erin, but those episodes had not resulted in any threats nor put anyone in danger. "At this point, we consider it to be a family matter. As far as we're concerned, he's on sick leave." I hated the way I sounded—like a soulless automaton doing a CYA.

"Oh, thank God. I was so worried." The sobbing started again. "His job means everything to him, and us. I-I only work part-time at a bakery. And we have a son who will be going to college in a few years. Oh, poor Justin." She glanced at her phone. "I have to pick him up soon."

The food arrived and she picked at it, not eating enough to sustain a small bird.

"I have IBS, so I have to be careful what I eat," Erin explained as she pushed her food around the plate. "And, of course, it gets worse when I'm stressed."

She surprised me by asking about Daniel with genuine interest. "I think it's so awesome you and your brother are trying to find a treatment. No one in my family would do something like that for me. Even if they knew how."

Erin looked dejected, as if she might be giving up. I thought she might suddenly blurt out an entirely different narrative, one aligned with what my own experience had taught me: Alex had been abusive for years, Erin had held it together for her son and for the financial support she'd lose if she fled. She'd hoped he'd change. Always the same backstory.

Instead, she stood to go. "Thank you, Neddy. For everything. You won't regret giving Alex another chance."

FIVE

"WAIT, Charles puts you in charge of investigating the dream program and you end up interviewing *the wife* of the *wife-beater*? That's gotta be weird."

"I know, but she contacted us and requested a meeting. Charles was out of town, so it was on me. Turns out her husband's been under the care of a mental health doctor."

"A lot of good that's doing."

"Carollyn, shush up. Let Neddy tell the rest of the story."

I was at dinner with my two best friends, Carollyn and Mindy. We'd been roommates in college and inseparable. After graduation we'd remained close, had vacationed together for several years, nursed each other through boyfriend dramas, and celebrated birthdays, weddings, baby showers. Now—though we'd matured, they were both still married, and our social interactions centered primarily around a monthly dinner—we still finished one another's sentences.

I shook my head. "Erin's a classic abuse victim. She's skittish, overly explains everything, denies, denies, denies. She's thinking only of *his* welfare."

The two exchanged a look.

"Okay, I *knowww*. That was me. It's why I recognize it."

"Nothing like a reformed sinner singing to the choir." Carollyn smirked, perusing the dessert menu.

"I should have listened to you both. You saw through Jeremy way before I let myself."

"You got sucked in by a manipulative jerk. It happens," Mindy said.

"If I'm honest, there was more to it. I wanted to hurt my parents. If not for Charles, they still might not be speaking to me."

Carollyn rolled her eyes.

"No, I'm telling you, Carollyn, he had to work on them. They were angry. Daniel was sick, and I was nowhere to be found. I dragged them through hell."

"I think Charles deserves a lot of credit and admiration for all he's done in his life, there's no question. But you're attributing something to him that would have happened anyway."

"How do you know?"

"Neddy, you're telling me if you had called your parents directly, the response would have been 'stay away'?" Carollyn asked. "Don't sell yourself short. Or your parents. The Ed and Myra I know don't abandon their children. Jeesh, you're their only daughter."

Only daughter. Neither Carollyn nor Mindy knew the depth of my deepest scar: My parents had wanted only boys, and a baby girl had been a disappointment to them.

"Neddy, the important thing is you *did* leave Jeremy." Mindy took my hand. "And I, for one, admire you every day for doing it." She gave Carollyn a *we're done with that subject* nod.

"You have an HR person on staff?" Carollyn asked.

"Yes, we have one HR manager, Leni Greenwood. We're small, remember."

"As your banker, I *know* how small you are. Anyway, Leni should be informed about this bum's arrest, and he shouldn't return to work until cleared by a doctor."

"I saw Daniel's Facebook page last night," Carollyn said later as we walked to our cars. "He posted the sweetest pictures of you all from your parents' thirty-fifth anniversary party. He looked so good, so healthy, his eyes were…just stunning." Her voice caught.

"Yes, he was on his way to becoming a real lady-killer. The perfect combination of smarts, athleticism, and humor."

"Do his old girlfriends ever call?"

"Not really."

"What about the guys? Do they visit?"

"Mostly phone calls. I think it's hard for his friends to see him now."

"That's a shame." Mindy sighed. "He had such a great group of buddies."

"Sickness has a way of exposing people for what they really are." Carollyn stopped at her car.

"Daniel never complains."

"I asked my mom to keep the prayer chain going at her church." Mindy smiled. "For whatever it's worth."

"It can't hurt. Thank you."

"Well, I say hire more engineers." Carollyn returned to her standard bossy mode. "God helps those who help themselves."

I would need to share the full details of our dwindling cash flow with Carollyn eventually, but I wasn't up to it that evening. She'd brought our business to the bank where she worked, vouched for Charles to her executives, and oversaw the line of credit we were so dependent on. Hiring more engineers was off the table, but I had to put a financial plan together before I alerted her to that reality.

I changed the subject. "Shall we pick a date for next month?"

Before I drove home, I checked my messages, reading a text from Erin, complete with heart and flower emojis. She thanked me again for my understanding.

"I understand you perfectly," I mumbled. But then with a pang of guilt I realized something. In addition to suffering physical trauma from our husbands, Erin and I shared another parallel track: We were both trying to keep our families together.

Charles came into my office Wednesday morning carrying two cups of coffee.

"Did you talk to Dr. Samson yet?"

"Whoa, I only read the labs last night. I stopped to see Daniel on my way home from the airport."

"I'm sorry. Welcome back."

"Daniel's in good spirits, but his blood work isn't where we'd like it to be." He handed me one of the steaming cups, sat across from me, and rubbed his eyes. The caffeine was no match for the jet lag and worry. He stared out the window, his gaze unfocused. "The disease marches on, as we knew it would. I think he's holding himself together for Mom and Dad. I doubt he feels as spry as he appears."

"Me too." Sadness rose in me. I hadn't let myself cry for Daniel in a long time, but what he needed most was for us to finish Alvee. I swallowed the ache in my throat.

Charles turned to me. "I'll talk to Samson today, but I doubt he'll have much to say beyond what we already know. There's not a lot to be done. We've got to get Alvee completed. So, what have you got for me?"

"First, I talked to Alex's wife, Erin. We had lunch yesterday."

"Really? Why?"

"She left a voicemail meant for you. It ended up in my message box. We need to get the voicemail directory fixed, by the way."

"I'll get Lupe on that. What did his wife want?"

"Her name is Erin."

"Sorry. What did *Erin* want."

"She was following up on a previous phone call to you." I summarized what Erin had reported about Alex's complaints in the weeks leading up to the attack—the headaches, moodiness, insomnia. "She's still shaken but has boundless faith in Alex. By the way, he was on some kind of medication before all this happened, and according to her, he was good about taking it. It sounded like psych meds. He claims not to remember any part of the attack. For her part, the primary concern is his job. She thought we were about to fire him."

"And you told her what?"

"Same thing we've told everyone. It's a family issue."

He nodded, then began scrolling through his phone. "What kind of psych meds?"

"I didn't ask. It felt too intrusive."

"Hmmm. What are your next steps?"

"I think Erin's in denial. Alex has probably been abusive before, but this is the first time it's bubbled over publicly."

"Did she tell you that?"

"No," I admitted, "but there's every sign of it. She defends him, overemphasizes his positive virtues, refuses to press charges —you know, all the crap I used to do."

He yawned. "I don't know if that makes me feel better or worse."

"It confirms for me the dream program had nothing to do with his violence. That and the rest of my audit."

I reported on the research I'd done on lucid dreaming, the conversation with Dr. Jorgensen, and the interviews with the sleep lab team.

"They all value the dream program and want to continue participating. The one thing they mentioned is the tea. They all said the same thing: It smells bad and tastes terrible."

"It's mugwort tea, totally harmless." He waved his hand, dismissing the topic.

"Right. I read up on it. Melody gave me some to try. Not my favorite, but not horrible like the engineers described. Didn't smell bad either, but—"

"It helps them relax. Why are we talking about this? It's harmless."

"As long as you're not pregnant. It's not medically pro—"
"What?"

"It's not medically proven, but many herbalists think it has an effect on the uterus, so it's not recommended for pregnant women. And I already let Stevie know that."

He shrugged. "Herbalists aren't doctors. But okay."

"It also has some psychoactive properties, at least according to the stuff online. So that made me think about Alex. Remember Kimberly said that the afternoon he was arrested, he'd woken up disoriented? And Erin said he'd been moody."

"Where are you going with this, Neddy? You just said Alex likely has a history of violence. Now you're saying something else?"

"No. I'm not saying the tea caused him to be violent—he's totally responsible for his own actions—just that he woke up that afternoon very agitated. And even if mugwort didn't cause his agitation, it has a reputation for affecting mood. So it doesn't look good for us to be using it. I mean, what if our engineers do their own research on it? And the pregnancy thing—we can't risk it. So I'm recommending we switch to another tea that also aids in sleep, tastes better, and doesn't generate red flags. Ginger tea seems to fit the bill."

Charles was quiet for a long minute. He rubbed his eyes, then his temples. "Mugwort is a very effective aid in lucid dreaming. It's a relatively new addition to the protocol, something they're still getting used to. I'd really like to keep it for a while before we give up on it."

"I can't agree to that. We told them their safety is our top priority."

He shook his head.

"As a doctor, aren't you concerned—"

He gave me a hard look before I could finish. Then he rubbed his temples again. "Okay, you win," he said, his voice heavy with fatigue. "I'll figure out something else. Send a message to the team letting them know they're clear to go back in the lab."

"And that we're going to swap out the tea for something tastier."

He scoffed, scrolling through his phone again. "Yeah, that's a good way to spin it. Anything else?"

"Just a reminder that we also told the team I would observe a sleep session."

"I'll have Lupe schedule that with you."

"Great." I turned to my notes on finances. "When I approved the vendor payments, I ran across one I didn't recognize: Ron Dorsey?"

"What about him?"

"He's received handwritten checks outside the AP system."

"He's a consultant I engage on occasion."

"On personal stuff?"

"Hmmm, no. Business-related."

"Any reason not to set him up in the payables system?"

"I don't use his services very often."

"He's been paid a few times this year."

"I won't be needing him for a while. Don't worry about it." He stood up and walked toward the door.

I turned to my laptop, feeling good about the progress I'd made in Charles's absence, yet glad navigation of the company was again in his hands. But as the day progressed, I found myself thinking of Erin over and over, unable to get her stricken face out of my mind.

SIX

AT THE END OF MARCH, two weeks after the engineers returned to the sleep lab, their dreams produced results again, generating five new theories for adjusting the medication dispenser. Our hopes were raised. I saw very little of Charles. He spent his days with the engineers, helping develop and test modifications to the device and participating in lucid dreaming sessions. After the team left each day, he sequestered himself in his office conducting online research, reviewing the financial updates I produced daily, and responding to demands from the board. Late Thursday, Charles stopped in my office as I prepared to leave for the day.

"Hey, I need your help." He took a chair across from me, sitting ramrod straight despite how tired he must have been. "I got a call earlier this week. A CEO of a technology company—they make some kind of hardware—called me about lucid dreaming. He wants me to consult with him. Help set up a sleep lab in his organization."

"Wow."

"Yeah. Clearly, I don't have time to do it. I told the guy I was flattered, but no. As it turns out, he knows Max."

"Oh no." I knew where this was going. As board chair, Max

was demanding, imperious, and sometimes manipulative. You didn't want to be on his bad side.

"You guessed it. Apparently, Max pretty much promised the guy. When I said no, Max talked to Dad, and Dad asked me to help the guy out."

"*Great* use of your time. All right, I can set up the accounting part of it. No problem."

"There's a bigger issue: This guy's business is in Atlanta, so I'm flying out Monday."

"Oh, you gotta be kidding. What is Dad thinking?"

"Dad didn't know about the location. I told the guy that after this first on-site trip I'll provide everything else remotely, and that's nonnegotiable. Melody will run the lab, but can you make sure nothing slows down? We can't lose any time."

"Of course, but why me? What about Kimberly?"

"I'm promoting her. I'll be announcing it in the morning."

"Oh, that's a surprise. But good for her. What's she going to be doing?"

"Heading up IT. We need to make sure all our systems are FDA-compliant so they can support production once Alvee is complete. She's worked in IT before, she's a stickler for details, so she's the right person for the job. And she's agreed to do it for a modest increase, less than two percent."

"That's great. It would cost a lot more to hire someone new."

"She's moving downstairs right away, so you can expect IT will tighten up considerably. Until I backfill her in engineering, I'll still be working closely with the team. And since I'll be gone next week—"

"No problem. Got you covered."

"Just keep things moving."

"Oh no." Flashing red and blue lights met me as I rounded the corner into our parking lot on the following Wednesday afternoon. My mind went to the worst possible scenario: active shooter. Then I saw a few employees milling near the front door and counted a single ambulance and patrol car. I relaxed a little —whatever was happening, the building was not in lockdown. I rushed into the lobby, where police and EMTs stood, talking with a few employees. In a corner, Kimberly spoke to an officer.

I rushed over. "Kimberly, what's happened? What's going on?"

"Neddy, it's Ryan. He had a heart attack, we think."

"Oh my God. Is he okay?"

"He's conscious. They're treating him upstairs in the sleep lab."

"I'm Neddy Emory," I told the officer. "I'm the CFO. What do you need from us?"

"Were you a witness to any of this?" the officer asked.

"What? Witness?"

"Were you here when the gentleman became sickened?"

"No. I was at lunch."

"Okay. He appears to have suffered a cardiac event. We're doing routine follow-up. You may want to speak to the EMTs, but he'll most likely be transported to Laguna Hospital."

I turned to Kimberly. "Has anyone contacted Ryan's family?"

"Yes, Leni called. His wife is on the way."

"Why didn't someone call me?"

"I asked Melody to, didn't she?" Before I answered, the elevator opened. Ryan was wheeled out on a gurney by three EMTs. Sitting upright, wearing an oxygen mask with an IV in his right arm, he was pale but alert. Stevie and Tim emerged from the stairwell and joined the escort out the front door and into the waiting ambulance.

"Do you want me to go with him to the hospital?" Kimberly asked.

"Yes, that would be great. I'd go, but you're closer to Ryan— he'll appreciate having you there. Please call me and let me know his status." She walked quickly toward the entrance. "As soon as you hear anything," I called after her. Several employees stood talking in low voices, looking worried. I walked over to them.

"Thank you all, for your concern about Ryan. Kimberly headed to the hospital, and she'll keep us updated. Are you all okay? Everyone doing all right?" They nodded, and a few thanked me. "Let me know if you need anything. I'll send out an email with an update on Ryan as soon as I hear anything. Thanks, everyone."

One of the EMTs came into the lobby and spoke to the police officer I'd met earlier, then approached me.

"I understand you're the manager here?" He was tall, with dark, serious eyes and a no-nonsense manner.

"I'm Neddy Emory, the CFO of the company. My brother, Charles, is the CEO. He's out of town."

"Okay. I'm Captain Cassaday. Can we speak privately?"

"Of course. My office is—"

"Let's go upstairs to the place where Mr. Belkey had his symptoms. I want to show you something I saw up there." We took the elevator to the third floor. During the ride, I peppered him with questions about Ryan's condition. His answers were general, lacking the specificity I sought. I must have looked frustrated.

"Look, Mr. Belkey is conscious. That's very good. No one thinks he lost consciousness during the cardiac event. His vital signs are good, and he isn't in pain. So they'll check him out at the hospital. I wouldn't worry too much. But—"

"But what? What do you want to show me?"

We'd reached the empty sleep lab. "I'll get to that, but first, why all the monitoring equipment in here?"

I explained we were a medical device developer and gave an overview of the dream program.

"So your employees sleep in here? All of them?"

"Oh no, only our research team. It's an unusual way to innovate, but we've been using it for over two years. We're near completion of a treatment for some very nasty diseases. And it's in great part because of what happens in this room."

He surveyed the room with a mix of confusion and skepticism on his face. "I guess it explains why Mr. Belkey was asleep and hooked up to all this…" He motioned to the monitoring equipment. "Which was good because we have a readout on his heart rate and pulse. We can see exactly what occurred and when."

"He's normally in here, sleeping for only a couple hours a day. I guess it's a blessing this happened when it did."

"Yeah. When my colleagues were working on him, I noticed more monitors with printouts. I guess Mr. Belkey wasn't alone in the lab?"

"No. Three other colleagues. Plus a lab assistant."

"So Mr. Belkey slept here." He pointed to Ryan's cot. "And the other three"—he walked across the room—"would have been here, here, and—"

"Yes." I was impatient at the forensic nature of his questions. "Why is this important?"

"A strange coincidence." He tore off the reports from the monitoring stations, then walked to where I stood and showed me the EKG printouts, pointing to a series of jagged lines representing the record of each heart rate.

"Okay… I can't read these. I'm not a doctor. What do you mean by coincidence?"

"Mr. Belkey had an actual cardiac event, what looks to be an infarction. Heart attack. But the EKGs from the other three individuals show they were also experiencing abnormal rhythms."

"What?"

"No one else reported feeling sick. They may have been unaware since they were sleeping. But it seems unlikely this is a coincidence."

"I'm sorry, I don't understand."

"I studied the other EKGs as I waited for my team to finish up with Mr. Belkey. It's odd. So you'll want to—"

"Are you sure?"

"I can tell by the printouts. Look, whoever oversees this needs to be aware something's going on. Your dream program may be problematic."

"Thank you. I was not at all aware of this. We'll get to the bottom of it, I assure you. My brother is a doctor. He'll be on top of this."

"Okay, now you know. Good luck with your research."

I shook with fury after he left. Where the hell was Melody?

I left a terse message for Melody, telling her to call me immediately. I then called Charles. As soon as he answered, I blurted out the story, how I had learned of the emergency upon arriving at the office after lunch, what the EMT had opined. "And Melody didn't monitor their heart rates, putting everyone at risk. If it weren't for the head of the EMT team, we would never know they were all experiencing irregular heartbeats. Charles, something's not right."

"Slow down. How's Ryan?"

"Kimberly is at the hospital checking on him. The EMT seemed to think all signs were positive—he was conscious, receiving oxygen."

"Okay." A pause. "Thank God."

"We have to stop using the sleep lab until we have this resolved."

"Hold on. The elevated heart rates—that's normal."

"Not according to the EMT."

"Neddy, I don't have the printouts in front of me, but if they show what I think, this has happened before. It's not uncommon during vivid dreaming. Look, I'm heading into a meeting. Anything you need me to do immediately?"

"I don't know. I'm worried about Ryan. And Alex is still an unknown. What are we gonna do? Melody is nowhere to be found."

"Neddy, Alex's disorientation has nothing to do with Ryan. And certainly his violent behavior is completely unrelated."

"I guess so. I don't know. I'm not thinking straight."

"I'll call you as soon as I'm done. But if you need to interrupt me, I'll keep my phone on. Okay? And have Melody send me copies of the EKG printouts."

"If I can find her!"

"Neddy, go in your office, shut the door, sit down for a few minutes, and breathe. Don't think about anything else except the inhales and exhales, like I taught you."

"I'm okay."

"I know you are. I trust you, but do it anyway. You'll feel more centered."

As soon as I ended the call, Melody walked into the lab. She glanced at me and then began tidying up. She wore an old Tom Petty and the Heartbreakers T-shirt with an orange heart-shaped guitar on the front over a pair of thin black leggings, which, when she bent over to pick up the debris left by the EMTs, didn't quite conceal the light-colored panties underneath. Ignoring me, she whistled to herself and reset the monitors. I took a deep breath, reminded myself to stay calm, and stood up.

"Melody, were you in the lab when Ryan got sick?"

"Yeah." She kept her attention on the monitoring equipment, punching in codes on each and making notations.

"Can you please *stop* for a moment? I'm trying to figure out what happened here."

She went to a workstation and sat down, facing me with a blank expression.

"Were you monitoring the teams' cardiac printouts?" I asked.

"Yes, like I always do." Her tone enraged me, but her eyes held no defiance.

I pushed down the impulse to yell. "Did you notice irregularities? Because the EMT said all four had irregular heart rates." I held out the printouts toward her. "All four were abnormal, not just Ryan's."

"I saw them." Melody did not take the printouts, barely glancing at them.

"And what did you— What type of SOP do we have set up for emergencies, or when the unexpected happens?"

"SOP?"

"Standard Operating Procedure." Was she stonewalling me?

"Yeah, okay. Well, this wasn't unusual."

"Pardon?"

"It happens a lot. Charles knows about it." Melody blinked several times, then looked down.

My jaw clenched. "But this time, someone had an actual heart attack. Which is not normal, wouldn't you agree?"

She shrugged.

I noticed her right leg jiggling up and down. I thought briefly of the female investor we'd met three weeks ago with the same tic, and the anxiety at our slow progress in securing funding heightened my unease. I needed to keep my worry in check.

I spoke slowly, enunciating each word. "Melody, when did you realize the situation was more serious? When did you call 911?"

"When Ryan woke up. He was short of breath, he had trouble sitting up and, uh, said he felt like he'd been punched hard in the chest."

"Okay. It's good you didn't delay."

"I looked at his printout and it was way off. So I called emergency. Then I called Kimberly."

I stared again at the squiggly, cone-shaped lines on the printouts. While the meaning was indecipherable, the graph representing the final minutes of Ryan's sleep did appear different than the previous hour of sleep. I had no choice but to assume

Melody had followed protocol. Still, I was unnerved at the lack of reaction or affect.

"One more question, Melody. Why didn't you call me? I would have come right away."

"I texted Charles."

I stared at her. Charles was two thousand miles away, in Atlanta. "Did you speak with him?"

"No. He didn't respond."

"So then why didn't you text me?" I fought again to keep my rage at bay.

"I thought Kimberly already had."

Was it possible the two had crossed wires, and each thought the other had texted me? Or had I misunderstood Kimberly? No, I didn't believe that. Melody had lied. I decided to bring my concerns to Charles. No matter what Melody had done or not done, Charles was responsible for the program and the health of the engineers. I relayed Charles's message, requesting the records for the team, and walked out.

Back in my office, I plopped in my chair, trying to empty my mind while simultaneously processing what had happened in the lab that afternoon.

I sent a text to Kimberly:

Any word?

The response came within five minutes:

He's stable. Doctor says he's in good shape but will need to take it easy for a while. Family here

"Thank God," I said out loud. My email pinged with a message from Leni in our HR department, requesting information on Ryan, including whether his condition was work-related. I responded with a carefully worded answer, indicating we didn't know enough yet. I'd begun to lose confidence in the safety of the dream program, but not to the point where I wanted HR to initiate a worker's comp claim.

As it turned out, my attention was immediately drawn to another call.

"Danny's in the hospital," my father said as soon as I answered.

———

I found my parents in the waiting room of the intensive care unit at UCLA Medical Center. My dad was on the phone with Charles, who was about to board a plane home. Mom walked toward me.

"What happened? How is he?"

"He's had a seizure. Worse than the last one."

Overnight she'd aged ten years, eyes rimmed in red, face drawn.

"Okay, okay." I hugged her. "Is he conscious?"

"He wasn't when the ambulance arrived, but the doctors were able to bring him around. He—" She stopped talking and sobbed. I held on to her, and then Dad wrapped us both in his big arms.

"Charles will catch a plane in thirty minutes." Dad let go of us. "He'll be home later tonight. Neddy, can you get him at the airport? He'll want to come straight here."

"Sure, Dad. When did you last speak with the doctor?"

"Dr. Samson is on his way in. The attending's stabilized him." Though Daniel had been cared for by an army of specialists over the years, we trusted Dr. Samson, our long-time family internist, to stay on top of the big picture. I felt better knowing he was en route; at least we'd be getting an assessment of Daniel's condition from someone who knew his illness and his history intimately.

We found the nurse's station and were allowed a five-minute visit.

Daniel's ICU room was dark, and my eyes took a minute to adjust. He dozed under a white blanket, which made his skin appear even more pale. His lips were chapped, large shards of skin hanging from them. Several monitors beeped and whirred. Electrodes were attached to his head and his chest, and he had an IV drip in his arm. We surrounded the bed. Mom leaned down and kissed his forehead. He stirred and opened his eyes.

"Hey," he murmured.

"Hi, darling." Mom squeezed his hand.

"Hey, buddy," Dad said. I waved at him.

"Dr. Samson's on his way. They're giving you fluids—you're dehydrated." Mom never took her eyes off Daniel, who gave a tiny nod.

"Just rest," Dad said.

"Yes, go to sleep. We'll be right outside." I turned toward the door.

"Sorry to be such a pain," he mumbled behind me. I turned to reassure him, but he'd closed his eyes again.

I'd held myself together all day, for my employees, for Charles, for my family. But hearing Daniel apologize as if his illness were an inconvenience he'd thrust on us—that was when I lost it. Dad followed me out and guided me to a chair in the waiting area, where I sobbed, doubled over.

"Don't cry, honey, please. It only makes things worse."

SEVEN

DAD WENT with me to the airport, making it impossible to query Charles about all the odd events surrounding Ryan's cardiac episode. I dropped the two of them at the hospital and went home. Waldo needed a walk, so I shoved my fatigue down and went out, running into Mrs. Gladstone in the parking area. She chattered nonstop about the weather and the latest headlines, expressing dismay at what she called the "lack of choices" in an upcoming local election. Normally I cut these encounters short, but listening to her mundane concerns distracted me from my heavy heart.

Later in the kitchen of my condo, I prepared Waldo's dinner and then opened the fridge, staring at its contents: rice, sliced tomatoes, and a scary-looking zucchini. I tossed the squishy vegetable, washed my hands, and closed the door. "I'm not hungry anyway," I said to the dog. I turned the teakettle on low, headed out to my balcony, sank onto my chaise lounge, and listened to the banter of my neighbors on their nearby deck as they played a card game. I checked my social media feeds until the teakettle screamed. In the kitchen I grabbed a bag of chips and considered the tea bag assortment.

"What the hell." I poured a glass of chardonnay instead and

sat in front of the TV. After an hour, I started nodding off. I sent a message to Charles for an update on Daniel. When he hadn't responded in fifteen minutes, I stopped fighting sleep and went to bed.

"We need to suspend the dream program," I said to Charles the moment he arrived in the lab the next morning. I'd texted when I'd woken at five thirty and asked him to meet me as early as possible. "There's something going on with heart rates when the engineers are dreaming, and I'm worried we'll have another incident like Ryan's. We can't—"

"Wait, Neddy. I know what happened with Ryan upset you, upset everyone. But it's not indicative of broader risk to the group as a whole."

"That's not what the EMT indicated."

"I'm guessing the EMT is not a doctor, much less a cardiologist. What he noticed was above the norm, yes, but not for active dreaming, not to mention lucid dreaming, where the sleeper is aware and directing the show, so to speak. The dreamscape can get very exciting." Charles opened his laptop and pulled up the EKG reports from the day before, then turned the device toward me.

I stared at the same graphs I'd seen yesterday, plus pie charts and column upon column of numbers.

"Dream periods are characterized—for all of us—by increases in cardiac activity. It's normal. And you can see"—he pointed at each engineer's individual EKG—"all have similar increases during cycles of sleep. And as we go back in time..." He scrolled through several months in the records. "The graphs are essentially the same."

There were peaks and valleys in each graph, but these were meaningless to me. With months and months of records, I had to assume if there had been nuances that spelled trouble, Charles would have made adjustments.

"And you didn't see anything in all of Ryan's prior EKGs that concerned you?"

"No, I didn't. There's no doubt he had a cardiac event yesterday." He looked again at Ryan's report. "But nothing prior."

"Okay, but it seems to be such a weird coincidence. Why all of a sudden are these things happening?"

"If we knew when heart attacks were going to happen, we'd save a lot more lives. Look, I think this incident upset you more than you realize, and then Daniel's situation piled on the stress."

"It's not only yesterday, Charles. After the audit I felt very comfortable with the dream program. But now, more than half the team has had some kind of unexpected illness—Stevie and her paralysis, Alex and his violent breakdown, and now Ryan."

He took my hand and looked at me, his gaze reassuring. "Stevie has epilepsy. Ryan had a cardiac event, all too common in our culture, and Alex… Well, we may never know what triggered his behavior. You said yourself you think he has a history with his wife. Don't you see, Neddy, these things *are not* related."

"Except they're all happening to participants in an unusual experiment."

"An unusual method of *research*. And remember, all agreed to participate."

"That's another thing, Charles. What happens if the engineers get spooked? This will all come to a grinding halt and where will we be then? Shouldn't we have a contingency plan for research? Something that doesn't involve dreaming?"

"There is a contingency plan." He closed his laptop and stood up. "Traditional research. But we won't be needing it, I assure you."

"Okay. Stevie, I get. Alex, who knows? But I'm still worried about Ryan."

"Let's go see him."

"Now?"

"Yes, right now. I want to see him too."

During the ride to the hospital, I thought about what Charles had said and remembered my call with Dr. Jorgensen. Nothing had come up about heart rates during lucid dreaming. I considered the pros and cons of calling her again to confirm what Charles had assured me. Did doing so mean I distrusted my brother? But I decided it wasn't necessary after seeing Ryan.

"I've been taking medication for high blood pressure and arrhythmia for about five years now," he told us. "And watching what I eat, too, so I'm kinda surprised this happened."

"I'm just thankful to Jesus you're still here," his wife, Robin, drawled from a corner chair. "The whole church is praying for you, hon."

"As are we," Charles smiled. "The whole Angiras family."

"The doc says I should be able to go home in a coupla days. And after a week or so I can work. Which I gotta do, cause we're waitin' on the adoption to be finalized, and that can't happen if I'm laid up."

"Oh, you're adopting a baby?" I was excited. Finally, some good news.

"Wow! Fantastic." Charles smiled again.

"You're gonna be fine, Ry." Robin blew him a kiss.

As we left the medical center Charles patted me on the back. "Okay. So, you see? Ryan was at risk for heart attack due to genetics."

He was smiling. But I couldn't help thinking that Ryan's predisposition to heart problems was nothing to feel good about.

"Do we—*did* we have the engineers complete a health history and an exam when the dream program started?"

I saw a flash of annoyance in his eyes. Then his smile returned.

"Of course. And each signed a release."

"And did Ryan's family's heart history get noted?"

"Melody knows. If Ryan reported it, then yes. Neddy, you're done with your audit, remember?"

"Not quite. I haven't observed a sleep session yet. We agreed to do that."

"You're right. There hasn't been a good time."

"I think we should make the time."

He shrugged. "Let me figure out a day in the next couple of weeks."

"And since we know about Ryan's history, shouldn't he be excluded from future sleep sessions?"

"No. Why should he? Did you not understand my explanation?"

"Because of the increase in heart activity of lucid dreamers. We know he's at risk, so shouldn't we move him off the sleep portion of the research?"

"Not necessary."

"Why?"

"The increases in heart activity during lucid sleep are no greater than what he might experience doing, I don't know, a brisk walk, or gardening, or playing with his dog. He's not running a marathon, Neddy."

"Aren't you worried though?"

"No, but I promise to keep careful watch on his rhythms."

"And will you be reviewing the health histories each submitted to be sure there are no more surprises?"

"I'll have Melody review them."

"Speaking of Melody, that's another discussion we need to have." We'd reached the car and he climbed in, turning the ignition.

"Wait. Let's talk about Melody and yesterday before we get on the road."

"If you insist." He turned off the car.

"Look, I realize she's loyal to you, but I suspect Melody withheld information from me. Yesterday, when I was at lunch and all hell broke loose, no one contacted me. I asked Kimberly why and she told me she'd instructed Melody to call me. When I asked Melody, *she* said the exact opposite—she thought Kimberly was calling."

"A misunderstanding in the heat of chaos."

"Maybe. But more disturbing, Melody showed no emotion at all. Until after Ryan went to the hospital, she wasn't even around. And when she came back, after I talked to you, it was like nothing out of the ordinary had happened. She just went about tidying up the place."

"Melody sometimes appears elusive, but she's good at what she does. I have faith in her." He angled the rearview mirror, met his own eyes, then straightened it again.

"I don't." I followed his gaze. "I think you should keep closer tabs on what she does and where she goes."

He laughed. "Oh wow! She's harmless, have no doubt."

"She's not cooperative. Not with me. When I questioned her yesterday, she provided the absolute minimal amount of information without volunteering any context or details."

"I'll have her look at the engineers' health records and if there's anything amiss, she'll let me know." Charles reached over and squeezed my hand. "Thanks for bearing all this. You were a great help while I was away. And now stop thinking about Melody. And for God's sake, stop worrying about the engineers."

Charles never mentioned the engineers' health histories again, and over the next week I wasn't able to follow up. My attention was on our dwindling finances. Though Alvee promised to be lucrative once approved and sold, until it was over the finish line, our cash flow was going in one direction: out the door.

Charles and Max had followed up with Frank Brazil, taking him to lunch and providing detailed engineering drawings of Alvee and a final set of projections, but the sage investor ultimately declined to fund us when we couldn't put Alex in front of him.

Max and I had met with Carollyn and her boss, securing an extension on our line of credit, and Charles was holding off on hiring a replacement for Kimberly, taking over managing the engineers directly. But those tactics were only going to take us so far.

Thursday afternoon I prepared a report for an important finance meeting with the board. I settled in at my desk with a cup of coffee for one last look at the presentation I'd fussed over all week. Over-preparing for these meetings had become standard for me. Two years ago, when Charles had been looking to hire a CFO, he bucked convention—and the board—by choosing me. They disliked the fact that I'd worked at very large companies in the past and argued for someone with life science experience. Even my father was on the fence, torn between supporting his children or his friends on the board, who'd provided a significant portion of the start-up costs.

But Charles had insisted. "Money is money," he'd told them. "Whether you're counting dollars for a widget-maker or a nuclear power plant. Neddy can learn the business along the way. And there's no one who will work harder to help us develop this product." Charles had prevailed and I was hired. And he was right, being part of a company working toward a life-saving therapy for Daniel and others gave me a motivation I'd never experienced before. And the resolve to prove the board wrong. Not only was I capable, but I was also an asset. Prior to each interaction with them, I crammed as if I was taking my CPA exam all over again.

The books were in good shape. The payables were straight forward, with one exception: Another handwritten check to Ron Dorsey, the consultant Charles retained, had cleared the bank the day before. But this time the payment was fifteen hundred dollars, almost double the prior amount. I pulled up the invoice, noting the description "consulting services" followed by three dates. Two of the three were days when Charles was in Atlanta helping Max's friend.

I dialed Charles, reaching Lupe, who said he was in the sleep lab and didn't want to be disturbed.

"He'll see you at the meeting. Unless you want me to interrupt him?"

I glanced at my watch. We had an hour. If he didn't surface before we started, I'd be unprepared should the board ask about Dorsey's payments. I decided to hedge my bet another way.

"No, Lupe, don't bother. But if you see him before the meeting starts, please ask him to call me."

I picked up my phone, hesitated for a moment, then called the phone number on the invoice. Reaching the voicemail of Dorsey, I left a message, detailing my question on the dates and the services and requesting a return call ASAP.

I finished reviewing the rest of the numbers and edited my notes. I was ready, save for the outstanding information about Dorsey's invoices.

An email arrived from Kimberly, announcing a series of mandatory IT compliance training modules for all employees. With a bit of time to spare, I clicked on the link, figuring I'd knock them out before the meeting started. But there were ten modules, each with an estimated completion time of ten to fifteen minutes.

"No way I'm doing that."

Instead, I called my father to check on Daniel, who had been moved from the ICU to a regular room three days before. Dad answered, sounding animated.

"He'll be released this afternoon." I heard the voices of nurses and technicians in the background. "We have to watch him. He's on a different… What's it called, Myra?"

"Anti-seizure," I heard my mother say.

"Yeah, a different anti-seizure medicine. Stronger. But this one has a lot of nasty side effects."

"Like what."

"Nausea, stomach upsets, maybe even ulcers. Has to be monitored."

"Okay." Another layer of complication in Daniel's care. "Maybe we should consider a home health aide. If even for a few hours a day. I can pay for it."

"No. We can take care of him."

"Dad, let's try for a few weeks, until he's settled in with the new meds. It doesn't have to be forever."

"No."

I rubbed my forehead. "When are you taking him home?" I asked.

"This afternoon sometime. I'll call you." The line went dead. I shook off the frustration, picked up my laptop, and headed upstairs to the conference room.

"So, as you can see, we've kept our year-to-date expenses below plan." I switched to the final slide in my presentation as the group listened, some jotting notes. "And remember, those expense projections were eight percent below last year's actuals. So we've netted a ten percent reduction in expenses over last year."

"And you feel you've done everything you can on costs?" Phil Harris, our board secretary asked.

"I do. Unless we start laying people off."

"We won't do that." Charles was emphatic.

"We're all burning the candle at both ends as it is," I said.

"And the additional line of credit," Max said, flipping through his notebook, "is a cushion we're not using at the moment."

"Correct. We're not going to utilize anything beyond the old limit on operating expenses."

"I convinced the bank to increase the credit amount and extend the life of the loan," Max boasted. "But only as a contingency. I don't want to have to scramble if we have a significant delay or get hit with some other unforeseen expenditure."

He left out the fact that I'd set up the bank meeting and we'd both made our case to the lenders.

The board asked a few follow-up questions before Max spoke again.

"I'm satisfied expenses are where we need them, but there's still no revenue stream." Max looked at the others. "Unless one of us wants to loan another half million or so in operating funds, and personally I'm not prepared to do that, I suggest we consider a longer-term strategy. We've been getting some attention from the press, and the exploratory conversations Charles netted at the biotech conference have led to plausible interest from a couple of life science firms looking to grow. On the surface, they look promising. One is a pharmaceutical firm working in pulmonary fibrosis. The other is a device company looking to expand its portfolio. Both think Alvee is worth a look."

"It will be a merger of equals, not a takeover," Charles interjected. "We'll make sure of that. What do you all think?"

"Look, in some ways, this is always where we were headed," Phil said. "Maybe it's a little earlier than we thought, but we need cash. How does your father feel about it, Charles?"

"He's agreeable with the caveat it speeds things up. He doesn't want to get bogged down in a complicated deal at the expense of getting Alvee over the finish line. None of us do. Max, let's you and I make a few calls and get the ball rolling."

"Hold on." Phil held up his hand. "I want to hear what Neddy has to say."

I couldn't help myself. "I thought you'd never ask."

The men exchanged glances.

Charles looked embarrassed. "Sorry, Neddy." He tented his hands and bowed his head slightly.

"Of course we want to hear what you have to say," Max sputtered. "Go ahead."

"Conceptually, it makes sense. It's a lot of work for everyone, but I've been involved in mergers before, of course on a much larger scale—"

"This won't be complicated." Max tapped his pen against his leg.

I looked at him, unsmiling. "No, not as complicated. I can help focus on the critical issues and avoid the time wasters and the time bombs. But mergers almost always take longer than you think. Because the devil is in the details, of course—"

"If we get to an agreement in principle, then you can map out a project plan and timing." Max gathered up his phone and papers.

"None of the legal wrangling will slow down the research team," Charles said.

"As long as we don't run out of money," Phil said wryly.

Max stood. "Let's get this started."

Given the focus on a potential merger, no one questioned the Dorsey payments, so after the meeting, I stopped Charles.

"How come this guy billed for the days you were in Atlanta last week? Is he helping you with the Atlanta firm?" We turned down the corridor toward the elevator. "If he's doing work for you on behalf of them, we should be passing those costs along."

"No, no. He's got nothing to do with Atlanta."

"Was he working with you on personal stuff? Is Dorsey your therapist, Charles?"

He laughed—genuine, surprised mirth.

I cocked my head.

"Sorry. It's so funny, the thought of Ron being a therapist."

"Look, I don't care. But if he is providing…personal coaching, it shouldn't be paid for by the company."

"No. Look, he's not really a consultant. Sometimes I think of him that way. He's a chemist. And he's discovered an interesting compound—a potential drug we may want to develop once we're done with the scope."

"And?"

"I didn't want to make a big deal of this with money being so tight, but I want the right of first refusal on his compound. So I decided to pay Ron to maintain it, and in exchange he won't sell to somebody else, until we opt out. We'll need another development project in the pipeline, Neddy. It makes Angiras a more attractive partner for a merger and keeps the playing field level. And once Alvee is launched, we'll have our next project already in the works."

We'd reached the elevator. "Okay, but wait. Why have the payments gone up so much in the last few weeks?"

He pushed the down arrow for me, then turned away and walked toward his own office. "I think the lease on his lab came due and he was hit with a rent increase. I'll make sure there's no further increases, okay?" He disappeared behind his door before I could respond.

Back in my office, I replied to routine emails, then noticed the blinking light on my landline. A voicemail had come in. I punched in my password and listened.

"Hey, Charles, it's Ron. Uh, somebody from your office—some girl—left a message asking about the latest invoice. I guess she's from your accounting department. Look, I told you it would be higher once we changed the formulation. I also purchased a case of those films you said to get. BioGrad doesn't sell them in less than a case. So unless you want me to do something different, that's why there's an increase."

I heard the sound of shuffling paper and then Dorsey's voice again.

"Uh, her name is Nellie something—didn't write down the last name. I left my phone in the truck, otherwise I'd have her number. So, yeah, just call me if you need to."

I rolled my eyes as I started to forward the message to Charles.

But then a text arrived from him:

> Spoke to Dorsey-- As I suspected his rent
> went up so he's passing a portion along to us.
> LMK if ?s

I tried to reconcile the two explanations. No matter how I looked at it, Dorsey's rang truer.

Instead of forwarding the voicemail, I went looking for Ron Dorsey online again, this time adding the search terms "chemist" and "pharmaceutical." I found an article from 2012 in which Dorsey was mentioned as a contributor, his name preceded by several PhD-level coauthors. Most of the content was indecipherable, full of technical chemistry jargon and illustrated with charts, graphs, and formulas. The bottom of the article contained a brief bio of Dorsey, and a chill went through me as I read it:

> Ronald Dorsey, BS, is a chemical analyst at Paramount Pharmaceuticals. This is his first contribution to the Journal.

I blinked and reread the bio, then checked the date. The article had been written during the period when Charles headed Paramount. So why hadn't he mentioned Dorsey used to work for him? And where did Dorsey work now? What "compound" was he maintaining for us?

After searching another few minutes, I hadn't found any indication of current employment for Dorsey. Then I searched Paramount Pharmaceuticals. Many results came up, including a defunct website, several articles about Charles I had already seen, and others about the company itself, its funding, and its then-promising new drug candidate, something called Lutense. I scanned through several of these before I found a brief article in a trade journal related to the drug's review by the FDA—specifically, the drug had not passed FDA scrutiny in its phase two trial. Although no reason was included, this was consistent with what Charles had said: The would-be hypertension drug had not shown sufficient results to warrant additional development. Other, existing drugs worked better. Lutense had come to an end, and with it, Paramount.

I thought I'd wasted a good hour, when I spotted an FDA report on the Lutense trial. The paper was lengthy, and like the previous article, full of scientific terms. But my eyes landed on a section of the report near the end, under the subhead "Side Effects." More technical narrative was followed by three bulleted items. I enlarged the image on my screen, my eyes no longer wanting to focus. It read:

- 12% of study participants reported mouth dryness.
- 14% of study participants reported an increase in urination frequency and volume.
- 60% of study participants reported vivid dreaming.

I stared at the screen, not moving, not breathing. A shadow moved in front of me, and I jumped. Charles stood in my doorway.

"You look like you've seen a ghost. What the heck are you reading? And why are your lights off?" He laughed. "That's more my MO than yours."

I stared at him. "Uh, yeah, my eyes were getting tired."

"Right. Did you receive my text about Dorsey's bill?"

"Yes, but I also have a message from him in my voicemail, which was intended for you."

"Damn."

"Lupe hasn't been able to get Dial by Name fixed, I gather."

"She tried. But it's an inexpensive system tied to our inexpensive landline that comes with the building. We can't give up the landline just yet, but we also can't afford to upgrade."

"Anyway, his explanation is different from yours. So I'm confused."

Charles crossed his arms. "What did he say in his message?"

"Nothing about rent increase."

"That's odd. Because I spoke to him an hour ago and he definitely had one."

I kept my eyes on Charles, but he didn't elaborate. I considered telling him what I'd discovered about Lutense and lucid dreaming but decided to give him one more chance to volunteer details. "Look, I'll forward Dorsey's voicemail to you, but what's going on with this guy? He sounds like a doofus."

Charles turned and walked toward the window. A flush of red crawled up the back of his neck. "As I said, he's maintaining a compound we started developing at Paramount. We were targeting hypertension and unfortunately it didn't really work on that, but it did show some interesting activity, including increases in dreaming. Hence the inspiration for what we're doing now."

I knew this already, but why all the secrecy? "Please tell me you haven't been buying this drug from him and using it on the team?"

He jerked away from the window, frowning.

"No, no, no. God, Neddy. First of all, it's not a drug. It never got that far. But it *could* be further developed, perhaps for psychological or neurological treatments."

He was quiet for a moment before he continued. "Second, I tried Lutense to stimulate my own lucid dreams, but that was more than two years ago, before we hired the engineers. No one else received it. Ever."

"What? That seems dangerous, Charles. Why?"

"To speed things up, of course. In case you haven't noticed, Daniel's not getting any better."

"That's uncalled for."

"Look, I'm sorry. I know we're on the same team. Lutense has a perfectly fine safety profile. No adverse events were ever reported in clinical trials. I wasn't putting myself at risk."

"Why did you stop?"

"It wasn't helping."

I nodded, relieved. But then a terrible thought struck me. "How do you know Melody didn't put Lutense in the tea in some misguided attempt to try to speed things up? She worked at Paramount too. She knows its side effects."

He bit his lip, shook his head, and walked toward the door. "Impossible. We haven't had any Lutense on site since before we hired the engineers."

"But what if she'd put something *else* into the tea?"

He laughed. "Okay! *What* in the world do you think she put in it, Neddy? Final answer."

"I don't know, maybe antihistamines—they make some people have crazy dreams. Melatonin? I read about it."

He laughed again.

"Melody is dedicated to you, and to your success, Charles. She could be doing the wrong thing for the right reasons. And it explains the weird smell and taste the engineers reported—*all of them* talked about the gross tea."

He sighed and shook his head.

"I *still* don't trust Melody, Charles. Haven't since Ryan's heart attack."

"You're done with your audit, remember?"

"You keep saying that, but I'm not. You were supposed to arrange an observation of a sleep session for me this week. And seriously, we did promise the team we'd do an observation."

"I think we can blow it off. Too much to do, and the engineers no longer—"

"*No*, Charles. It's a loose end for me and it's disrespectful to the team. We've put it off long enough."

He turned to face me. "Okay. Tomorrow Max and I are

meeting with a company called Salton-Winstrom. They look to be a pretty good fit for us. So I need you to start preparing for a financial evaluation as early as next week, if all goes well."

"Really? We're that far along?"

"I think so. Max is pushing ahead, and we need to be ready."

"That sounds awesome." It also meant a lot more work. But if we made a merger happen quickly, we'd be able to hire more people and speed up the development of Alvee.

"Once you get past the due diligence, your time will be more freed up and we'll arrange an observation."

"I'm going to hold you to that."

"Don't I know it." He closed the door and left me alone.

EIGHT

"SORRY I'M LATE, GIRLS," I rushed to the table where Mindy and Carollyn sat, already sipping their cocktails as a waiter hovered.

"Heeere's our friend," Mindy said to the waiter, who greeted me and left to get a menu.

"What kept you?" Carollyn sounded more annoyed than I knew she was.

"Work. What else."

"You need more help. When are you guys going to hire?"

"Soon." The waiter came and took my drink order, an Old Fashioned. "We had a big finance meeting this afternoon. Before that I had a call from my dad. Daniel's been released from the hospital."

"Oh, some good news," Carollyn said.

"I'm trying to get my parents to hire a part-time aide to help with his care. So far, they've resisted."

"Isn't that expensive?" asked Mindy.

The waiter arrived with my drink.

"Yeah, but Charles and I can only be there sporadically to help—too much going on at the company."

"You've got a lot on your plate, girl," Mindy said. "Drink up."

"Ooh, this is delicious." I took another, smaller sip. "Carollyn, it's even better than the ones we had last week."

"Wait, you guys went out for drinks without me?" Mindy whined.

"It was business." Carollyn waved her hand. "Neddy and her board chair came to our office for discussions about their account. Afterward, he and my boss decided to get a drink and pretty much dragged us along."

"Dragged is the right word. I would rather not go drinking with Max if I can help it. By the way, thank you again, Carollyn, for advocating for us. The whole conversation was seamless."

Carollyn laughed. "Oh, you don't know the half of it."

"Really, did you have to twist arms?" I turned to Mindy to explain. "We asked for a credit extension and Carollyn came through."

"She's such a good friend," Mindy purred.

"Oh, you guys won't believe this," Carollyn giggled. "You know, Max made a big pitch about how Angiras was on the verge of *the* research innovation of the century." She air quoted. "'Its brilliant leadership will change the way medical devices get created in this country.' On and on."

"He was referring to himself and Charles," I corrected. "Max does *not* think I'm brilliant."

Carollyn smirked. "A good ole boy if there ever was one. And my boss, Peter, is… Well, let's just say he and Max had a grand time massaging one another's egos. They both see the world through the same outdated lens."

Mindy laughed.

"Anyway, Neddy, the thing is, Max thought he'd finessed a huge concession from us."

"And?"

"And Peter let him believe it. Of course. Like I said, gotta feed each other's egos. But the truth is…" She leaned in close and lowered her voice. "The *real* reason Peter extended the loan is because we don't want to go to *our* board and tell them yet another one of our small business customers is nearing default. They'd flip."

"You are kidding me!" I laughed.

"I'm not." Carollyn brushed away tears of laughter.

"Oh my God, Carollyn! Is the bank in trouble?" Mindy asked.

"No, no," she gasped. "We're the small business side of things. The parent bank has plenty of assets. But the board is watching our unit closely because it's new. So we extended the Angiras loan and voila! Everybody's happy."

"And Max and Peter are heroes," I laughed. "Cheers!"

———

"C minus. That's how I'd rate the Angiras financial picture. It's not acceptable as far as I'm concerned."

I looked straight ahead at Dennis DuPres, the CFO of Salton-Winstrom. I wasn't going to let him intimidate me. I'd sat in the conference room on the twenty-third floor of their downtown Los Angeles suite all week, reviewing financial reports they'd provided as well as giving detailed answers about our own. Dennis and the CEO, Marie Becksall, and several of their senior staff members had been in and out all week as we worked to understand the financial results of a combined entity. Three-ring binders full of scientific and marketing data related to their pharmaceutical products, sales projections, and regulatory documents were stacked on both sides of the table.

Marie sat next to Dennis. She'd arrived a few minutes into our meeting at his request, perhaps his attempt to maintain the upper hand while he passed judgement on our suitability as a merger partner.

"I'm not faulting the way you've done your job, Ms. Emory, I want to be clear. Everything is in order. Most small companies don't keep such tidy books," Dennis went on. "But there isn't much financial wiggle room. A single large, unexpected cash outlay will derail your entire operation."

"Our board is committed to infusing more cash, if necessary. They are confident we'll get to commercialization in under a year," I responded. "And you've agreed the revenue projections for Alvee are conservative – it's likely to do much better. I'm not disagreeing we're in a cash flow crunch." I looked at Marie. "And yes, we need your resources to get beyond it. *You* have to decide if it's the right opportunity for your company in the long run."

Marie was quiet for a moment, turning to look out the window before speaking. "There's no perfect situation, Den. We have more cash right now than we need, a very nice position to be in. But it won't last. The patents are expiring on two of our products within three years. A new delivery system provides opportunity to extend the patent life. It's win-win."

"If it all works out," Dennis said. "I'm telling you, there better not be any surprises."

She tapped her fingers on the table. "Fair enough. Wait for me in my office—I want a couple of minutes with Neddy, then I'll join you and we can debrief."

Once Dennis left, Marie smiled at me. "His bark is worse than his bite."

"Not at all, he's doing his job."

"I'll be honest with you, Neddy. I was very impressed with Charles, but I was skeptical of the company. When I learned his sister is the CFO I thought, uh-oh, a small family business, funded by family board members. That profile usually scares me off."

"We do have two founding members who are not family."

She paused and I waited, hoping the correction hadn't offended her.

"After spending some time with you earlier this week, and after what Dennis said—"

"You mean about Angiras being a C-minus candidate?"

"No. What he told me in private yesterday. Despite the… let's call it less than ideal financial situation Angiras is in, he saw great experience, talent, and most of all integrity in what you all are doing. And in how you've managed to keep things going on a shoestring. Most family businesses are much messier."

"And how do *you* feel about us?"

"I'm a scientist. I get energized by science and innovation, not only Alvee itself, which will be a huge game changer for us once it's finalized, but the dream program holds all kinds of fascinating possibilities. But I'm also a huge fan because of your mission. It's hard not to root for you guys given your brother's condition." Marie stood up. "Thank you for all your time this week. And so that I'm clear: I'm a fan, but I agree with Dennis about no surprises. I won't be able to justify any unexpected changes in the pro formas with my board. Don't forget that."

It was close to four thirty, and I had one more meeting before I left for the day—a follow-up with the head of pharmacology, Adam Rich. He'd spent time earlier in the week patiently describing the science behind their products, which treated arthritis and other inflammatory illnesses, including respiratory inflammation. Their products could potentially be delivered by Alvee. Dr. Rich had an easy conversational approach, answering my layman's questions in straightforward language, giving examples and analogies which made the complex material understandable to my untrained ears.

He arrived in a white lab coat right on time and sat where Dennis had been a few minutes earlier. The late afternoon April sun, softened by the blinds, lit his face and his gray-blue eyes. I pulled my list of questions up on the laptop and we went through them, Dr. Rich making the technical nuances of the science more understandable. He clarified the three phases of testing a drug in humans, what happens in each phase, and how each builds on the prior studies. Our conversation gradually drifted to more general topics.

"I understand you used to work for a large telecommunications firm," he said.

"Yes, I was a small cog in a very big machine. Now it's the opposite."

"What was that change like?"

"To be honest, it was a very big learning curve. I used to have a staff of people to delegate to—of course, I wasn't at the C-level then, but still. I had people!"

I threw my arms up in surrender, and we both laughed.

"Now I'm the CFO one minute, the bookkeeper the next, and the janitor when it's needed."

He chuckled again, and this time I noticed his eyes laughed along.

"Seriously, I love it. I'm thrilled to be working on such a personal mission. The job itself is the hardest and most challenging I've ever had. We have fewer than two hundred employees, so we all wear a lot of hats. But I don't mind the long hours. My work used to be so structured and routine in the big companies. Always process, process, process. Now, no two days are alike. Except for keeping our heads above water."

"It sounds like you have a ton on your plate."

"Two tons, but since you've started me talking about it, I realize how much I enjoy the variety. And all the things I've learned. It's amazing."

"Yeah, as a scientist learning's what's always driven me too."

"We're working very, very hard to get this product finished. We have great hope for it."

"How is your younger brother?"

"Daniel is up and down. Mostly just okay. His prognosis isn't great, so you can imagine the stress we're all under."

"Boy, that makes things personal. Wow, I so admire what you're doing."

A lump rose in my throat, so I changed the subject. "What about you? How long have you worked here?"

"This is my fifth year. I've been in development—sorry, drug development—most of my career. Primarily in large firms, but I really appreciate the size of Salton. We're not as small as you guys, but I do feel I have impact on our products. I can see the results of my work in a direct way. At least most days. And Marie is a fantastic boss."

"She seems tough, but very fair."

"Marie has great instincts and doesn't suffer fools. Something I needed when I was hired here."

"Every once in a while, the right people come along at the right time."

"Yes, they do." He stood to leave, then turned. "Would you like to have dinner with me tonight?" The question caught me off guard, but my appetite… I hadn't had a real meal in three days, and those gray eyes overruled any hesitation.

On the way to the restaurant, I debated with myself about whether this was a business dinner or a date. Was Dr. Rich being polite to a business colleague, suggesting dinner after a very long day in an even longer week? Or was it more?

At seven I walked into the El Segundo Grill, where he waited. The host escorted us through the indoor dining room, past the large grill where steaks, chops, and seafood were attended to by the kitchen staff. The aroma made my stomach growl. We sat at a table on the patio.

"It smells wonderful. This is a beautiful spot. Thank you for the invitation."

"My pleasure, and it's my treat."

He'd changed into a dark gray V-neck sweater and a pair of slacks with a subtle plaid. I was glad I'd decided to change into a black jumpsuit I'd recently purchased. The gold trim gave it some polish without fuss. "I hope you'll expense the meal?"

"It depends on how much we talk shop."

I laughed. "Fair enough. I'll try to ask a lot more questions. Although it's hard for me to think of many. You've been very helpful, Dr. Rich."

"Call me Adam, please. Do you think our two companies will merge? Off the record."

"Do I think the two organizations are compatible? Yes."

"Compatibility. A good start." He smiled and we picked up the menu. After ordering, I took in the decor of the restaurant. Large cacti and other potted desert plants lined the terra-cotta tile floors, complimenting the floral upholstery on the seats. The night was warm with only a slight breeze. I was grateful I wouldn't need to wrap my shoulders in the shawl I'd brought along. We read the wine list and agreed on a sauvignon blanc, then settled into easy conversation.

"Angiras is embarking on some very interesting research. The lucid dreaming program—how exactly does it work?"

I shared how we'd developed the lab, the processes, and the good results we'd had so far.

"And I understand, from what Marie has shared with our team, at the moment there's a bit of a hiccup?"

"Yes. We've been trying to resolve a glitch with the dosage tube, and so far haven't come up with a solution. But our engineers are very dedicated. I'm confident we'll get there."

"All medical advances require confidence and a great deal of perseverance. Not to mention good science."

The wine arrived and we sipped. "This is delicious."

"Hmmm."

"So, is the 'hiccup' worrying to you all?"

"Not really. Your team has already overcome bigger obstacles."

"How do you feel about it personally? A potential merger?"

He didn't hesitate. "Scientifically, it's very exciting. The technology you guys are working on ties in with what we're doing, so if it goes through, it will be a match made in heaven." Adam leaned forward and I caught the slightest trace of bergamot. "A huge step forward," he said.

"But might your job be affected?"

He smiled sideways and tipped his head slightly. "Heck, everyone's job will be affected. I've lived through two of these before. Once, a company I worked for was gobbled up by a larger firm. The second time we were the gobblers."

Bergamot again. I inhaled deeply.

"So I'm not afraid of being let go, if that's what happens down the road," he went on. "I've done a job search before. It's kind of the nature of the beast, at least in the pharma world."

"It's a very practical way of looking at it. Of course, there will be people impacted on our side as well."

"Here's to equal opportunity pain." Adam lifted his glass, his long fingers curling around the stem.

The waiter came around, took our orders, and then our conversation drifted to more personal topics. I talked about my marriage and found myself sharing even some of the most painful memories.

"I was rebellious. I knew Jeremy was abusive before I married him, but I went ahead anyway, thinking I could change him and prove my parents wrong. And guess what? They weren't wrong. But I damaged my relationship, accusing them of wronging me in all sorts of ways. It took a long time before they'd accept me back. I credit my brother, Charles, for getting them to listen. I'm not sure what I would have done without him."

Adam listened to all of this without interrupting, never taking his eyes off me.

"Charles must be an awesome brother. But I suspect you might have found your footing eventually. You sound like a very determined person."

"Oh, I'm determined all right," I laughed. "You have no idea. That's what got me into trouble in the first place."

"A strength overdone can become a liability."

"Exactly. I'm the Jack Russell terrier in our family. 'Got a tough job? Toss it to Neddy, she'll never give it up.'"

"I'll bet you never give up on people either."

"Hmmm, my ex would beg to differ."

"Your younger brother wouldn't."

"No, you're right." A heaviness released from my shoulders. Was it the wine? Or this man I barely knew who recognized me nonetheless. Either way, I wasn't ready for the evening to end. "Tell me about you."

He opened up about his own life: twin boys bound for college in two years, and the financial sacrifices he'd been forced to make during his divorce.

"I may have to work the rest of my life. But it's worth it. My ex-wife was great with the boys, but somewhere along the line, I stopped measuring up. Took me a long time to make peace with it. I believed in marriage, family. I still do. But…it turns out to be better for everyone, including me. And now we live happily apart. I have joint custody of the boys."

The food came, the conversation meandered: we were both dog lovers, we loved classic rock. We talked about new movies we'd seen recently and old favorites. Before I knew it, the waiters were loitering near the server station, and I realized we were the last two customers in the place.

I glanced at my watch. "Holy cow. It's eleven thirty."

"No way," Adam said, looking at the other tables.

"My gosh, I've got to get going." We stood up, thanked the wait staff, and apologized for keeping them. They were gracious but no doubt relieved.

In the parking lot, Adam walked me to my car. "Will you be at Salton tomorrow?"

"Yes, I have some things to wrap up in the morning. Listen,

this was so lovely. Thank you for the great dinner and conversation. I really enjoyed myself. This was…a great treat."

"My pleasure. I'll see you tomorrow, Neddy." He turned and walked to his car.

Once in the driver's seat, I checked the mirror. "I don't look half as tired as I thought I would," I said out loud." Then I realized something—I no longer felt tired. "Adam Rich, how did you manage that?"

The next morning, Friday, was my last at Salton-Winstrom. I had a final meeting with Dennis, who was cordial and seemed to have lost yesterday's disdain, and their board chair. I thanked them for the preparation they'd done to make my work easier and the open communication.

Alone in the conference room, before packing up I checked my email. Mostly routine questions from the Accounting Department, an invitation to a professional association dinner, an urgent reminder from Kimberly to complete the IT compliance training.

"Ugh. I guess that's not going away. Maybe I'll do it over the weekend."

"Ah, good, you're still here. I was worried I might miss you." Adam stood in the doorway. "Were you talking to someone?"

All morning I'd hoped to see him again. Once he arrived, I was tongue-tied. I busied myself stuffing files into my briefcase. "You almost did, I'm about packed up," I finally managed. "And no, I talk to myself. A bad habit."

"It's a sign of genius, you know. Neddy, I had such a great time last night. It's been a long time since — Well, no matter. I'm hoping you enjoyed yourself too."

I met his eyes. "Yes. For sure."

"I'd really like to see you again. I'm hoping you feel the same."

NINE

LATE THAT NIGHT, I lay in Adam's arms amid a tangle of sheets, not wanting to move or speak lest I break the spell of contented drowsiness. Muted light from the streetlamp filtered into his large, high-ceilinged bedroom. My eyes scanned the furniture, a mismatched collection of oversized pieces—dressers, side tables, and outdated lamps—furniture chosen for functionality rather than aesthetics. The room smelled of milled soap and his bergamot aftershave—subtle, masculine. I'd always been sensitive to fragrance. I applied it with a light hand on the rare occasions I wore it, and appreciated it when others did the same.

Adam stirred. "Hey," he whispered.

"Hey yourself."

"I started to doze off."

"Hmmm. I'm fighting sleep too."

"You're welcome to stay." He kissed my forehead.

"I have a dog waiting for me."

"Lucky dog." He yawned. "I'll drive you home. But not just yet."

"No, I can get a ride." I reached for my phone. Twelve forty-five.

"No way. I insist. I'll feel horrible if you leave in a Lyft."

"I'm a big girl."

"I know. But I'm a little old-fashioned. You must have figured out I don't do this kind of thing often." He turned over and propped up on his elbow, blinking several times to wake himself.

"I like the old fashioned-ness," I said. "And neither do I—do this often. Have we been indiscreet? I have no idea how adults date anymore."

He laughed. "Neither do I. I won't tell if you don't."

I smiled, then got serious. "Adam, I like you. And being with you tonight was a huge surprise for me. But it all kind of happened fast. Super fast. So, again, whatever happens or doesn't happen after tonight, I'm a big, grown-up girl."

Adam gave no sign if I'd insulted him or provided the out he might be hoping for.

"When I was married," he said, "I only thought about the future. I was oblivious to the here and now, you know? So, when my marriage ended, I decided to work harder at appreciating the present. It's where life happens. So, I think"—he stroked my arm—"yes, we've only known each other a week. But I feel a real connection with you, Neddy. Like I said, I don't do this very often. Partners have to mean something to me. I hope that doesn't scare you. And we can slow everything down if it does."

Was I scared? Did anyone have the answer as to what an "appropriate" time frame was for courting, for dating, for love-making, for sharing deepest thoughts and fears?

"Adam, I've told you things I haven't shared with anyone, at least not anyone I've known for such a short time. But it felt natural and right. So I'm also going with that feeling. I say, let's enjoy one another's company and not worry about what stage we're supposed to be at and when."

He smiled, a big, honest un-self-conscious grin. "I was hoping you'd say so."

It was two a.m. when we set out in his car toward my condo. I pulled my jacket tight around me.

"Are you cold? I've got a blanket in the back seat."

"Thank you. I'm almost always cold." He pulled the flannel throw into the front and I wrapped it around my legs.

On the 405, I scrolled through my email, silently vowing not to respond to anything until morning. But an item from a news feed related to a Salton-Winstrom product caught my eye and I read the headline to Adam.

"'Salton-Winstrom's "Ivanta" Receives Approval to Move to Phase Three Trials.'"

"Yeah, we heard from the FDA late yesterday."

"That's good, right?"

"Yes, very good. We can move to phase three—sorry, long-term studies. And if everything goes well, in about three years we can apply for approval."

Long-term studies. I leaned against the headrest and closed my eyes, my body warming and giving up the fight against fatigue. As I drifted into the twilight of sleep, my mind fused the real with the abstract, conjuring absurd combinations. How long was Lutense studied? Did they test it on pugs before it was given to people?

I was sound asleep when Adam pulled up in front of my condo.

"Time to go in, sleepyhead." He squeezed my arm, walked me to the door, and kissed me goodnight.

On Monday afternoon, I finally observed a sleep session. When I arrived, Melody was attending to the engineers, connecting their monitors, and ensuring the feeds were linked to her laptop.

Ryan, Tim, Jeff, and Stevie had been given a heads-up I'd be observing the proceedings as the final step in my audit. The four were in good spirits and joked with me, promising not to snore or drool excessively during their naps. The last few days had been productive for the team, with several new technical ideas making their way through concept testing.

"Anybody craving the ever-popular mugwort tea?" I joked.

They all groaned.

Charles came into the lab and chatted with the engineers for a few minutes. I caught bits and pieces of their discussion—something technical about the shape of the trigger on the Alvee prototype. "See if you can focus there this afternoon," he said.

I sat at one of the workstations while Melody lowered the black-out blinds and the engineers settled down, each donning an oxygen mask in addition to the cardiac monitors. The masks looked like the same style Daniel used, so I asked why the engineers wore them.

"We're not giving oxygen, but we measure the amount of carbon dioxide exhaled," Charles replied, "to ensure they're not falling into chronic sleep apnea. It's a precaution."

"I gather you're no longer participating yourself."

"Had to cut back. Too much going on."

Charles settled himself in an oversized, pillowy chair near the door, selected music from his iPad, and provided a guided meditation for the engineers.

"Take three deep breaths, and exhale through your mouth," he began as the room filled with a soft piano composition. "Let go of what has happened or not happened today. Let it go."

I silenced my phone and waited, my mind wandering to thoughts of Daniel, Waldo, and finally, Friday night with Adam. I smiled to myself, remembering the ease with which we'd fallen into each other's bodies, how my self-consciousness had melted away. For once, I'd let myself be carried along with no thought of right or wrong, savoring the sweet realization I might—just might—be able to trust another man again.

"As you inhale, silently say 'peace' to yourself," Charles

instructed in a soothing monotone. "As you exhale, think: release."

The music played on at a low volume. Then Charles spoke again in the same measured, soothing cadence. "Now, we're going to relax each part of the body. Starting with your feet and toes, let them melt into the bed. Let your ankles and calves release." He guided the group to relax every part of the body, pausing briefly before each prompt.

I felt myself concentrating on his words, noticing the tension in my own feet, calves, knees, and hips in turn holding and then releasing tension. I grew sleepy, as Charles approached the end of the meditation.

"You are safe. Let your mind drift into the lucid zone between conscious and unconscious. Tell yourself, 'I'm dreaming' as you drift away. You can control the dream state. You can direct the dream. Direct the dream."

Charles rose silently and went to his office. The music continued at an even lower volume.

Once the four were asleep, I moved my chair closer to the workstation where Melody sat. I asked her questions occasionally, in a low voice, but she never volunteered anything or initiated an exchange.

"How long do you expect they'll sleep?"

"We usually wake them after about an hour and a half. They put the ideas into their laptops, right when they wake up. And you'll need to be quiet then."

"I understand. I'm curious about something. I noticed they didn't have any tea before they got started. I thought Charles was switching to ginger tea?"

Melody gave me a funny look. "No, the tea is gone."

Just then, Charles came in and approached each cot, checking the monitors and the masks.

"I have to pay close attention." Melody watched Charles, then glanced furtively at me, though I wasn't sure why.

I took notes on what I observed. The sleep session created an odd scene: four employees sleeping nearby, wearing masks and connected to a series of electronic wires. Occasionally, one twitched or exhaled deeply.

I opened my laptop, connected my earphones, and clicked through to the compliance training Kimberly had set up. She'd called me that morning, polite but adamant: Every employee was required to complete the modules. I'd procrastinated well past the due date, so I figured I had time to kill as the team slept. The modules consisted of short videos depicting business scenarios that exposed individuals and teams, portrayed by actors, to cyber security and data privacy threats. These were followed by multiple choice questions on how the workers should handle the dilemma. I completed two of the ten, then grew bored.

I decided to text Adam:

Guess where I am?

No clue

Observing the sleep lab. It's mind-numbing

Why are you observing?

I bit my lip. Should have anticipated that question. I didn't want to answer in a way that implied a problem with the program.

In case I ever have to run it. Yawn

Lying to him felt wrong, but I was in no position to reveal the truth at that moment.

Is there an extra bed or cot where you can curl up?

> No such luck

> Want to curl up later? I know a nice quiet place...

> Let's try mine this time. The dog feels neglected

> I'll bring some treats for the little guy. Seven?

Melody stepped out from the workstation, caught what must have been a lascivious expression on my face, and frowned. I flushed, embarrassed.

"Melody, thank you for letting me observe and answering my questions," I whispered. Of course, she'd had no choice about my visit, but I wanted to melt the ice that seemed a constant obstruction between us.

She nodded crisply and walked to the other side of the room, busying herself rearranging an already tidy cabinet.

Charles appeared twice more as the afternoon wore on, and both times Melody's eyes never left him. She sat straighter and fussed with her hair. Was she enamored with him?

The session ended when a low-volume alarm sounded, and the engineers began to waken. Jeff and Tim reached for their laptops and started typing. Ryan sat up for a few minutes, rubbing his eyes before he took his laptop and typed a few characters. Stevie sat on the cot for a few minutes longer. She appeared to need a bit more time to fully wake. The others chatted among themselves. I walked over.

"Have you solved all the secrets of the universe?" I joked.

"Almost." Ryan smiled.

"It must feel good to be back in the saddle."

"It does."

"Were you here the whole time?" Stevie asked.

"Yep. The snoring almost drove me away, but I stayed till the bitter end." They laughed. "Did you have any *interesting* dreams?" I avoided the word "successful" —it sounded judgmental.

"Nothin' useful, at least for me." Ryan stood up. "We'll try 'er again tomorrow.

"Well, you've just returned."

"I had a thought or two I jotted down," Jeff said. "Might not amount to much, but we'll see." I followed his gaze toward Charles and Melody, whose heads were bent over a printout. I couldn't see their faces, but he stood a little too close to her.

"What about you, Tim?" I asked quickly.

"I had a weird dream about hypodermic needles," Tim said. "I was handing them out at a drug clinic and the police came and raided the place. I ended up in jail, except the jail turned out to be Dodger Stadium during the World Series. And the guards kept bringing me all this ballpark food—hot dogs with sauerkraut, sodas, ice cream. Tons of crap. My cell was full of it." We all laughed.

"That's not a weird dream, dude, that's a wet— Never mind." Jeff stopped right before he embarrassed himself. He turned red and glanced at Stevie and me.

"Shut up, Jeff." Stevie shook her head.

I turned to the rest of the group. "Whatever you all glean from your session, thank you for letting me observe it." I turned to leave, walking past Charles and Melody. I raised an eyebrow and looked at them a second longer than necessary. I wanted him to know their tete-a-tete, if that was what it was, had not gone unnoticed.

"Neddy, do you have a minute?" Tim called from behind me in the corridor.

"Of course." I stopped and turned.

"Can we speak privately?"

We took the elevator to the second floor and walked to my office at the far end.

"What's up?" I closed the door behind us and motioned for him to sit.

"I know today is supposed to mark the end of your investigation."

"Audit. Yes."

"I hope you'll keep your eye on it in some way. Alex, Stevie, Ryan—I'm worried about them. Us."

His question caught me off guard.

"Did something else happen? Oh my God, did something happen to Charles when he was asleep?"

"What? No. Charles?"

"I thought he was joining you guys in the lab until Alex returned."

"No, he's never joined us. He's too busy. Look, three of us have missed work with some kind of episode." Tim's brow was deeply creased. "In some cases, serious enough to require hospitalization. Doesn't that seem odd?"

It was the same question I'd asked Charles after Ryan's heart attack. I needed to be careful not to reinforce Tim's fears. So I answered the same way Charles had answered me.

"The conditions are not related to one another. Stevie said her paralysis is due to her epilepsy, Alex's emotional crash—we may never know what triggered that. And Ryan had a heart attack."

"It doesn't worry you?"

"If it worries you, Tim, you are free to decline going to the sleep lab. Same goes for all the engineers."

He pursed his lips. Was he fighting to keep from saying something he might later regret? "Look, I know I have no right to ask you this, but I'm really worried. More for the team than for myself. So I hope you'll keep looking at…or at least keep an open mind."

"I don't want you to think we're unconcerned about the well-being of everyone in the group. But I'm curious about something. If you're so worried, why not stay out of the lab? We gave you a green light to do so."

After a curt nod, he stood and left.

TEN

BEFORE I LEFT the office that afternoon, my mother called to tell me Daniel had to be admitted to the hospital again. His last stay in the ICU had been only a month before, and while he'd been weak, he seemed to stabilize once at home.

"Mom, what's happening?"

"I had to call an ambulance. Your dad was out, and Daniel started vomiting. He was struggling so—" Her voice caught.

"Is Dad with you?"

"Not yet. He's on his way."

"Okay. Has Daniel stopped vomiting?"

"Yes, but we can't go in yet. The doctors think it's a reaction to the new medication."

"Damn. Okay. Listen, Mom, I'm on my way. When I get there, I want to talk again about getting you and Dad some help."

"Your dad won't hear of it, Neddy."

"*You need help*. You can't keep up with the work! It's killing you."

"I told your father we can manage it…" Her voice trailed off evasively.

I rubbed my forehead. "Okay, I'm going to get Charles and we're coming down."

On the way to the hospital, I urged Charles to talk to our parents about getting a health aide for Daniel.

"Their situation is untenable," he said. "But for them, getting an aide is crossing a line. Once Mom and Dad acknowledge they can't provide a hundred percent of the care, it's the point of no return, psychologically."

"As if they're giving up on him."

"Or accepting his disease progression as inevitable. Right now, they still have hope he'll recover, hope we'll find the solution."

Denial. What a potent force, often destructive but sometimes underrated. Had it served my parents and Daniel well, allowing the three of them to acclimate to each "new normal" phase of his decline? And thus kept the façade of managing his illness intact? Perhaps. But my parents were constantly struggling, constantly homebound, and it was time to move forward.

"You have to convince them, Charles. They don't listen to me."

"I'll talk to them."

We drove most of the way in silence. Before we turned into the hospital parking lot, I turned to Charles. "Are you involved with Melody?"

"No! Are you crazy?"

"She's enamored with you. I want to know if it's mutual."

"Absolutely not. That's ridiculous." Crimson crawled up his neck as he pulled into a parking spot. I didn't believe him, but I also didn't want to argue about Melody when our family was inside waiting.

It was two hours before we were allowed to visit Daniel. While we waited, Charles took my parents to the cafeteria for food and coffee, and I sat vigil, pulling out my phone to check emails and text Adam:

Hey, wanted to let you know I'll be with my family tonight at the hospital. Daniel was admitted today

Oh, sorry to hear. How is he?

Stable. Haven't seen him yet. Long night ahead

Need help? Waldo?

Thanks, I'll let you know

I'm here. Call as late as you need to

Thank you!

When they returned, Charles gave me the slightest nod, letting me know he'd been successful in getting through to them about hiring a health aide. My father looked defeated. He sat, unspeaking for many minutes. But Mom seemed nonplussed, chattering about the nursing staff and their caring attentiveness to Daniel. I figured she must have been in favor of the aide all along.

I walked outside to the small balcony adjacent to the waiting room, leaned on the railing, and stared at the sprawling medical complex, with floors and floors of rooms, clinics, labs, and mechanical equipment. Beyond the buildings were several parking lots, so far from the main entrance, shuttle buses were required to transport visitors to the hospital itself. I turned and gazed through the glass door at my parents.

"They're onboard with the aide," Charles said as he stepped outside to join me.

"Congratulations."

"You set the stage for it, Neddy."

"Exactly my point. I wish—just once—when I bring up an

idea, they'd agree without seeking validation from you or Daniel. They've never taken me seriously."

"I've never experienced them that way."

"You've never experienced them that way because you're—"

"What? 'The golden-haired firstborn'?"

"Firstborn *son.*"

"Okay." Charles raised his hands in resignation. "We're not having this discussion yet again. You're upset and it'll go nowhere."

"Look, I've learned to live with the fact that Mom and Dad wanted boys."

"You don't know that."

"Charles, they named me after Dad. I mean, come on."

He looked away.

"Don't pretend otherwise. Pretending makes it worse."

He opened his mouth to respond, but then Dad stuck his head out the door. "The nurse says we can go in now."

Daniel sat upright in the bed, propped by pillows. We circled around him.

"You doin' okay, buddy?" Charles asked, squeezing Daniel's shoulder.

"Yeah." His voice halted, and he took a deep draw from his oxygen mask. "Better than this m-morning." He put his head back and met my gaze with glassy eyes.

I watched my two brothers with an aching heart, one the picture of health, trying to save lives. The other pale, weak and struggling for every breath, losing the battle to hold on to his own.

"I'll take the first shift," I said, volunteering to sit with Daniel overnight and let my parents and Charles go home and get some rest. Over the next several days, we'd all take turns staying at the hospital and interfacing with the caregivers who came and went during their shifts, checking on his breathing, his heart rate, and ensuring he was comfortable. That night I sat on a faux leather recliner and read while Daniel slept. After an hour I texted Carollyn:

> At the hospital with Daniel

How's he doing?

> Sleeping now

Hang in there

> Thx. Fam finally agreed to an aide...

Go Neddy!

> ...thanks to Charles

Wasn't it your idea?

> Yeah – you know how we roll

Lunch next week? I'll send dates

> Not sure. I'll get back to you

OK. Get some sleep if u can

At about eleven, a respiratory therapist arrived, woke Daniel, and prepared him for treatment. I waved at Daniel, mouthed "I'll be back," and stepped out to phone Adam.

"How's it going?" he asked.

"Overall, he's comfortable. They're treating the nausea, and right now he's getting respiratory therapy. But he's weak, and I'm worried about him."

"I'm sorry. Is there anything I can do? Who's taking care of Waldo?"

"My parents went by my place and picked him up."

"Oh, good. How are you holding up?"

"I'm tired, but once his therapy is done, I can try to sleep. There's a recliner here, and the nurses gave me a blanket. So I'll try to get a little rest."

"Make sure they give you two blankets. Can I bring you something? Did you eat?"

"No— I mean, yes, I ate, but thank you, no." I yawned.

"What about tomorrow? You're not working, are you?"

"Yeah, I'll go in for a few hours."

"Okay, listen, I don't want to badger you with a million questions. I'd love to fix dinner for you tomorrow if you're up for it. If not, I get it. I can imagine how exhausting this is."

"I'd like to try. Let's see how I hold up tomorrow. I may head straight home and crash."

"Wouldn't blame you. Call me or text me, whenever it's convenient. I'll hang tight."

In Daniel's room I slid into the recliner and pulled the blanket up to my shoulders. I took one more peek at him, closed my eyes, and held the image of his pale face in my mind. Before I knew it, my thoughts shifted to Adam, and how easy he'd made it for me to care for my family. Had I still been married to Jeremy, he would have insisted I come home. I realized my teeth were clenched and opened my mouth to relax my jaw, then let my shoulders drop away from my ears.

I awoke with a start when a doctor came in to check on Daniel sometime after two thirty.

"Hello, I'm Dr. Morris. I'm here to check on Mr. Emory. Sorry to wake you."

"It's okay. I'm his sister, Neddy."

I watched as the doctor moved his stethoscope around Daniel's chest, assessing the heart and lobes of his lungs. Daniel's eyes fluttered open, and the doctor asked him a few questions in a low voice. After the brief exam, I followed the doctor out the door.

"Dr. Morris, what's happening with Daniel?"

"As near as we can tell, he's experiencing stomach upset due to one of the medications he's been taking. Most likely the anti-seizure drug. It doesn't play nice with his anti-inflammatory."

"'Doesn't play nice?'"

"Sometimes drugs cause a reaction directly, a side effect. Other times, two drugs don't work well together."

"I see."

"Your brother will be staying with us for a few days until we get the meds straightened out. It's best if he has very small amounts to eat, several times a day. If he's hungry, by all means he can eat, but only offer small bites spaced out over twenty or thirty minutes."

When I returned, Daniel was alert and had raised the top of the hospital bed to sit up. He looked around at the room and the elaborate medical equipment.

"What time is it?"

"Late—three-ish."

"Why're you still here." He coughed.

"We didn't want to leave you alone."

"It's okay, you don't need to stay all night."

"I'm not leaving." I walked to the bed and squeezed his hand. "How are you feeling?" I held my hand to his forehead, checking for fever—an automatic gesture without any benefit, since his vitals were being monitored and recorded.

"Not horrible. Not like before." His breathing was still raspy, but his color was better. "I guess I freaked Mom out."

"She called an ambulance, which was a good thing."

"Yeah, I guess. I can't remember." Daniel took a deep breath, but no cough erupted.

"You look better now, your color is good. Do you feel like eating? There's a patient fridge near the nurse's station. You know, the standard mushy fare: applesauce, juice, yogurt."

He laughed. "Yeah, for people without taste. Or teeth. I'd love a sandwich or something."

"Yeah, the doctor just gave me the word: small amounts of food. I'll see what's available."

The selection in the fridge was minimal, and I knew the cafeteria wouldn't open for a few more hours, so I grabbed two yogurts and went in search of vending machines. I returned with chips and Oreos.

"Oh! You're awesome."

"Eat slow. Tiny bites."

"Yes, Mother." He mimicked a small child.

As we ate together, I wondered how many more nights like this we had ahead of us—rushing to a hospital waiting room, passing hours in worry and sadness. Daniel was not improving, and that night for the first time, I doubted Angiras would find a solution in time to help him.

ELEVEN

EMPLOYEES WERE SPEAKING IN SMALL, huddled groups and stared at me as I arrived late the next morning. Something was clearly up. I found Charles in his office. He was on the phone when I arrived, and pointed me to a chair.

A moment later he ended the call. "Good morning. How's Daniel?"

"He was wide awake at three, wanting food."

"Really? Sounds like a step in the right direction." He rummaged through some papers on the large table that doubled as his desk.

"Yeah, it might not last, but we had a couple hours of good conversation, and I let him have some junk food."

"Hah! If nothing else, he'll cherish getting to eat something wicked-bad."

"Yes, and I'll have indigestion for a week. So, what's going on here? The place is buzzing."

"Right. Listen, I didn't want to call you last night, but I had to let Melody go."

"Wow, okay. That explains the busy bees."

"She'll be receiving severance pay, but she won't be back to work."

"What happened? Did you find out she dosed the team? I knew it!"

"No, Melody wasn't dosing them. I wish you'd drop that. She was insubordinate."

I almost laughed out loud. Melody had barely managed to be civil on her best days. I wondered what the tipping point had finally been for Charles.

"In what way was she insubordinate?"

"Not following protocol in the lab. Taking shortcuts, not completing entries into the database. I'd spoken to her about it several times. Today when I pointed it out, she blew up. Her reaction was… Well, let's just say totally uncalled for."

I knew this wasn't the complete story. He'd defended Melody's work repeatedly and assured me she was "harmless."

"It's very sudden."

"Like I said, she blew up."

"And she's never acted out before?"

"No. Not like this. Completely unprofessional."

"She's been less than professional for some time, Charles. The way she dressed, the insolence, the lack of communication—"

"It's over. I don't want to talk about it anymore." His patience was thin.

"You put up with it for so long—"

"Neddy! Please." His fist landed with a thud on the table.

I stared at him, considering what to say. He was exhausted and trying to save face. Whatever had happened, he'd never admit it to me. But it didn't matter. If Melody had been messing with the sleep program, I would no longer have to worry about it.

"What kind of announcement are you planning?"

"I already sent out an email. Didn't provide a lot of details, but the word is out."

I thought again about the atmosphere I'd encountered when I entered the building. "I bet people were surprised."

"Yes, and I imagine some will be angry or upset." Charles tapped at his phone, scanning messages. "I talked to the engineers. So, at this point, I think everyone's informed."

"Okay. Need any help finding a replacement for her?"

"No. We've used a medical employment agency before. They'll send resumes."

"Have them send some managerial resumes too." He looked up. "Kimberly's replacement? You can't do it all, Charles. You look like you haven't had a decent night's sleep in a month. Start now, find the right people, and then you're ready to hire once the merger goes through."

He nodded. "I've forwarded the severance agreement for you to read. You're going to have to finesse it with Salton-Winstrom."

My stomach lurched. "Uh, why? How much money are we talking about?" I'd warned him a large cash outlay could stall the merger.

"It's a chunk, but payable over five years. That should ease their worry. Now get out of here. Go home as soon as you can, get some sleep and a decent meal."

I opened my mouth to ask more about the severance but decided to wait until I'd read through it. Charles wasn't himself, we were both exhausted, and I didn't want to agitate either of us further.

Walking out, I thought about Adam and his invitation for a quiet dinner tonight. I hadn't yet told Charles I was dating because I wasn't sure where the relationship was headed. But more importantly, I was determined not to make the same mistake I'd made with Jeremy: introducing him to my family before I truly knew him.

I grabbed coffee and a bagel at the snack bar, then noticed Ryan, Jeff, and Tim huddled at a nearby café table.

"Good morning. May I join in?"

"Sure." Tim moved over to make room for me. I sat, stirring my coffee before I spoke.

"I understand from Charles Melody's no longer with us."

Tim's brow furrowed.

"I know you all were friends, and this must be a shock, so if there's anything you want to say to me or Charles please don't hesitate."

A funny look passed between them. Were they happy to see her go? Did they suspect the same things I did? After an awkward moment, I changed the subject. "How are you all doing? Ryan, you look rested."

"Yeah, I'm cleared to come back full-time. The doc has me on a pretty strict eating plan. I'm sticking with it."

"That's great."

I asked about progress on Alvee.

"We made some headway in the last coupla days," Ryan said. "We tested cooling the medication and it seems to move through the scope better. We'll have to keep testing it, but it looks like it's working."

"Yeah, that part looks good," Tim said. "But we still have the problem of incomplete disbursement."

"We'll get there, Tim. The dreaming has really helped," Ryan said.

"But at the same time, all this stuff that's happened…to you, to Alex—" Tim was still worried.

"Hey, I have a heart issue," Ryan said. "Don't be blamin' the dream program."

"I know."

Tim tried to hold my gaze, but I stared down at the last bite of my bagel. Convinced that with Melody out of the picture the program was safe, I was desperate to keep them in the lab. Daniel's life depended on it. I chose my next words carefully, the way a good trial attorney poses a question to a witness, all the while knowing the answer—and knowing that the answer will strengthen their case. "The different events that have happened among you—they don't seem related, do they?"

"Not to me. No, ma'am." Ryan was adamant.

"No. They. Do. Not." Jeff turned and tossed his empty cup into a waste bin. "Tim, knock off that paranoia shit. Look, Neddy, we're all committed to this. We can see the light at the end of the tunnel, and we're going for it."

I stayed at the office until about three, when my eyes blurred from fatigue. I stopped at my parents' to pick up Waldo, who sunbathed on their patio. Dad had walked him already and I was grateful because, while I loved our daily strolls, today I planned to get home and crawl into bed.

"Mom and I interviewed a couple of aides today," Dad said as I hooked up Waldo's leash. "The social worker at the hospital sent them up to Danny's room."

I was too tired to call him on his behavior. "Good. Anyone promising?"

"We liked one of them. Once Danny's home we'll have the guy come to the house for another chat."

"Is Mom staying at the hospital tonight?"

"No, I think she'll come home later. Danny insists on it. His sleep is a little restless because he's sometimes nauseous, but at least he's stable."

"You need a good night's sleep yourself, Dad."

"I'm fine. How's the research coming."

"I spoke with the engineers today, in fact. They've had some good breakthroughs lately."

"And?"

"It's very encouraging, Dad. And the team is committed to finding the solution." I didn't have the energy to elaborate, and my answer wasn't satisfying. Then again, nothing short of a guaranteed cure would be.

When I arrived home, I made scrambled eggs for myself and gave Waldo his dinner, which he picked at. I realized Dad had already fed him.

"Did you eat already, you little stinker." He looked up, wagged his funny spiral tail, and licked his mouth before returning to the bowl. "At least you'll sleep well. No begging Mom for a walk or a biscuit." I yawned.

I went upstairs and turned on the bathwater. While the tub filled, I flopped on my bed and dialed Adam.

"Good afternoon." His voice was buttery but without pretension. "How are you?"

"I'm good, a little tired."

"And Daniel?"

"He's about the same. My mom is with him now."

"Do you know when he'll be released?"

"I guess when he's stable enough to be moved. And when we're equipped to care for him. On the bright side, my parents have finally agreed to a health aide, so that will be our next step."

"Hmmm. Did you work today?"

"For a few hours. Listen, I hope you understand, but I feel like death warmed over. I'm going to crash."

"'Death warmed over.' That's funny. Yes, of course I understand. Don't fret."

I yawned. "What are you doing? How was your day?"

"I spent most of the day on a very boring conference call with the FDA and several attorneys. I was there for technical clarification only, but the attorneys haggled and haggled with each other, and they never asked me a single question. I had a hard time staying awake."

"No one gets to slay a dragon every day."

"True. By the way, from the scuttlebutt I'm picking up at work, sounds like the merger will move forward. A few more steps to get through, but everything looks good, I'm hearing."

"Great." I said a silent prayer of thanks that Melody was gone. Then I remembered the damned severance agreement. I hadn't yet looked at it. I grabbed my laptop and scanned my emails, looking for the one Charles had sent with the attachment.

"What are you doing now?" He must have heard my keyboard.

"Looking for something to stream. Something nice and mindless." I felt a pang of guilt for lying to him. Again.

"Listen, Neddy, when can I see you next?"

"Can you give me a couple of days to get my head above water at work?"

"Of course. Let's try for dinner sometime this weekend."

"Sounds perfect. Thank you for understanding." I'd located the email and clicked open the attachment, half listening to Adam as I read.

"No problem. I'll call you near the end of the week. Take care of yourself."

"I will. Going to bed soon."

"A quarter of a million dollars?" I shouted into the phone not two minutes later.

"Yes, that's what Dr. Emory wanted," Leni assured me. "Payable over five years. Believe me, I double-checked. Because it's far more than we've ever paid a severed employee in the past."

I made a choking sound.

"I a-assumed at the t-time, you and Dr. Emory had agreed to the amount, but it sounds like—" she stuttered.

"No," I cut her off. "Never mind. I-I think I must have misunderstood when we talked. Thank you for the clarification, Leni."

Charles had committed to pay Melody a huge sum of money. Far, far more than we'd paid before. The kind of money people are paid for only one reason.

"So, what has Melody got on you?" I demanded, once Charles returned the three calls I'd made to him that evening.

He sighed. "I know. I screwed up."

"That's an understatement. How long were you involved with her?"

"Long enough for her to have me over a barrel."

"*How long*, Charles?"

"Since before she came to work here. Since Paramount."

"You lied to me. I asked you directly and you swore there was nothing romantic going on."

"Yes. It wasn't my finest hour."

"Oh, that's brilliant." I swallowed hard. "So this goes back a long while." I thought about all the possible repercussions—the impact of the severance payments on the merger, the PR disaster if Melody went to the press, the embarrassment to our family. "What the hell were you thinking?"

"I didn't think it would end like this."

"How *did* it end? Who broke it off?"

"I told you already. She went off when I spoke to her about the lab protocols. Things escalated, and I fired her. I should have seen it coming."

"Oh, you think so? Duh. Now we're stuck with this *unbelievable* severance arrangement." I hated the venom in my voice, but I was furious. "Damn it, Charles. This is going to be impossible to explain to Salton."

"We can't let this mess up the merger, Neddy."

"And how am I supposed to stop that from happening?"

"I know, I made a huge miscalculation. I'm sorry. But I had to make sure she wouldn't expose—wouldn't go to the press. My reputation would be ruined. I had to give her something substantial."

I was quiet, thinking fast.

"The severance agreement is airtight," Charles implored.

"We've always made sure anyone working with the research team had the strictest confidentiality agreements, but this one has several other layers of protection. And Max had his attorney look it over. She said—"

"Are you kidding me? Max agreed to this? Did it *ever*, even remotely occur to the two of you to ask me about this first? I'm the fucking CFO!"

"Stop yelling."

"I'm the CFO, Charles, and I warned you: no surprises. You two have put the entire merger at risk. I'm not sure it can be salvaged."

"No, no. We *have* to find a way. We can't stay afloat without it."

I was quiet again, my head throbbing.

"Neddy?"

"I'm going to get off the phone now. I have to figure out how in the world to explain this without it all blowing up in our faces."

"Can't you just bury it? Until after Alvee launches? It's easier to get forgiveness than permission—"

"Oh my God. Intentionally withhold disclosure of this obligation to our merger partner? And our bankers? You can't be serious."

"It's not optimal, but—"

"Getting off the phone now," I growled at him through gritted teeth. I shook with anger at his arrogance, his ridiculous, childish suggestions to remedy the mess he'd made for all of us.

"Okay, wait, one minute. I get it. I'm really, really sorry I put you in this position. I don't deserve redemption. But if anyone can find a way, it's you. Put your unrelenting stubbornness to work, Neddy, please. Not for me. *Not* for me. For Daniel."

TWELVE

"IT CAME to me in a dream, so it must be a good idea." I smiled at my own joke.

Charles sat at his desk, stirring his first coffee of the morning and staring at me. "I don't know about this."

"It's the only reasonable, immediate, and, if we're lucky, substantial mitigation I can think of to offer Salton and keep the merger on track. If we're lucky."

"Explain, please."

"You sign an agreement committing to pay half the severance yourself. Out of your own personal funds. For the first two and a half years of the five-year payout, you'll be providing the funds from your personal assets. And it's ironclad," I went on, almost enjoying myself. "Whether you continue to work at the company post-merger or not, you're still responsible for it."

"So, the obligation of the merged company is halved."

"One hundred twenty-five thousand. It's a hell of a lot easier to sell than a quarter million dollars."

He was quiet for a moment, frowning. "Are you doing this to punish me?"

I laughed. "Really? Make it work, Charles."

He sighed. "I will. Somehow."

"And I'll call Dennis DuPres to set up a meeting."

"What about Marie? And don't you want me or Max to go with you?"

"No. I want to keep the initial conversation between Dennis and me. Bringing you all in—I don't like the optics. Makes it an even bigger deal than it already is."

"Hmmm, yeah, I see." He sighed heavily. "You're a lifesaver."

"Don't thank me yet. This could go either way. We are not out of the woods. So harness all your karmic Chi or whatever you call it, and send it to me. We're going to need it."

It took over a week to get on Dennis's calendar. He was away on a long-planned family vacation out of the country, and interrupting it to lay this mess at his feet would not serve us well. Besides, I wanted an in-person meeting. I needed to both hear *and* see his reaction to gauge the likelihood of keeping the merger on track.

On his second morning back, I sat in his office, watching as he read the severance agreement. His brow moved up and down, alternating between furrowed and stretched, as if he were doing facial exercises. A tic percolated on his cheek.

When he'd finished, he tossed the document on his desk and leaned back in his chair, rubbing his forehead.

"Okay, who did what to Ms. Wilson?" he finally asked.

"Charles had a…long-term affair with her."

"Why did she leave? What happened?"

"They had a significant disagreement about the work, which ultimately led to a break up of the relationship. Melody's work was, in my opinion, shoddy for some time—"

"Doesn't matter."

"I know, we're still where we are. Charles takes full responsibility for it."

"Apparently, he's only taking half responsibility. The rest will be on the company."

"But the corporation's liability is significantly reduced this way."

"From a financial perspective, yes. You're assuming it's only money. But I'm worried about what else is at risk. She might decide to go to the press or share the whole mess on social media. Make herself a victim, a 'Me Tooer.' It's impossible to estimate the potential damage."

"I believe the agreement is tight. Comprehensive and—"

"Did you ever think, when you were drafting this, Ms. Wilson might not go away quietly? What's her state of mind, does anyone know? Has anyone been in touch?"

"I have not personally been in touch with her, no. You can see from the language in the agreement she's not allowed to communicate with anyone in the company."

He snorted. "I'd be willing to bet she's already talking to friends inside. What kind of damage control have you put in place?"

"That's in process," I lied. "Look, have your attorneys review the contract. They'll find it very tight."

"Oh, have no fear, Neddy. This thing will be put under a microscope. If *any* holes are found, we're calling off the merger."

"I feel good about this, Dennis. We had some very smart people working on it."

"You better hope so." He stood, pointing at me. "I'm not signing off on this until I'm satisfied Salton won't end up with egg on its face."

"Any word?" Charles stood in the doorway of my office.

"No, nothing." Two days had passed, and we still had not heard from Dennis. A press conference was scheduled for the next afternoon, Friday, and we had no idea if we could go through with it.

"It's excruciating," he said.

"I warned you at the beginning of all of this—mergers take longer than anyone thinks. Have you phoned Marie?"

"I did. She explained the delay. She's waiting on what their in-house attorney has to say before deciding anything. They ran it by outside counsel first, and I guess it passed muster. She wasn't unfriendly, but she also wasn't gracious."

"Gracious?"

"If the situation was reversed, I'd at least be a little understanding. I'd be trying to expedite the decision."

"Oh my God. You'd be understanding because you think it's okay to mess with a female employee, as long as you don't get caught. 'Happens all the time'," I mimicked. "It's different for women, Charles. If Marie were caught doing something like this, she'd be fired. Not to mention she's probably been on the receiving end of unwanted attention more than once. So she takes this crap seriously."

"I simply meant I couldn't read her." He sounded hurt.

"She's probably pissed but needs to keep her shit together."

The irony was not lost on him. "When are *you* going to stop being pissed?"

"I don't know. When this is all behind us, I guess." I *was* angry at him, but I was even more terrified. If this merger were to fall apart, the company wouldn't survive.

Lupe came in with a delivery. "Neddy, this arrived for you."

"Huh? I wasn't expecting anything." She handed me a large manila envelope. The return address was a post office box in Redondo Beach, but included no sender name.

"I'll leave you to it." Charles stood. "Lupe, let's go get lunch and review the arrangements for the press conference."

I opened the envelope warily, pushing aside memories of headlines blaring "Mail Bomb." Inside I found an orange plastic flash drive and a pad of orange Post-it notes with a message on the top sheet:

Neddy, everything you seek to know is here.
Melody.

I stared at the note. What the heck? I placed the flash drive into my laptop and checked the directory. A single file—a video with no title—was the only content. "Uh-oh," I groaned. "What is she sending me?"

I pulled up the antivirus tool on my system and scanned the file.

Clean.

I called our IT department.

"Do you know who sent it?" the technician, Bailey, asked. Before I answered, she continued, "If you ran the virus scan and if you know the sender, it's probably okay. A hacker wouldn't sign a note."

"What if the sender has a beef with us?"

"It would have to be a pretty sophisticated program to go undetected. If you want, I can come up and run a more comprehensive scan, but not until later today. Unless it's an emergency." She lowered her voice. "In the old days we could have let you jump the line, but unless the issue prevents you from working or has crashed your laptop—"

"No." I had no idea what was on the video, but I was sure I didn't want anyone to view it before I did. A chill went through me as I remembered Dennis's warning, envisioning all the awful things that might be on it—a soon-to-be viral rant, an interview with a tabloid reporter, or worse. Surely Melody wouldn't have recorded Charles and herself in bed together?

"The safest option," Bailey said, "is to save whatever you've been working on today, then disconnect from the network before you view the video. Worst case, if it is malware, the infection will be limited to your laptop and the network won't be impacted."

So that's what I did. I moved to my comfy chair, took a deep breath, backed as far away from the screen as my arms allowed, squinted, and clicked. The sleep lab appeared. Then Melody entered the frame, prepping the cots. I relaxed a little when Ryan appeared, then Tim and Stevie, and lastly Jeff. Melody prepared their monitors as they arrived. Then I was shocked to see myself come in, chatting first with the engineers and then with Melody and Charles, and finally settling into a chair.

"This is the day I observed the sleep lab!" I said out loud. I hadn't realized a camera had been placed somewhere, it must have been mounted near the ceiling. Both Charles and Melody moved in and out of the camera's view, while the engineers remained visible on their cots. I noted the elapsed timeline at the bottom of the screen: less than five minutes of the two hour and ten minute total. I read the cryptic note again.

"What the hell, Melody?" I muttered.

I considered my options. Watching in real time meant committing hours to the task, and I didn't relish that prospect. I picked up the mouse and advanced the video, keeping careful watch when anything on the screen changed or someone entered the camera's range. I saw exactly what I'd seen that afternoon but from a different angle: Melody behind a cubicle, monitoring the proceedings; me sitting with my laptop, typing away and occasionally checking my phone; Charles entering and checking on the team, then leaving again.

Repeat.

I hated watching myself—I looked bored and stiff. At one point, I watched the video version of me typing out a text, smiling and leaning back, my body visibly relaxing. Then I remembered: Adam. On the screen, my face held a candid, unconscious grin for several seconds. It had been a long time since a man made me smile like that.

I advanced the video again, watching as Charles entered the room once more, checked the monitors and masks, and left again. Nothing. Edging the image forward, mercifully I reached the end. I checked the drive's directory again in case I'd missed something. No other files. Nothing.

Why had Melody sent me this? Why had she recorded it in the first place? I picked up the note for the third time.

Everything you seek to know is here.

Charles advanced and reversed the video on his own laptop in his office a half hour later, as I looked over his shoulder.

He leaned forward several times, paused near the end and squinted. Then turned to me, shaking his head.

"Beats the heck out of me. I don't see anything."

I noticed a slight tremor in his hands as he removed the flash drive from his laptop and tossed it into his credenza drawer. Was he also worried about Melody's motivations?

Remembering the press conference scheduled for tomorrow, I put my hand on his shoulder. "Let's not worry about Melody. We need to call Marie again."

"No."

"We have no choice."

"No! That makes us look desperate."

"We *are* desperate, Charles. The press conference is tomorrow."

"Tomorrow at five. We'll wait till the last minute to postpone if we have to."

"Postponing is bad for everyone. Press speculation flies, and the bank will get scared off. I say we call Marie."

"If we let Marie and Dennis call the shots now, it's all over."

"What are you talking about?"

"It sets up the exact dynamic we must avoid. Instead of equal partners, they become dominant." His hands continued to shake, and he finally sat back, crossing his arms.

"Are you all right? When's the last time you had a full night's sleep?"

"I'm fine."

"No, you're not. You're overdoing it."

He was silent.

"Why haven't we seen any resumes from the medical employment agency? We need to fill those two positions to give you some relief."

"I haven't seen any good ones."

"Do you want me to—"

Lupe flew through the door, panic on her face. "Stevie's collapsed."

THIRTEEN

STEVIE LAY on the floor of the Hovel, motionless except for her twitching right hand. Her mouth gaped open. Ryan and Jeff stood staring, while Tim sat on the floor next to her, speaking softly.

"The ambulance is on the way, Steves." He held her left hand.

"What happened?" Charles asked Ryan in a low voice.

"I don't know, I didn't see."

"She was at her desk, and the next thing I know, I heard her hit the floor," Jeff said.

Charles knelt on the opposite side from Tim and felt along Stevie's limp wrist for her pulse. "Your heart rate is good, Stevie. Can you speak?"

"Yeah." Her voice was weak but audible.

"Stevie, what day is it?"

"Wednesday."

"That's right."

"Where do you work?"

"Angiras"

"Excellent. Lupe, please run to the lab and get my medical bag, and a couple of blankets."

I stood behind Tim and laid my hand on his shoulder, leaning closer. "Hey, Stevie. Try not to worry. We're all here for you." She looked at me, her pale lips quivering.

I felt helpless.

Lupe returned and Charles dug into his medical bag, pulling out a finger thermometer, a stethoscope, and an otoscope. He shifted positions, examining Stevie's neck, eyes, and ears without moving her.

"Do you remember falling?"

"Yeah, I fell, but I don't remember why. I don't remember tripping."

"But you remember falling?"

"Yeah."

He was quiet as he pressed the stethoscope to her chest and ribs.

"Do you remember if you hit your head on anything?" he asked as he pulled the earpieces off.

"I don't think so. My head doesn't hurt."

"That's good."

"Nothing hurts. I can't feel my legs."

"It's probably a seizure. You'll get a full workup at the hospital."

A tear ran down the side of her face. "Yep," she whispered.

"We've got Thomas," Jeff called from somewhere behind me, then tapped me on the shoulder and handed me a phone. "Hold it for her." He nodded toward Stevie.

Tim shifted to the right to make room. I knelt and put the phone to her ear.

"Hey, babe." Stevie smiled at the sound of her husband's voice. "I'm okay. I didn't pass out but can't feel much. Okay. Okay."

Suddenly, Tim scrambled to his feet, nearly knocking me over. His face was ashen as he made an odd motion with his hands toward Stevie, then rushed out of the room. When I turned back to her, I saw what had unnerved him. Blood, a lot of it, had begun spreading down the inseam of her jeans.

Charles was still palpating Stevie's neck.

"Charles." I jerked my head toward her torso.

"Shit," he muttered. "Lupe, get towels. And somebody find out when that ambulance will be here."

"I'll see you soon," Stevie, unaware, assured Thomas. "Yeah, it's okay, I can't feel anything. Just drive carefully. I love you too." She turned to me. "Can you let him know what hospital I go to?" Her voice cracked. "He's at least an hour away."

"Of course. We'll stay in touch with him."

"Stevie, when was your last period?" Charles asked.

"Uh, a while ago. I just found out I'm pregnant." An embarrassed smile turned to anguish as she suddenly understood. "What's going on?"

I tried not to stare at the growing puddle and grabbed her hand, looking directly into her eyes. "Can you feel my hand, Stevie?"

"What's going on," Stevie demanded again, beginning to cry.

"A little bleeding," I lied. "Can you feel anything?"

Her eyes flew from me to Charles and back again. "Sit me up! Sit me up!"

"No," Charles tried to soothe her. "You need to remain as still as possible. In case there's a head or neck injury."

Lupe ran in with a stack of paper towels from the ladies' room, shoved them at Charles, then knelt opposite me.

"*Por favor Dios,*" she prayed, stroking Stevie's hair, "*no permitas que Stevie sufra. Alivia su dolor y dale fortaleza.*"

Stevie began crying loudly, big heaving sobs. Lupe lowered her head next to Stevie's and whispered in her ear.

I looked at Charles. Sweat dripped from his nose as he knelt, trying to stem the flow from her groin with the already saturated towels. I smelled the iron in the viscous mess and hoped I wouldn't be sick. "Hang in there, Stevie, you're going to be fine."

"Am I losing the baby," she screamed at me. "Tell me!"

"I-I don't know."

Suddenly, the EMTs were in the room. "Everybody out," Charles called to us. "Make room for the gurney."

I stood, pulling Lupe up with me, and we went out into the corridor. Tim sat on the floor against the wall. He stared straight ahead, unblinking. Ryan and Jeff were at the end of the corridor talking quietly.

I heard Charles barking orders at the EMTs as they worked on Stevie, something about a CT scan and starting an IV. I walked back and propped myself against the doorjamb, light-headed, praying I wouldn't be needed further.

"Keep her neck stable. Who's the head neurologist at Laguna?" Charles demanded.

The EMTs lowered the gurney, its legs and wheels folding under the flat board-like mattress. One technician started an IV drip. The other, a formidable-looking woman, clamped a neck brace on Stevie, then spread fresh sheets on the gurney's bed before turning to her. "We're going to lift you onto the gurney now, okay? Are you ready?"

Stevie bit her lip. "Okay."

After Stevie was loaded, strapped in, and the gurney raised, the EMT gently lifted Stevie's legs, propping pillows under her knees. "We're going to keep your legs a bit higher, dear."

But with her legs raised, Stevie caught sight of her blood-soaked jeans. "Oh my God," she shrieked. "There's so much blood! Oh my God, oh my God."

The woman technician wrapped sheets around Stevie's waist and legs, cocoon-like.

"Get her in the ambulance," Charles bellowed.

The EMT ignored him, keeping focused on Stevie. "You're being very brave. Try to stay calm. I know it looks like a lot of blood, but don't worry. How far along are you, sweetie?"

Stevie inhaled deeply. I knew by the look on her face she was losing the battle to keep herself together. I turned away, back into the corridor, just before I heard her anguished wail.

FOURTEEN

"YOU'RE NOT SERIOUS. After what our staff went through this afternoon?" Charles and I stood in his office an hour after Stevie had been loaded into the ambulance. We'd sent the rest of the engineering team home for the day and arranged for our HR department to reach out to them. During all the chaos, Marie Becksall had phoned and left a voicemail for Charles, confirming the merger was on, and that she planned to attend the press conference the following day.

Charles was giddy with excitement. "I don't want to give Salton-Winstrom even one minute to change their minds."

"Tell them we had a medical emergency here today. My God, they're not heartless. Waiting a couple of days isn't going to derail anything."

"I can't take that chance."

"It's a press conference announcing the *intent* to merge. Nothing binding."

"Once it's announced, it's a lot harder for them to weasel out of it."

"Did you *see* Tim's face before he went home? He's in shock. Watching Stevie miscarry right in front of him. God."

He picked up the landline and punched in four numbers.

"Lupe, the press conference is *on* tomorrow. Make sure you have plenty of help for setup. Call me back if you need anything."

"Lupe is *traumatized*, Charles. The entire staff is worried sick about Stevie. And the engineer's office… God, they can't work in there until its professionally cleaned. That won't even start before tomorrow."

"I can't delay a press conference because the Hovel is unusable."

"It's insensitive to the staff."

"Sensitivity won't matter if the deal falls through. We'll all be out of jobs. And think of Daniel."

I flopped down in one of the chairs, dropped my head against the wall, and closed my eyes.

"If this was a slam dunk, Neddy, I wouldn't insist. But Salton waited until the last possible moment to tell us yes. I can't give them even one day to reconsider."

I shook my head, eyes closed.

"We'll keep it short. I promise."

When I didn't respond, Charles came over and sat in the chair next to me. "You're not worried about a stained carpet. What's bothering you?"

"I thought Melody had messed with the sleep program, but she's been gone two weeks. Yet this stuff keeps happening." I started trembling again. "But if we delay at all, we might lose Daniel."

"There's nothing happening. *Stevie has epilepsy.*"

"I can't see the connection yet, but it's there. Just beyond my reach."

"You're imagining it."

"*Imagining it?* Oh, of course." I stood.

"I didn't mean it like that."

"I'm tired. I'm worried."

"Look, how about some good news: Alex will return to work on Monday. He's been cleared by his doctor and the court after completing an anger management program."

"That's good," I said, looking at Charles. But it didn't feel good.

Charles smiled down at the group of reporters and business analysts gathered in front of him. Standing behind the podium in our transformed conference room, dressed in a cream-colored V-neck cashmere sweater, black wool sports coat, and dark blue jeans, he evoked confidence, optimism, and sincerity, as he talked about the synergies of the two firms and the meshing of their cultures. A group of executives from Salton-Winstrom stood with Charles, smiling for the cameras. Our board members, Max and Phil, sat with my father in the first row. Max looked around the room, caught my eye as I stood at the rear, and nodded tersely. Marie and Salton-Winstrom's board chair took turns speaking at the podium, showing solidarity and enthusiasm for the coming marriage of the two firms. I barely listened, biting my lip as I thought about what I needed to do next.

"Penny for your thoughts." Adam appeared at my side.

"Oh, Adam, I didn't realize you'd be here."

"I tried to reach you last night," he murmured.

"I'm sorry, I haven't been feeling great. Some stomach bug, I guess." I was still lying to him. I vowed to myself I'd not do it again.

He stepped closer, keeping his voice low. "Neddy, do you need to tell me something? Do you want me to back off?"

"No!" My voice was much louder than I'd intended. A couple of people seated in the nearest rows turned to look in our direction.

"Let's step out," I whispered. Once we were in the corridor, we took the elevator to my office, and I closed the door. "I'm sorry. I haven't been myself the past few days."

He stared for a moment at the disarray of my office, strewn with paper, used coffee cups, and electronics.

"And I haven't spent much time in here. Sorry it's such a wreck. We had a medical issue with an employee yesterday. It shook us all up."

"Is the employee okay?"

"She will be. Her husband called earlier today. She'll be out in a week or so, but— Look, Adam, I have some pressure on me related to my brother. I mean Daniel. And my parents. But I want you to know it has nothing to do with how I feel about you."

He stepped closer to me. "I'm very relieved to hear that. But I am worried about you." He took another step toward me and I found myself in his arms.

That wonderful smell of him again, taking me back to his bedroom on the first night we'd slept together. I held tight to him and, for a moment, my worry and confusion seemed manageable. Adam didn't move or speak. Perhaps I wasn't so alone after all.

I kissed his lips. "I need to get back."

"Do you want to try for dinner? Once you're feeling better." He stroked my hair.

"Early next week? I have some things I have to do over the weekend."

"Can I bring you some dinner on Saturday? I'll drop it and run, I promise."

"No, you won't," I laughed. "If you come over, I'm not going to let you leave."

"I'll be your prisoner, then." He kissed me again. "Call me Saturday and let me know how you're doing. And get some rest, Neddy. Whatever bug's bitten you, you have to take care of yourself."

We hugged again, then stepped into the corridor, holding hands until we rounded the corner toward the elevator and ran into Charles.

"Charles! This-this is Adam — Dr. Adam Rich, from Salton-Winstrom."

"Dr. Rich? Sorry, are you on the executive team there? I don't think I recognize you."

"No reason you would." Adam smiled. "I'm a pharmacologist. They don't let me out of the lab much," he joked.

"Ahh, a pharmacologist." Charles looked him up and down. "So then, how did you two meet? Neddy's neglected to mention you."

My face burned. "Adam was kind enough to answer questions about Salton-Winstrom's pipeline during due diligence. And we've since become friends."

"Well, great. We'll all be one happy family soon enough, won't we? Or perhaps you object to the merger, Dr. Rich?"

I saw a flicker of surprise at the veiled challenge, but his eyes remained steadily on Charles.

"Not at all, Dr. Emory. On the contrary, I look forward to it. I find the prospect of our two families coming together to be quite stimulating. Scientifically speaking."

"Touché." Charles gave me a hard look and excused himself.

I leaned against the corridor wall and shut my eyes. This was not how I'd wanted Charles and Adam to meet. "I should have told him about you. Us."

"Why didn't you? If for no other reason than you're the CFO. And our two firms are about to merge."

"Oh, Adam. I needed to be sure." I reached for his hand. "And the crazy thing is, I'm more sure about *you* than anyone or anything on this earth right now. Look, can you be patient with me? Can you trust me when I tell you I really, really care for you, and nothing I'm doing or not doing is because I'm not interested? But I need some space and time to sort out a few personal things—family things."

"Sure. I'm— Well, there's no second shot at a first impression, and I'm not sure Charles and I got off to the best start."

"He's protective of me because of Jeremy. He'll be fine once he gets to know you."

"I hope so, Neddy. I want this to work. Call me in the morning and let me know if you want me to bring you dinner." He touched my cheek, turned, and left.

Back in my office, voicemails waited on my landline. Figuring they were from reporters who'd attended the press conference and wanted a follow-up interview, I decided to ignore them for the moment. I attacked the heap on my desk, moving the laptop and iPad to the credenza before sorting through the paper detritus. The manila envelope that had held Melody's video and notepad was on top. As I went to toss it into the recycling bin, a slip of paper fell out.

"What's this?" I muttered, unfolding a packing list from Ron Dorsey, addressed to Angiras, c/o Charles Emory, and dated March 29.

I scanned the page to see what items had been shipped: twelve vials of Lutense.

I gasped, staring at the description, then double-checked the date again. The shipment had been sent to Charles a little over a month ago.

***

"Where did you get this again?" Charles asked after I'd barged into his office a minute later.

"In the same envelope as the video. I didn't notice it before. Charles, what the hell? You told me you'd stopped using Lutense two years ago, before any of the engineers came to work here. Why is Dorsey shipping this stuff to you?"

"Hold on. Did you look at this thing? It looks homemade."

I looked closer. True, the document appeared amateurish, as if created by an inexpensive, off-the-shelf receivables program. "You think it's a fake?"

"Or doctored. Maybe it's an old document from two years ago and it's been altered."

"My God. What is Melody up to?"

"I don't know, but I'm going to put a stop to it." He picked up his cell phone.

"Wait, Charles, let's think this through. Why do this? To blackmail us, or you? She's already getting paid off."

"Hmmm."

"If she goes to the press"—I shuddered when I remembered Dennis's warning about this risk—"it violates her severance agreement and the payout is voided. So it's not money."

"I'm calling."

"Wait. Melody sent three things to me—*to me*. That's weird in and of itself."

"Neddy—"

"I *need* to work this out, Charles! She sent the video, which shows nothing at all. She can't do anything to us based on that."

"Correct."

"She sent a Post-it pad, not a single sticky but the *whole* sticky pad with a note on the top sheet. Also weird. Why the whole pad? And then the packing list."

"*Fake* packing list. *What am I waiting for here?*"

"Her motive."

"I don't care what her motivation is. I'm taking her out right now." He punched at his phone, his face ablaze.

"Melody, I'm only going to say this once: Stay away from us. Stop sending mystery packages and riddles and half-baked messages. You have an NDA and a severance agreement."

Whatever her response, it was brief and, I assumed, nasty because Charles began pacing the room, his face twisted.

"Back off," Charles shouted into the phone. "You're fucking crazy." Charles generally avoided cursing, but as unusual as his profanity was, the tone of his voice was nothing short of vicious.

I waved at him, motioning to calm down or hang up.

"I'm warning you, Melody. Back the fuck off. Angiras is not

your concern. And if I find out you're talking to anyone here, you'll be very, very sorry."

A feeling of sickness washed over me. His reaction signaled the worst: Melody was threatening us, and his counteraggression made the situation more volatile. Again, I signaled him to cut off the call. Together we could piece together the puzzle of her motivations and prepare for a response. He ignored me until I grabbed a piece of paper off his desk and scribbled, "HANG UP NOW!"

He jerked a nod toward me, listening to Melody the entire time, then took a big breath.

"I told you, it's not up to you. You are nothing now. You're just someone who used to work here—"

I grabbed the phone out of his hand and ended the call.

"What are you doing, speaking to her like that? If she wasn't pissed at us already, she sure is now."

But he was somewhere far away. "I took care of it," was all he said.

"By bullying her? What exactly did she say?"

"Claims she's not in violation of the severance. And she was under no obligation to talk to me."

"What else?"

"Nothing of substance." He sat down on one of the armchairs and ran his hand through his hair. His breath was heavy, perspiration forming on his upper lip.

"Hold on. She must have said *something* to get you so riled up. That's not like you."

"She accused me of dishonesty—no, the word she used was 'dishonorable.'"

"Meaning?"

"Look, I don't know. I don't know what her end game is, I really don't."

I suspected she'd said something far worse, something very personal he didn't want to share with me. "We need to prepare for the worst. I'm thinking she'll go to the press."

"She won't." Charles looked past me, out the window of his office at the tree canopy. He was calmer now, or perhaps just spent.

"How can you be sure?"

"Severance agreement. Plus the NDA."

"She doesn't seem to think she's in violation of either. Do you *really* think Melody has the sophistication to understand when she crosses the line?"

"You make a good point. I'll have Leni call and remind Melody again of her obligations. In detail. And I'll have her coordinate with that PR consultant we've used a few times."

"Good, because we can't afford any surprises. We can't be blindsided by an accusation. If she's going to weaponize something you did, or said, or promised her—"

"Affirmative. I'll take care of that piece. Can you pull together all the documentation on your audit, so everything is in one place? That will help us prepare a press response."

"I'll do that over the weekend. And we *must* get you more help in the lab. Do you want me to call the agency?"

"No, I'll take care of it, now that I'm done with the Atlanta work. I know best what I need."

FIFTEEN

"WHAT SITUATION WITH MELODY WILSON?" Leni asked the following Monday, as we walked toward the building. Her parking space was next to mine, and by coincidence we'd arrived at the same time that morning.

I stopped and stared at her.

"I'm sorry, did I miss something?" She grabbed her phone from her pocket. "I checked my messages over the weekend."

"Charles didn't call you? On Friday?"

"No, unless I missed his message. But he would have followed up if I wasn't responsive." She scrolled through her phone nervously. "What-what do I need to know?"

I thought about my conversation with Charles on Friday, his intense anger during the call with Melody, followed by a complete lack of urgency about her possible actions. Why wasn't he as worried as I was?

"Never mind. Let me talk to him."

She nodded and held the door for me.

"You go ahead." I leaned against the wall of the building, trying to collect my thoughts and keep my anger in check.

"Are you okay? You look…not quite yourself."

"I…didn't get a lot of sleep over the weekend."

"Take care of yourself, Neddy. And if you need me to do anything, I'm happy to help."

A few minutes later, composed enough to face the day ahead, which would be kicked off by a very unpleasant conversation, I crossed the lobby to wait for the elevator. The place was alive with activity. Two couriers unloaded packages from carts while our receptionist, Anna, sorted them, all the while navigating incoming calls and creating visitor passes. Sales reps from supply companies perched on the sofas and chairs, waiting to be ushered in for their appointments.

"This one requires a signature." The UPS driver handed an envelope to Anna, who scribbled on his clipboard.

"Neddy," Anna called to me, holding out the envelope.

I stepped over to her station and reached for it.

"Wait, sorry. I have to log it in." She pulled the package back and searched the countertop. "Where's my scanner?"

Impatient, I snapped at her. "Isn't it enough the delivery people scan it?"

A look of surprise crossed her face for an instant. "All part of our security protocols," she chirped. "We track everything coming into the building. Ah, there you are." Anna grabbed the scanner, and a second later, I had the envelope in hand.

The return address was a post office box I recognized.

"Anna, is Charles in?"

"Lupe said he's coming in at ten."

"Thank you. And sorry for the attitude."

"No worries."

Once in my office, I opened the envelope. Inside was an odd "gift"—a package of Listerine Pocketpaks breath freshener. Scrawled across the package's top in neon orange ink was another cryptic message:

It's in the film.

"That's it?" I demanded, staring at the breath freshener, as if it might explain itself. Then I dug out the first envelope Melody had sent a few days before and dumped its contents on my desk. The packing list and pad of Post-it notes with the message on top:

Everything you seek to know is here.

"And the flash drive with the video," I mused out loud. "Why is she sending this stuff to me?" My eyes fell on the packing list. Was it a fake? If Melody planned on going to the press, why send manufactured evidence, knowing we could disprove it?

Or could we?

I pulled up the accounts payable files and found what I was afraid of. Then I called Kimberly.

"Is it possible to find out when a particular package was delivered?" I kept my voice as innocent as possible. "I understand from Anna every delivery gets scanned in."

"Well, that depends on when it arrived. We started scanning every incoming shipment in...I think late March, early April. Before that it was hit and miss."

"About the time you took over IT, right?" I figured flattering her might help.

"It was an easy fix. We just needed to set up a few protocols."

"Sorry to be a nuisance, but can you check and see if a particular package arrived sometime March thirtieth or thirty-first? I have the packing list if you need it."

"Nope, just tell me who it's from and give me a few minutes."

When she called back, I hit another wall.

"We have several packages scanned in that day," Kimberly said, "but none were addressed to you."

"Yeah, I'm talking about a shipment addressed to Charles."

"Okay. Then either he or Lupe needs to request the tracking info."

"I understand, but he's away this morning. Can you tell me if something came in from this person, Ron Dorsey?" All the reasons I'd been happy Charles had promoted Kimberly—her efficiency, diligence, being a stickler for details—were haunting me.

"I'm not able to do that."

"I promise I'll observe all protocols in the future." I waited, praying she'd give in. "And I'll complete the remaining compliance modules to assure you I'm reformed. I do respect you, Kimberly, and I know I've been very remiss."

"Those modules are not a bargaining chip. They're required. Required by the FDA."

"Yes, and you've been more than patient with me. I haven't set a good example and I've made things difficult for you, having to remind me over and over. That shouldn't have happened."

I waited. Would she give me a break?

"Okay. I don't see what harm it can do."

"We need to talk. Now." I stood outside Charles's office when he stepped off the elevator a few minutes before ten.

"Okay." He unlocked the door and stepped in, turning on the lights. "Take a seat."

I closed the door behind me. "Thanks, I'll stand." I handed him the packing list. "This is not a fake. It corresponds to a shipment of Lutense we received on March 31. And an invoice we later paid. So let's cut the crap, Charles. If you've been using Lutense on the engineers to enhance their dreams, *now* is the time to stop. No one will be the wiser. It's not too late."

"We're not having this conversation again."

"Then let's have a different conversation. You told me

Lutense hadn't been in the building in two years because you'd stopped using it. That's a lie, Charles."

"I did stop using it. But we purchase vials nearing expiration to ensure proper disposal. That's an agreement I have with Dorsey. I used to have Melody take care of it. And that must be what this packing list is for."

"Why didn't you tell me earlier?"

He shook his head and threw up his hands. "I didn't think about expired vials when you showed me the packing list. Melody used to take care of all this. Do you not believe me, Neddy?"

I sat down, frustrated. "Do you know what I did over the weekend, Charles?"

"I suspect you did what I'd suggested: put together documentation to help us in the event Melody decides to trash us to the press. Which I don't think is likely." He shrugged.

I stared at him. "I created a spreadsheet with all the health information we have on each engineer, including medications and known history of illnesses or family predisposition. I recorded symptoms or ailments they'd experienced since the dream program's commencement. I pulled together my audit notes, including their assent to continue voluntary participation, and my notes from observing the sleep session. It's all in one place finally, everything we need to respond to a PR event."

"I appreciate the thoroughness."

Anger rose in me. I'd postponed Saturday's dinner with Adam and backed out of a brunch date with Carollyn. "I worked all weekend, Charles, then I find out this morning you didn't even bother to give Leni a heads-up and failed to connect her to the PR guy."

"You're right. I dropped the ball on that piece."

My mouth hung open as I shook my head, mystified. "Why?"

"Because *I* spent the weekend with Max and our attorneys, hashing out the details of the merger. And there's a huge amount of work still to be done. But more to the point, I'm not going to let Melody control us. Any fuss she stirs up will be pure speculation. No one will look at the data you've organized and see anything untoward." He stepped into his kitchen and started brewing coffee.

I followed him, furious. "Are you kidding? If she accuses us of using an unlicensed drug on our employees—and we, very unfortunately, have documentation that yes, we did indeed purchase some of that drug—how do we defend ourselves? 'Oh dear, what an inconvenient coincidence'?"

He turned on me, red-faced. "I told you, she's not going to accuse us of anything. Her hands are tied. And I never drugged my team! Why the hell did you dig up this paper trail, anyway, Neddy? Nobody asked you to. It's a huge distraction. Are you totally bent on ensuring Daniel never recovers?"

"Oh yes, Charles. You're on to me. That's my plan." I fought back tears. "You sent me on a wild goose chase. Why didn't you call and let me know you weren't going to follow through on your end?"

"I should have. I'm sorry. But the work you did isn't wasted, Neddy."

"It is. I canceled all my plans for the weekend. For nothing. It's like I don't even have a life of my own." As soon as I'd said it, I regretted it. Every day Daniel fought for his actual life, and I sounded like a spoiled teenager.

"It isn't for nothing. I can get Leni and the PR spinmaster up to speed in no time if I need to. The work you did probably won't be needed. But if we do need it, it's ready. And I'm grateful to you for the work. Now, I'm late. I've got to get over to Max's. Can you handle things here?"

I nodded, still angry but also determined.

Back in my office, I phoned Adam.

"Hey, I finally came up for air."

"Good to hear it. I hope you managed to get some rest in."

"A little. Listen, I wanted to apologize again for canceling Saturday night. Now that this project is behind me—sort of anyway—I hope we can reschedule. I want to see you, Adam."

"I'd like that also. I have the boys this week. They'll go to their mom's on Friday. Can we do dinner then?"

"If I have to wait till then, I'm going to need to stay over. And maybe stay over again."

He laughed. "You can stay the whole weekend, but you may not want to. On Saturday, I'll be helping my niece out at her school science fair. You can come with me if you don't mind being surrounded by a gaggle of fourth graders."

"Believe it or not, an elementary school full of noisy kids sounds like a great change of scenery. And cast of characters."

"Then it's a date. I'll see you Friday, Neddy."

I texted Carollyn:

Lunch next week?

Her response came right away:

Wed works

Would you mind checking with M? I have
news to share with you both

OOOh – intriguing. What's his name?? Spill!

You'll have to wait till then – gotta run

I was not going to cancel on my friends—and myself— again, no matter how difficult the week ahead.

Charles's explanation about the expiring Lutense vials didn't make me feel better. I wanted very much to believe him, but he had misled me initially about Dorsey's role and his connection to Angiras, and then his explanation about the increase in Dorsey's invoice amounts didn't square with what Dorsey himself had said in the voicemail. At the same time, I had to prepare for the very real possibility we were being set up by Melody, though if true, she risked loss of a huge payoff. Was she so bent on revenge she didn't care about the money?

I considered again the odd assortment of items she had sent me.

"'It's in the film.'" I read her second message out loud. "*What* is in the film?"

I picked up the phone. "Charles, before you go to Max's, can I pick up the flash drive Melody sent us? I want to watch her video one more time."

He took a moment to respond. "Why? What are you looking for?"

"I don't know. I can't stop worrying about Melody's motives. Maybe there's something in the lab we didn't notice the first time we watched it, something sitting on the counter, or in some corner of the room she set up to catch us—"

"Neddy—"

"Charles, please! It's part of the audit record. You said you wanted everything in one place."

He paused again. "No. No more sleuthing. And something else. Stay away from that guy—the pharmacologist from Salton. Your little fling might jeopardize the merger."

SIXTEEN

"HE'S STILL at Max's office." Lupe looked up, watering can in hand as she tended to the plants in Charles's office. "Is there anything I can help you with?"

"No, I was just walking by and saw the door ajar."

In truth, I'd been going upstairs and walking by his office repeatedly for the last two days, hoping for an opportunity to slip inside unseen. But until today his main door had remained locked. The only other way into his office was through the Jack and Jill kitchen, accessed via a door off the main corridor into a short hallway. But this door was routinely locked as well.

The flash drive containing the mysterious video was in the drawer of his credenza, just behind me, but I dared not rummage through it while Lupe was there.

I needed to stall.

"Who supervises the sleep lab while he's gone?" The afternoon before, I'd been surprised to find the shades on the interior windows to the sleep lab were closed, which meant the lab was in use.

"He's here for a couple of hours each day so the engineers can go in."

So Charles wasn't stuck at Max's all day, every day. Another lie.

"As long as I'm here, do you mind if I pilfer some of his coffee supply? He has the best beans."

"Help yourself."

I walked across the carpet to the adjoining kitchen, where I took my time, hoping she would finish and leave me alone to accomplish my stealth mission.

Instead, she joined me. "I talked to Stevie today."

"Oh, how is she doing?" I fake-quickened the coffee preparations.

"She's having a really hard time. The pregnancy was a big deal for her. For them."

My heart broke for Stevie and Thomas. "Of course it was." I thought again about that awful day she'd miscarried. I knew we were somehow responsible. "Do you know if Charles has been in touch with her?"

"He sent a gift basket the day after she lost the baby. But he hasn't followed up. Would you mind asking him to? I don't want to pester him again."

"I'll remind him." I was embarrassed she'd needed to prompt the two top executives to carry out this basic decency. "Would you like some coffee?"

"No thanks. I locked his main door, so we can go out this way instead."

Damn.

We headed into the short hallway that connected to the main corridor, passing what had been Melody's office, still cluttered with files, binders, and an abundance of mementos.

"What's going to happen to this space?" I asked.

"That's tomorrow's project. I'm cleaning it out."

"She left a lot of personal stuff."

"I'll box it up and ship it to her. I wish I knew where to store all those binders and files. Charles wants it all put away."

I nodded. "Has Melody been in touch with you?"

"Nah, we were never close. I think the engineers were friends with her."

I nodded again, glanced back, and calculated. At some point the next morning, when Melody's office was being cleaned, I'd have my best shot at slipping past it, down the hallway, and through the kitchen where I'd just made coffee, to my destination: Charles's office.

I woke up early on Thursday morning. Before I left home, I completed the remaining compliance modules I'd promised Kimberly. At least that was one loose end tied up. Once in the office, I stopped to talk to the engineers. I hadn't been in the Hovel since Stevie fell ill. The carpet had been cleaned, and Stevie's workstation had been tidied. The men appeared comfortable. I'd had their well-being on my mind for the past several days, and seeing them at work in good spirits lifted my mood. But I was also there for another, more covert reason.

Tim greeted me at the door. Alex was there, talking to Jeff, who appeared disinterested in the conversation. I chatted with them and welcomed Alex back. He spoke politely, but more slowly than I'd remembered. I assumed he must be on new medication. The men shared their most recent assays with me. They were still struggling with the major technical glitch, and though several new approaches had been tried, they hadn't yet succeeded.

"Keep up the good work. You'll get there." I made a show of looking around the room and asked the question I already knew the answer to. "Do you have room in here for storing a half dozen or so boxes of files, binders, that kind of thing?"

"Yeah, you can use those cabinets." Tim pointed at the wall opposite the windows. "We only use about half of 'em."

"Great. Lupe needs a home for files from Melody's office. I'll let her know."

Tim motioned me into the corridor, and we stepped out, beyond earshot of the other engineers.

I thought of his anguish after Stevie had collapsed. "How are you doing, Tim?"

"Not great. When I saw Stevie bleeding, I thought we might lose her."

"That was hard to watch."

"Yeah. Really hard. Listen, I'm going to take a leave of absence for a few weeks."

This was terrible news. Another slowdown. I swallowed hard. "Really?"

"Yeah, I told Charles this morning. I can't focus here, so I might as well take some time to clear my head. I want to come back when things are more settled. When I feel more like myself."

His eyes never left mine.

"Are you experiencing anything unusual in the sleep lab?"

He shook his head. "No, I would tell you that. It's just that, since Stevie got sick, I've really been struggling."

"I understand. You need to take care of yourself. Are you getting help?"

"Yeah, HR gave me the green light to take the time and they referred me to a counselor. Anyway, I wanted to tell you because you seem to be..." He paused while a couple of employees walked past, then lowered his voice. "You seem to be the one person in this company who pays attention to the dream program," he continued. "If something weird *is* going on, you're the one who will figure it out. You're still looking at it, right?"

"I completed the audit, what makes you think I'm still looking at it?" Melody must have been in touch with him.

"I—" He blushed. "I dunno. I guess I'm *hoping* you're still looking at it. Especially since Alex has returned."

"Tell me, have you been in touch with Melody? I'm wondering how she's doing, that's all." I hoped my question would prompt him to open up even more.

"As far as I know, she's okay." He turned and went back to the Hovel.

I dropped my laptop in my office and climbed the stairwell to the third floor. My pace quickened when I rounded the corner and saw lights on in the dream lab, and the door to the hallway ajar.

"Lupe?" I stuck my head in. A half-packed box, shipping tape, and bubble wrap sat on Melody's old desk. I continued past the kitchen door and into the lab. "Lupe," I repeated. "You here?" I peeked around the corner where the cots sat, then turned toward the dark kitchen.

I hesitated. If Lupe happened to find me in the dark, she'd become suspicious. But I didn't dare turn on the lights—a guarantee she'd come looking.

"Screw it." I slipped through the kitchen into Charles's office, waiting a few seconds for my eyes to adjust to the dim light that filtered through the windows. I crossed the room toward the credenza behind the conference table.

As I reached for the drawer, I heard Lupe in the corridor, not three feet away on the other side of the main door.

"Hey! I wanted to be done with this packing before you got back."

"We finished early."

Charles. I froze.

"Finished? With all of it?"

"Yep. The lawyers have more to do, but I'm off the hook, at least for the moment."

I heard his key in the lock and the door opened a crack. I closed my eyes and held my breath. How would I explain myself?

"What's going on?"

I opened my eyes, prepared for a confrontation, but Charles had stepped back into the corridor.

"Melody's personal stuff. Remember, you asked me to clear it out," Lupe said.

"Oh yeah. I did, didn't I."

My heart raced. In a split second I crossed the office, traversed the kitchen, and tiptoed into the still fully lit dream lab, berating myself for being such a fool. Kneeling behind one of the cots, barely concealed, I listened as the two talked, first about storage options for the boxes, then a meeting Charles wanted to set up, then her vacation plans.

Finally, Charles went into his office. His phone rang and then I heard him in the kitchen, rummaging through the cabinets as he talked to someone—Kimberly?—about his laptop. He was closing the distance between himself and me, and I was stuck, sure to be discovered by either him or Lupe if I tried to exit the lab. Squatting on the floor, I heard her pack and tape shut two more boxes, my left leg growing numb.

"You going to need the lab again today? I can have it cleaned." Lupe's voice was muted. At last, she'd stepped into Charles's office.

"Yes, definitely. We'll be using it every day."

I stood up and almost fell over. My left leg could bear no weight. Silently cursing, I waited while painful prickly sensations made their way toward my foot as circulation returned.

Keep talking. I tested a little weight on the foot, steadied myself against the cot and took an awkward step forward, pausing to let my foot recalibrate. I prayed Lupe remained with Charles for a few more moments and that nobody walked down the corridor to catch sight of me through the windows. I inched past the kitchen door, down the remaining few feet of the hallway and hobbled into the safety of the main corridor. I heard Lupe laugh at something Charles said.

"I'm outta here in five. I'll be at my station if you need me." She emerged from behind his door.

"Hey, Neddy. Charles is here if you need him." She walked back toward Melody's office.

I joined her, my foot still aching. "Actually, I came by to let you know I've found a place for you to store all this stuff. In the engineers' office." I was out of breath, my heart pounding.

"Oh. Thanks." She looked confused. "You didn't need to take time to do that."

"I was down there this morning and noticed they have some extra space." I glanced at the address label Lupe had affixed to the carton—the same post office box number in Redondo Beach Melody used as a return address on the packages she'd sent me. At least I knew it wasn't a fake.

Lupe watched me reading it.

"A post office box? That's kind of strange." I feigned ignorance.

"That's where she asked me to send it. Probably because it's several boxes. She doesn't want those left on her doorstep."

"Oh, I see."

"Lots of people do that. Neddy, is there something else?"

"No, no. Sorry to keep you. Just wanted to let you know about the storage."

"Okay, great. Thanks again."

I turned, my face burning, and hurried to my office.

On Friday, after the near miss of the day before, I mailed a certified letter to Melody at the PO box Lupe had unknowingly confirmed for me, requesting she phone me immediately. The letter was a long shot; Melody had avoided direct contact with me even when she'd worked for us, but I needed to try. My hope was that she had kept a duplicate of the video. It would take a few days for the letter to reach her, but she was expecting the cartons Lupe had prepared, so I figured she'd be checking her mail regularly.

Now that Charles was no longer tied up at Max's it was impossible to get into his office. Instead, I needed to figure out a rationale that would convince him to give me the drive as I waited for the unlikely call from Melody. I pulled out the large envelope with all of the items Melody had sent to me, still perplexed at their meaning but hoping I'd find something useful with which to approach Charles. I turned to the spreadsheet I'd created over the weekend and studied it, looking for similarities in the engineer's experiences. I needed to find the common denominator. Once I did, I could convince Charles to make adjustments.

But instead, I saw what Charles saw: a whole host of unconnected conditions and symptoms. And two of the team, Tim and Jeff, had not exhibited any negative health effects at all. Frustrated, I turned to the medical histories. I started with Alex, since he'd exhibited the earliest and, so far, most perplexing behavior. Under medications he'd listed Chonaptic, along with more pedestrian medications I recognized—an anti-hypertensive and a cholesterol drug. I researched Chonaptic and found it to be an anti-depressive medication, sometimes prescribed for psychosis. If Alex was psychotic and had stopped taking his medication, it could explain why he'd had a meltdown and injured his wife. But Erin had insisted he'd been compliant.

As for Ryan, two cardiovascular medications were listed on his form. I turned to the forms for Tim and Jeff. Neither had listed any medications.

Stevie had one medication listed for epilepsy, an anti-seizure medicine, different from the one Daniel had been recently prescribed.

"Stevie," I groaned. I closed my eyes and massaged my temples. I picked up the phone and called HR to get her number. "And can you also give me Melody Wilson's street address and phone numbers? Both cell and landline, if you have them."

I called Stevie first.

"Hi, Neddy." She sounded sleepy.

"Stevie, it's so good to hear your voice. How are you feeling?"

"Physically, okay. Each day I feel a little stronger." I heard a female voice in the background. "My mom's staying with us to help out."

"Oh good. I'm sure she's a great comfort."

"Yeah, it helps a lot." She paused. "I'm still very sad. About the baby." Her voice shook.

My heart broke for her. "I wish I could say something to make it better, Stevie."

"Everyone tells me not to give up. My doctor says it's fine to try again. But I'm scared my body can't handle it." I heard soft whimpering.

"All I can tell you is we're all thinking of you and praying for you."

"Yeah, I know. Thanks. The guys stay in touch with me. And I talked to Melody today."

"Oh." I tried to keep my voice casual. "I hope she's doing okay."

"Hmmm."

"Stevie, do you recall anything about your episode at the office? I know at the time you didn't remember falling. Have any memories surfaced?"

"What kind of memories?"

"Oh, I don't know. Does your doctor have any idea why this happened?"

"She says sometimes there's breakthrough events."

"What are those?"

"She says I must have missed a couple of doses of my medication. But I don't think I did. I was so diligent because of the pregn—" She sobbed into the phone.

I was stunned, remembering what Erin had said about Alex. I half listened to Stevie choking out her story.

"He says…it's like a-a 90 percent thing."

"Sorry? He? Your doctor?"

"Thomas. He read medications don't work a hundred percent of the time. There's ten percent when it misses or something…" Her voice trailed off.

"Nothing's perfect," I heard Thomas say in the background.

"All I know is, I didn't miss a dose."

"Right." I took a deep breath. "Stevie, take as long as you need to rest and recuperate. We'll be happy to have you back, but only when you're ready."

"Thanks for calling, Neddy. Say hi to Charles for me."

I stared at my hands after we'd finished the call. Ryan had been surprised by his cardiac event. He'd been on medication for more than five years. Erin was insistent Alex had taken his medications. Had Stevie, Alex, and Ryan *all* missed enough doses of their respective medications, within mere weeks of one another, to create a suspicious but benign pattern? The odds seemed astronomical.

I picked up the phone and dialed Melody. I still needed to exclude Lutense as a factor, and as much as I wanted to believe Charles, something was off. Neither number was in service. I studied my spreadsheet, thought about the video again. Then I grabbed my blazer and handbag.

I banged on the apartment door. The building, a U-shaped three-story structure, was neat and smelled of fresh paint. Its open hallways meant all the tenants' front doors faced the inside courtyard and swimming pool. I leaned on the railing to see if perhaps Melody was sunbathing but saw only an older couple and their grandchildren using the pool. I rapped on the door again.

"Melody, are you in there?" I called. No response. I tried to peer through the window, but curtains had been drawn, blocking any view of the interior of the apartment.

"You looking for Miss Wilson?" a voice called from the opposite hallway.

I spun and faced a bearded man in a tank top and tropical swim trunks. "Yes, do you know when she might be coming back?"

"I don't think she's coming back." He spoke with a slight accent I couldn't place.

"Oh. Why?"

"She moved out. Didn't say where she was going."

That explained the post office box.

"When? Do you mind me asking?" I walked toward him.

"I'm not sure if I mind or not. What's your business?"

"She, uh, Melody—Ms. Wilson worked for my company, and I wanted to talk to her about some company files she has." I handed him my business card. He glanced at it and seemed satisfied.

"If she comes back, I'll tell her you were here."

"Thank you. And tell her I won't take much of her time."

"Right. But just so you know, she left in a hurry. Her boyfriend came by one night and they had a big argument. I went over there and told the jerk to leave. She wrote me a nice note thanking me the next day. But I didn't realize she'd moved out till I saw the manager locking up over there a coupla days later." He looked past me at what had been her door. "Sure hope she's okay."

I drove to the office, furious Charles had gone to Melody's apartment and confronted her. I imagined their encounter, recalling the terrible way he'd spoken to her over the phone the prior week. No wonder the neighbor had intervened.

Since I hadn't been successful in finding Melody, I saw no reason to tell Charles I had attempted it. He'd asked me to stop looking into her mysterious communiques and to halt the "sleuthing."

For the time being, I'd let him think I had.

SEVENTEEN

"I RESERVED A PRIVATE ROOM. I know you've been under a lot of pressure." Friday evening had finally arrived, and Adam and I were ushered into a tiny dining room at Begonia, an old converted bungalow tucked into the hills of Malibu. Once seated, we ordered chardonnay and a bottle of purified water.

The room was lovely—colorful planters bursting with begonias of several varieties created a simple, calming decor. Jazz played at a very low volume, and while not my favorite genre, that evening it provided the right delicate embellishment.

"Thank you for this. This place is beautiful. I hope I'm decent company tonight."

"Do you want to talk about it? Any of it?"

The waiter arrived with the drinks. I waited until he'd finished pouring and disappeared into the kitchen.

"Not right now. Let's let the wine find its way to my brain first."

He laughed. "Drink up!"

The waiter returned with menus and described the chef's specials. We spent a few minutes considering the options, then ordered.

Adam took my hand. "You okay?" he asked.

"Yes. I know I haven't given you the attention you deserve. I don't want to disappoint you."

"You're not. Look, I know you have huge family responsibilities, I get it. Not to mention a heck of a big job. We're going to go slow, you and me. Until you're ready and—"

"Adam, I want to sleep with you tonight," I blurted. Thank God we were in a private room. "I don't want to be alone. But that's not the only reason."

He smiled. "That did not disappoint." We laughed and he lowered his voice. "Nothing sounds better than sleeping with you tonight."

"And tomorrow, I want to go with you to your niece's event."

"Ah, the science fair. It's noisy, hectic, and truth be told, the same experiments are repeated every year." He poured more wine. "Just remember, you were warned."

"I need the distraction."

"Yeah, you do. What's going on, anyway? Is Daniel doing okay?"

"He's declining. Slowly, but it's happening. He isn't going to get better without some major intervention. I'm worried we may not…be in time."

"Oh, Neddy, I'm so sorry."

I started to choke up, but then our food arrived with great fanfare. Once the staff left, we both laughed at the over-the-top pretentiousness. But the meal was delicious, we couldn't argue that.

"Let's enjoy the meal. If I talk about Daniel, I'll lose it."

"Okay. What about work?"

"Busy. Lots of moving parts with the merger."

"I'll bet. Is there anything I can help with? If it's appropriate for me to be involved."

"I can't think of anything."

How I longed to unburden myself to him. Could he help me reconcile my growing suspicions of Charles and the dream lab and my nonstop worry for Daniel? I couldn't risk it. The one thing I knew for sure: If the development of Alvee stalled, Daniel was doomed.

"How's your employee—the one who had the seizure right before the press conference?"

"Stevie. She had a seizure and a miscarriage."

"Oh, that's horrible. How is she?"

"I talked to her yesterday. Her doctor thinks she missed a dose of her medication, and it caused this breakthrough event— a seizure. But she swears she didn't skip any doses. Have you ever seen that kind of thing happen?"

"Not in the clinical trials I've run. But then again, it could happen in a later phase. I don't want to second-guess her. But most likely the medication was either skipped or diminished by something else. Maybe the pregnancy impacted it."

"Tell me again, what's the difference between the phases in drug development? I promise I won't ask you again." I pulled out a small notebook and a pen.

He laughed. "You don't need to take notes, ask me anytime. Everyone gets confused, so don't worry." He set his fork down and took a sip of wine. "After a compound—what we call the chemical mix that ultimately becomes a drug—undergoes scores of tests in the lab it can move on to the first test, or trials, in humans."

His eyes lit up when he talked about science. Here was a man who had true passion for his work but managed not to let his career get in the way of his life.

"That's phase one," he continued, "and we're assuming the compound has passed the rigors of the lab tests, and of course not every compound does."

"Right," I said, returning to my scribbling.

"Phase one tests the drug in a small group of healthy adults for a short period of time to make sure it's not toxic and to determine dosage levels. This is where I come in. I look at what the drug does to the body, what the body does to the drug, how much and how well it's absorbed."

"'What the body does to the drug.' Wow, I never thought about that."

"If all goes well, we move to phase two, also a short study, but this time with patients—people who have whatever condition the drug targets. I'm still involved here for the same purpose. If all goes well for this small number of patients—they show some improvement and they don't exhibit any unacceptable side effects—it goes into phase three. In phase three many, many patients need to be studied over a long period. We're talking three years or more."

"And this is the phase where patients get recruited. I've seen posters in the hospital sometimes when I've visited Daniel."

"Yes." The waiter arrived to check on us, but Adam shooed him away. "Phase three is primarily about efficacy—does it work on the patients' condition over the long haul. Getting to phase three is pretty exciting, but a lot can go wrong. The drug might not work as expected, or it might cause problematic adverse events over time that outweigh the benefits the patients are receiving. Until phase three is finished, and the data analyzed, the whole picture isn't complete So, it's not a sure thing. But it's the only path to approval."

"And the picture's not complete until phase three is done?"

"Correct. And all along the FDA evaluates everything. The efficacy, the side effects, the adverse events. The FDA asks the sponsor for all kinds of reports and statistics."

"Sponsor?"

"The pharmaceutical company that's developing the drug. It's FDA-speak."

"Got it."

"Neddy, why *are* you taking notes?"

"I don't want to forget, in case I'm ever asked by a reporter or something." I sounded lame. My mind turned over and over what Charles had said about Lutense: that it had a perfectly good safety profile. But Adam had unknowingly revealed that couldn't be true. The safety profile wouldn't have been complete until the end of phase three. Lutense had failed in phase two.

"Why would a reporter ask you about— Does this have some relevance to the merger?"

"No, no, sorry." I forced my attention back to the present. "I'm interested because Charles has been keeping an old compound from Paramount on the back burner. He plans to develop it sometime. And I wasn't sure what's involved, since a prescription drug is different than a medical device like Alvee. What you've told me helps. Thank you."

The waiter appeared with the dessert menu. Adam raised an eyebrow at me, and I shook my head no. He winked at me and turned to the waiter.

"I think we'll skip it. We'll take the check."

We arrived at the school Saturday morning and made our way to the booth where Karen, Adam's sister, and his niece, Jessica, were setting up. Jessica bounded up and down, squealing with excitement as Adam approached.

After introductions he took charge, helping Jessica set up four mini stations inside the booth with beakers, mixing bowls, utensils, and a small hot plate. Karen and I stood ready, occasionally assisting by plugging in an extension cord or filling a water bucket. I watched Adam with Jessica, his patient explanations and jokes eliciting giggles and enthusiasm. How I wished to enjoy the day, but I couldn't stop thinking about Charles's lies.

Out of the corner of my eye, I noticed Karen appraising me. To avoid small talk, I feigned great interest in Adam and Jessica's preparations, smiling and nodding as they put the finishing touches on the rudimentary lab. But Karen, oblivious to my distraction, or perhaps challenging it, chatted at me until another parent she knew came along. Soon they were deep in a conversation about the school's volleyball team, her attention away from me as she walked with the woman toward an area where parents were setting up a bake sale. I kept my eyes on Adam and Jessica, but my mind tumbled over the growing crisis I faced.

At ten o'clock the science fair opened, and within minutes, four or five kids approached the booth, asking questions, pointing, and elbowing each other for a closer look. Adam invited the students into the booth, handed each a paper cup of vinegar, and directed one boy to add his to a beaker of cooking oil and watch the concoction separate. The kids seemed unimpressed but moved to the second station, where another boy, a stocky kid in a baseball jersey, dumped his paper cup into milk.

"Oh, gross," he declared, squinting at the curdled mess.

"That's nasty," said another.

The third station was the biggest hit—the classic volcano erupted the moment baking soda met vinegar.

"Cool!" two girls said in unison. The children crowded around the foaming beaker as it bubbled and spewed.

At the final station, a beaker of vinegar changed color after a handful of pennies were added.

Sadness washed over me as I watched Adam with those kids. The innocence, excitement, and laughter on their faces under-scored my misery. I longed to meander through the fair, enjoy the home-baked goods, and take in the simple pleasure of the beautiful day. I looked at the happy crowd. Surely none of these people had any worries.

Karen appeared, offering a steaming cup. "Adam thought you might need coffee."

"Thank you." I took the cup and smiled at her. She nodded, giving an obligatory smile in return, then turned to survey the group of children in front of us. I was making a horrible impres-sion on her.

"He's great with kids," I tried.

"Yes. He raised two of the best." She looked at me. "Do you have any?"

"Kids? No. I was married once but no children. Hope to someday though." Her face turned quizzical. I was nearly past child-bearing age, but I'd simply meant I'd welcome children into my life if they came attached to the right man. I opened my mouth to explain, but as I did, three boys ran past us, laughing and shoving each other.

"Slow down, guys," Karen called after them, then turned to me. "How long have you and Adam known each other?"

"Oh, not long. We met because our two companies are in talks. Potential merger."

"Potential? I thought it was a done deal."

I hadn't expected her to be so well informed. Adam must have filled her in. "It's not finalized, but yes, it's going well. I'm the CFO so, you know, always a bit cautious. Nothing's done till it's done." My stomach flipped. The merger date loomed, and I had some very tough decisions to make.

"How much of a bloodbath will it be?"

My mind twisted for a crazy, irrational second. What did Karen know about Lutense?

"Sorry?"

"How bad? Assuming the merger goes through. Because that always means layoffs."

"Right. It's still being negotiated," I lied.

She frowned. "I'm surprised. Those discussions usually take place early on."

I cocked my head.

"I'm a labor attorney," she explained, "so I've seen a few of these."

I flushed, feeling exposed. I'd underestimated her knowledge. "Then I'm sure you can appreciate the need for discretion at this point."

"Mom, come here!" Jessica called. Karen and I walked closer to the booth. Adam had begun ushering a second group of students through the stations. We watched the kids, Jessica whispering at each stage of the experiments, parroting Adam's descriptions as the vinegar mixed with each element in turn. Adam turned to the students.

"So, what did we learn?"

One boy, shorter than the others and carrying a binder, shouted out, "The vinegar does different things, depending on what you mix it with."

"That's right," Adam said to the children, "the same substance can react differently depending on what it's mixed with. That can happen outside, like what we just observed. But it can also happen on the inside of our bodies, with things you put in your body. Which is why it's so important not to take any drugs—anything at all—unless it's given to you by your doctor or your parents."

I stared at him, frozen. There it was. His words made the final connection in my brain, the one that had been teasing me with urgency yet staying just beyond my reach. I no longer heard anything but the meaning behind those words—not the chatter of the children, not even the music coming from a bandstand where a local rock group had started up.

Distant sirens grew louder, closer, jolting me to awareness. I stepped away from the booth, jabbing at my phone as I ordered a ride. I watched the slow progress of the driver on the app, cursing under my breath.

Karen stared at me.

"I'm sorry, I have to go," I mumbled, walking past her toward the exit.

"Wait here with Uncle Adam," I heard Karen call to Jessica. She caught up with me when I stopped in front of the school to wait for the ride.

"Hey, I hope you're not messing with my brother."

"What?" She was distracting me. I needed to be alone, to think.

"Listen." Karen grabbed my arm, coming close to my face.

Her breath hit me, acrid from the coffee. "He's had a hard time. His divorce. His ex-wife strung it along for almost two years. Made him think she was back to stay. So don't fuck him over."

I stared at her gray eyes, like Adam's but darker, unforgiving. "What are you talking about?"

She let go of me. "Don't hurt my brother. If you're not interested—and it doesn't look like you are—cut him loose now." She turned and disappeared into the schoolyard.

EIGHTEEN

ONCE IN THE LYFT, I called my father and asked him to meet me at the Starbucks near his house. Then I dialed Dr. Samson. After a few transfers and a lengthy hold, we were connected.

"Dr. Samson, it's Neddy Emory. I'm sorry to be calling instead of asking you in person, but there's something I need to know."

"Is Daniel alright? I just saw him yesterday."

"Yes—I mean nothing's happened as far as I know. But I need to ask you to be honest with me about his prognosis. Given where his health is today, and assuming there are no new medical interventions"—I closed my eyes, bracing for both my question and his response—"how much time does he have? Approximately?"

"Neddy, as I've said before, it's very hard to say for sure. We do know most patients at his stage generally do all right for about two to six months. Then things often deteriorate rapidly. But we've talked about this before, with Daniel and with your parents. Why the urgency today?"

"I'm, ah, thinking about an extended trip away. And I don't

want to not be here…" I choked up as the reality of the conversation gripped me.

"I see. It's only my best guess."

"I understand. One other thing. When Daniel was in the hospital the last time, one of the doctors there talked about his medications 'not playing well together.'"

"But I thought we'd gotten on top of that with Daniel. Is he having some symptoms leading you to think—"

"No, no. I wondered what the technical term is. 'Not playing well together.'"

"He was probably referring to drug interactions. To put it simply: Drug A impacts drug B, causing drug B to either become amplified or underutilized. In other words, too much of drug B or not enough of it. I can give you online references to drug interaction data if you're looking for what interferes with what or—"

"Thank you, Dr. Samson. You've helped me more than I can say."

He was silent, perhaps wondering what in the world I was fishing for.

"Thank you again, Doctor."

"Uh-huh. Goodbye now."

By the time Dad arrived at Starbucks, I'd already secured a table in the rear, far away from other patrons, and purchased a plain coffee for myself and a cappuccino for Dad.

"Hi, honey." He sat down across from me and reached for his cup.

"I talked to Dr. Samson today."

"What? Why?"

"I need to know Daniel's prognosis, –short- and long-term. How-how much time he has."

"Neddy! What are you saying? What's going on?"

"Something's wrong, something Charles has been doing with the research."

He stared at me, silent.

"And listen, this is super important—you can't say anything to him. I mean it."

He nodded. "Start at the beginning."

I detailed my investigation of what we'd been experiencing —from Alex's psychotic and violent break, Ryan's heart attack, Stevie's collapse and miscarriage, and my suspicions about Melody through my discoveries about Lutense and the likelihood of drug interactions causing all of it. My father listened, asking questions along the way and alternating between frowning and shaking his head as the story unfolded.

"Once Charles fired Melody, I was convinced it was over. But nothing changed." My voice cracked. "We have to stop putting the engineers at risk. We can continue with traditional development or try lucid dreaming without the doping—"

"Doping?"

"Yes. We can't risk anyone's health any longer, Dad. And that may mean we...we're too late for Daniel." The tears came relentlessly. I buried my face in my hands.

Dad moved closer to put his arm around my shoulders. "Calm down, honey, please. Don't cry. Take me through this one more time, I want to make sure I understand what you're saying."

When I'd composed myself, I went through it again. As I finished, he stood up. "I don't think you have anything here."

"Dad!"

"No proof."

"Dad! I have proof Lutense was in Charles's possession during this time. And each of the engineers who became sick— they were all on different prescriptions. I couldn't figure out for the longest time why they didn't have similar reactions if Lutense was being used. But now, there's no other explanation. We have to do the right thing."

"You have no proof, Neddy. You think you're connecting dots, but they don't draw a picture of anything. And we're not risking Danny's life on some emotional conclusion you've drawn. You're not talking to his doctors again. Forget it. You're imagining it."

I stared at my father. "Charles already talked to you about all this! Why didn't you—"

"I wanted to hear your side of it. Weigh each viewpoint." He looked away.

I knew he hadn't weighed anything. Once again, Charles's opinion was the only one that mattered.

"Dad, I'm begging you. I don't want to stop Alvee. I want to stop the risky way we're going about it. We can't do this—it's unethical. Worse, it's criminal—"

"That's it!" he shouted, banging on the table and knocking over my cup. "Charles knows what he's doing, for Christ's sake." Several customers stared at us. The barista, a slender young man with long hair pulled into a ponytail, took a few steps toward us, then stopped, hands on his hips. The hot coffee dribbled onto my jeans.

"Dad, I want you to think hard about this. Think about what I'm saying, the implications for the engineers and their families, the business itself. And yes, for Daniel. I'm trying to figure out a way to get out of this mess and still help Daniel, but I need you, Dad. I need you to help me get Charles to see reason. And I need you to talk to the board because we'll need their support."

"The board? No! Drop it, Neddy. I don't want to hear any more about this, you understand?" He pointed an accusing finger at me, his face twisted with pain and anger. "It's a nonstarter." He threw a wad of napkins toward me onto the table and left.

I still have no recollection of the drive home that afternoon, recalling only that I trembled so badly I had to use both hands to insert the key into the door of my condo. Once inside, I didn't know what to do with myself. I collected Waldo from Mrs. Gladstone and took him out to the common area adjacent to the parking lot. "No long walk today, buddy. Mommy is sick."

In the kitchen, I made chai and then went upstairs to draw a hot bath. Right before I sank into the steamy water, I checked my phone. Two messages from Adam and a couple of group chats from neighbors who wanted to set up a dinner. I responded quickly, telling Adam I'd had a great time at the science fair, apologized work had called me away, and promised I'd be in touch the next day. And to the dinner group, I tossed out a few dates, far enough into the future to keep them at bay.

On Sunday, Waldo woke me, needing to go out. I pulled on my sneakers, grabbed my wallet, and walked an extra half mile to a pastry shop, where I tied Waldo outside while I went in to get breakfast and coffee. Once home, I sat at my kitchen table, buttering the bagel while Waldo chewed his kibble. I would talk to our board whether Dad wanted me to or not. I was sick at the thought of doing so, turning away from my family, again, and sealing Daniel's fate, my beautiful, innocent brother. But I had a duty to the company, its board, its employees. A runaway freight train bore down on us, and I needed to get us off the tracks.

I texted Carollyn and Mindy, canceling our planned lunch for Wednesday, explaining work would keep me away, again not daring to share the truth of what I faced. Carollyn responded, demanding to know "your dating news." I promised to call that evening, a promise I knew I would break.

I called Phil Harrison, hoping to secure him as an ally. Though not the most assertive personality, Phil was the one board member who had been consistently supportive of me as CFO, and I wanted him beside me as I approached the much more formidable Max. I left a message on both his mobile and office numbers but did not hear back. Late in the afternoon I sent a text, and when that went unanswered, I knew he wasn't going to get involved. I went to bed without contacting Adam as I'd promised. I couldn't bear lying to him again.

On Monday, I phoned Max to say I was stopping by on my way to the office. He told me he was leaving for a business trip at five and that the only time he could see me was four o'clock. I would only have a few minutes to plead my case. As board chair, Max had primary fiduciary responsibility for Angiras. He'd also led his own company, so I prayed his business savvy would prevail and he would agree to help me force Charles into a temporary hold.

I worked from home until it was time to meet him. His office downtown was in a beautiful stone and granite Art Deco building. In the lobby I waited while the receptionist texted Max. An ornate mural on the ceiling featured Zeus throwing a lightning bolt toward a crowd of cowering mortals. Granite columns gleamed, reflecting light from the original brass chandeliers.

"They don't make 'em like that anymore." Max entered the lobby, nodding toward the elegant fixtures.

"No, they do not."

He ushered me into the elevator and in a moment, we'd arrived at his office on the top floor. He wore dark trousers, a custom-tailored dress shirt with monogrammed cuffs, and no tie. The travel bag near the door reminded me I had little time. Worse, I knew Charles had already gotten to him. And to Phil.

Max settled behind his large antique desk, and I sat across

from him. He looked at me over his reading glasses. "How can I help you, Neddy?"

I described my investigation, the evidence I'd unearthed, what I'd learned from Adam, being careful not to reveal my relationship with him, and what I'd discovered from the FDA website. "Charles has acknowledged he used Lutense, though he denies using it on the engineers."

"And you don't believe him," Max said, poker faced.

"No. At first, I thought Melody was dosing them—"

"'Dosing?'"

"Yes. Dosing. Or if you prefer, doping. It's not pretty, but that's what it is. Somehow, he's administering Lutense without their knowledge to optimize lucid dreaming. Melody has been gone for several weeks, and nothing has improved."

I was still livid about the separation agreement he'd approved for Melody but kept my tone professional—I needed Max's support to stop Charles, and showing my anger would only complicate matters.

"I've analyzed all the evidence multiple times and I always come to the same conclusion. I searched for a common denominator, something beyond the symptoms each engineer exhibited, because of course their symptoms were all different. But the thing is"—I kept my eyes on him—"their reactions to Lutense *are* all the same. Each had a recurrence of a chronic illness they'd been taking prescriptions for. That's the link. Lutense interferes with each of their medications. We can't ignore it."

"What are you going to do?" The question surprised me.

"I need your help, Max. You're the chairman of the board."

"What are you planning to do?" he repeated. "Because you can't prove this."

If he had even an ounce of trepidation, he wasn't showing it.

"This can't be a coincidence, Max." I took a deep breath. "We need to halt the dream program, or at least ensure the engineers no longer get dosed. And we'll need different resources to continue development of Alvee."

Max shook his head, then stood up and walked toward his travel bag.

"We're about to merge with Salton-Winstrom." He slipped his jacket on. "I'm not inclined to screw that up based on some unfounded accusations."

I bit my inner lip. "I've brought you evidence of unethical, perhaps even illegal research. Aren't you *inclined* to at least follow up?"

He turned and glared at me. "Don't be naïve, Neddy. Medical research is fraught with trade-offs. Have you ever read one of those pamphlets that come with prescriptions? About all the side effects? Nausea, diarrhea, suicidal thoughts. And those are for drugs the FDA actually approved. There's always risk. Every drug, every medical device is imperfect, and so is the research behind them. You have no proof. Get over it."

I stood and walked closer, never taking my eyes off him. I kept my voice even and low. "Get over it? Charles is making our employees sick, and I'm probably signing Daniel's death sentence by trying to stop that from happening. My brother's going to die, my entire family will blame me for it, and you're worried about a merger? You pompous ass."

NINETEEN

BY THE TIME I arrived at the office at five thirty, the building was starting to empty out. I found the lab vacant, so I took the stairs down to the Hovel, finding Jeff and Ryan with their heads bent over an Alvee prototype, adjusting the instrument with a diminutive tool.

"Hey guys." I kept my voice low, not wanting to startle them.

"Hi, Neddy." Ryan straightened up. "How's it going?"

"Okay. How's the scope?"

He sighed and rolled his eyes.

"Sorry, you must get tired of that particular question."

"I wish we had a different answer for y'all. You got a minute?"

"Of course." We moved away from the table toward a corner of the office.

"Sorry for the mess." Ryan cleared empty coffee cups and leftover doughnuts from the table. "I'm glad you stopped by today." He glanced in Jeff's direction and lowered his voice. "I know you wanted us to let you know if anything unusual happens in the lab? Well, I think Alex has started to..." He lowered his voice again, to just above a whisper. "...act funny again."

I fought to keep my voice even and matter-of-fact as panic consumed me.

"What have you observed?"

"He was agitated today when he woke up."

"Like before?"

"Similar. Maybe not as disoriented, but not himself—"

"Where is he now?"

"Charles took him up to his office."

I walked back up to the third floor, my heart pounding. On the way, I phoned Erin and told her to come take Alex home. "Bring someone with you."

Then I dialed the front desk and directed them to have Erin wait in the Engineering office.

When I knocked on Charles's door, I heard muffled voices from within. After a moment, I knocked again. The voices stopped, and I waited.

"It's Neddy," I said, loud enough to be heard. Another ten seconds passed. "I'm not going away."

"One moment," Charles called from the other side. The door opened a crack and he peered at me. "Yes?"

"Is Alex here?"

"Yes. Alex and I are meditating. And you're interrupting."

"Let me in."

He hesitated, then opened the door with a faux flourish.

"You *are* interrupting," he repeated. I ignored him and surveyed the room. Alex sat on the floor near the alcove, knees drawn up, rocking slightly.

"How is he?"

"He's okay now. He woke up agitated. I've been helping him relax."

"I called Erin."

"Who?"

"*His wife!*"

"Why?"

I was incredulous. "He needs to go home. And she needs to be aware of his state of mind."

"He's fine."

"This is exactly what happened last— Let's step out for a minute."

Once in the corridor, I took a big breath and lowered my voice to a near whisper. "Look, Charles, we need to figure out another way to move the research forward. Tim is still on leave, probably because he's scared to be in the lab, and Ryan spoke with me today. He's very concerned about Alex. It's only a matter of time before they'll all refuse to participate. With Tim, Stevie, and Alex now out—"

"Alex isn't 'out. '"

"You can't be serious!" I looked up and down the corridor but saw no one on the floor. "He might be at the beginning of another psychotic break. It's criminal to ignore that possibility."

"Criminal? Are you insane? I'm a doctor, remember? I'm the one qualified to assess his fitness to continue or not."

"You're not a shrink," I whisper-yelled at him. "And even if you were, *I don't believe you.*"

I turned, bumping into Erin, who'd just rounded the corner at a near run. She looked from me to Charles. She must have overheard at least some part of our argument.

"Where's Alex?" she demanded. Charles glared at me.

"Erin, I asked for you to wait in Engineering," I sputtered.

"Ryan said Alex is up here. I want to see my husband."

Charles switched to his most soothing cadence, smiled, and opened the door. "He's inside. You're more than welcome to come in, Erin."

We filed into the office.

"Alex said he felt a little agitated when he woke up from the dream session," Charles purred, "but he's doing fine now. I guided him through some meditation, and he's had some juice."

Alex had stepped down to the yoga alcove and sat on a cushion facing away from us. Erin approached him, speaking in a low voice.

"Hi, sweetie. How are you feeling?"

He looked at Erin but said nothing.

"Neddy called me and asked me to come by. Maybe drive you home? You're not feeling great?"

"I…don't know." His voice was hoarse.

"Do you want me to call Dr. Rogers?"

"What? Why?"

"Sweetie, you seem a little…confused." Erin touched his shoulder.

"No, I'm annoyed."

"Okay, about what?"

"I'm tired of answering questions." His voice rose and she took a defensive step back.

"Erin," I said. "Can I speak with you for a moment?" She walked toward me, keeping her eyes on Alex.

"You need to take him home. Can you call someone to help you?"

Charles moved closer to Alex and knelt, his gaze benevolent.

"I-I don't understand what's going on." Erin turned to me. "He's been feeling so much better. The doctor changed his medication, he's been taking it every day, every dose. I make sure."

My chest tightened, and I realized I'd stopped breathing. How could Charles continue this charade?

"Erin, will you be all right here for a few minutes, while I speak to Charles? We'll be right outside if you need us."

She nodded.

I motioned to Charles. He rose, gave me an annoyed look, and then we stepped out into the corridor and into a conference room. I closed the door behind us. I was desperate to convince Charles. We couldn't leave Erin and Alex alone for more than a few minutes.

"Charles, you must stop the Lutense. It's interacting with his medication."

Surprise flickered in his eyes before they turned stony, his voice low and remote. "We're very close to completing Alvee. I'm not stopping anything."

"You must." I reached for his arm, but he turned away.

"You don't know what you're talking about." His voice was slightly below a shout. "Have you ever seen me administer anything to the engineers without their consent?"

He walked the length of the table, rounded its end, and didn't stop until he'd reached me again on the other side. "Tell me!" he demanded, grabbing me by the arm. His fingers tightened, and a memory of Jeremy twisting my arm threatened to panic me.

"No." I wrenched myself free. "But it's the only missing piece."

He stared, his lips twitching, his breath heavy. Would he do the right thing?

"Get away from me."

I walked out of the conference room, shaking. I wanted to leave the building, but I didn't trust Charles with Alex and Erin. I smoothed my hair, adjusted my sweater, and stepped back into Charles's office. Alex was agitated, wild-eyed.

"Can't get them to shut up," he repeated over and over, hugging his knees to his chest.

Erin pulled a vial of lavender oil from her purse, rubbed it her into palms and massaged Alex's temples and shoulders.

"I'm gonna put the lavender on your wrists, okay? So if you start to feel anxious, you can sniff it."

He nodded. After another tense moment, he quieted.

"EMTs are on the way." Her hands were shaking. I could nearly see the anxiety, as if it smoldered just under her pale skin.

Erin approached us. "I gave him another dose of his meds. Hopefully, that'll help. I'm calling his doctor." She grabbed at her belly. "I'm sorry but I *have* to use the ladies' room right now, before the EMTs get here. I may be a few minutes."

"No problem. Go ahead. It's at the end of the hall. I'll sit with him," Charles said.

Erin glanced back at Alex one more time and then headed into the corridor toward the ladies' room. Charles stepped down into the alcove and offered Alex a second bolster to prop against his back.

Alex's eyes searched the room, as if he'd awoken in a strange place. "I'm cold."

Charles crossed the office into the kitchen. "I'll get you some hot tea, buddy."

I heard him humming as he prepared the tea. I looked around the room devastated, recalling our early days building Angiras. How many plans had we made in here? The long hours, the long odds of success. Our optimism and determination drove us even when we were petrified of failure.

But I had never been more terrified of the future than at that moment.

My eyes fell on the credenza, and without a second thought, I walked over, glanced toward the kitchen, then opened the drawer. I spotted it immediately: Melody's signature bright-orange flash drive stood out from the drab contents strewn across the bottom. I slipped it into my cardigan pocket and closed the drawer, then walked toward Alex and stood looking at him, the lavender assaulting the air. I'd been convinced this man had been abusive before he'd ever come to work for us. But here I was, holding the proof I was wrong in my sweater pocket.

Charles brought the tea to Alex and the irony hit me.

"What kind is it, Charles?" I didn't even try to keep the snark out of my voice.

"Mint," he replied evenly, setting the mug down near Alex, then stepping close to me. "If you don't believe in what I'm doing, you're free to resign," he whispered, then moved away.

I followed. "I'm aware of my options, Charles. But I won't abandon our employees as long as I believe they're in danger. Not like you, not like Max."

"You're insane."

Alex stood, a little unsteady. "What's wrong with you two? Don't you like each other anymore?"

Whatever spell the poor soul was under, he nonetheless sensed the tension between us.

"Where's my wife? Where'd Erin go?" Alex clenched and unclenched his fists.

"Just went to the restroom." Charles crossed to the alcove and touched Alex's shoulder. "Why don't you sit here and wait for her?" He patted the bolster.

I walked toward the door. "I may be insane, Charles. But I'm no criminal."

I heard a horrific sound behind me, like an animal bellowing. Alex grabbed me by the hair and yanked my head backward, pressing a knee into my spine. Pain seared into my neck, my back, my scalp. Another hellish snarl exploded in my ear. Self-defense tactics lurched single file through my mind. My arms whipped behind me, grabbing for Alex—his arms, his torso, anywhere. But he kept pulling me downward, until I was on my knees, bending backward. I reached blindly forward, flailing for a chair or a tabletop to steady myself, desperate to right myself and wrench away. His fingers circled my neck. His grip tightened and my breath snagged. I heaved a trickle of air into my lungs, my thoughts sprinting, random and frantic. *Where is Charles? He can stop Alex. Is he hurt too? Am I going to die now?*

I gagged, then inhaled with great effort. A tiny wisp of air crept into my lungs. I tried again, then fell forward, an enormous weight on my back. I tried to crawl, but the heaviness kept me in place, fingers relentless against my throat. Flat on the floor, I tried to move side to side several times, but even the slightest wriggle required enormous effort. I stopped then, concentrating only on taking breaths, as shallow as they might be. It was cooler on the floor—maybe I wouldn't need as much air if I lay still. Then, sharp pain in my chest, radiating down my arms. Soon, I lost sensation in my hands and fingers. Finally, images: a sailboat on a calm sea, an elephant herd running, dust flying, my grandmother singing. I relaxed, no longer fighting. Sleep was coming.

"Stop! Stop! Let her go." A voice, distorted, as if traveling through water. "Let her go!" Then the monster's hands released my neck, and I was coughing, heaving big gulps of air, clawing forward. From behind I heard grunting, cursing, and then glass breaking. When I reached the door, still on hands and knees, I turned to see Alex and Charles on the floor, shards from the shattered coffee table scattering beneath them.

Alex sat astride Charles, pinning his arms against the floor. "Stop fighting, man!"

I heard Erin at the door, pounding to be let in. "What's happening? Open up!"

Charles bent his knees, and with his feet grounded, thrust his hips high, catapulting Alex over his head toward the windows. Charles twisted and scrambled upright, a deranged look on his face, the backs of his arms bloodied. He lunged for Alex. The next instant they were on the floor again, rolling toward the alcove, a grotesque human tumbleweed. When they ran into one of the side chairs, Charles yelped and let go of Alex, who slid sideways and stood.

He glanced from me to Charles and in that instant, I saw the slightest shaking of his head, a fleeting frown. He was confused but no longer aggressive. "That's enough, Charles," Alex panted. Charles stood, glanced at me, then lunged again.

Alex took a step back, stumbling on the steps to the alcove.

His arms windmilled as he tried to regain his balance, but he fell straight back, smacking his head on the marble altar with a horrendous pop. I turned, jerked the door open, and saw Erin running toward us, with Ryan and Jeff right behind her.

"He tried to kill me, he tried to kill me!"

TWENTY

I WAS HOSPITALIZED, sedated, and kept for observation. Assigned to a private room, I slept for hours until I woke with a throbbing head. When I tried to rub my forehead, I found my arms constricted by IVs and monitors. My mouth felt like a squadron of desert troops had marched through it. The lights were dim. My father slept in a recliner in the corner.

"Dad," I croaked. He started, then stood and rushed to my bedside.

"Honey, how you feeling?"

"Like crap."

"You gave us a helluva scare. Thank God you're all right. The doctors checked you out real good."

"What time is it?"

"Almost midnight. Sweetie, do you want anything? Water? Are you hungry?"

"My head. It's splitting."

"I'll get the nurse." I must have dozed off again. When I opened my eyes, he stood next to a nurse, who checked my pulse.

"Do you think you can swallow a pill?" she asked. The question seemed absurd, but when I tried, I almost gagged. My throat was sore and every muscle in my neck revolted. I forced myself to drink some of the water, then swished another mouthful to moisten my parched tongue.

I began to recall bits of what had happened, all the while not wanting to. My argument with Charles, Alex mumbling. Had Erin been there? Mostly I relived the terror and desperation when I'd thought I was dying.

"Is Charles okay?"

"Yes, he pulled you out of that room."

"I can't remember. What happened to Alex?"

"I think— Honey, he hit his head real bad. Thank God because he might have killed the two of you." He choked up, bending over me.

"Oh my God. Did he die?"

Dad nodded, wiped his nose.

"Oh my God. This can't be happening. Dad! We could have stopped this!"

"No, no, Neddy. Don't talk like that. Alex was dangerous."

"Where's-where's Charles?"

"He had to talk to the police for hours. They had to go over the whole mess with him."

"Did Alex hurt him too?"

"No, he's fine. Shook up though. He'll be by to see you tomorrow. You'll feel better by then. You'll get a good night's sleep and tomorrow, have your perspective back."

How I wished he were right. "Where's Mom?"

"Home with Danny. Shall we call? They'll want to talk to you."

"No, it's too late. Let them sleep." I closed my eyes. "Dad, can you stay tonight? I don't want to be alone."

"I'm not going anywhere, pumpkin."

No matter how exhausted one is, hospitals are not ideal places to get a good night's sleep. The nursing staff checked my vitals every two hours. The smell of disinfectant was constant and conspired with incessant pinging of monitoring equipment to ensure I slept fitfully.

Dad, true to his word, stayed with me all night. In the morning, as I finished the bland breakfast I'd been provided, Charles came in, hugged me hard, then picked up my chart and flipped through it.

"Good, no sign of concussion. You'll be sore for several days. But how are you feeling? Emotionally?"

"Oh, lovely, never better," I croaked.

He grimaced.

"I guess I'm still in shock." My eyes wandered, as if the answer to all this madness lay written on a tiny piece of paper, tucked up somewhere into a corner of the ceiling. "I keep seeing it in my mind again and again, but some parts are fuzzy. I can't believe he freaked out the way he did. He was agitated earlier, but then he seemed to—"

"Yeah, he... I underestimated his mental state. Immensely," Charles cut in. "I'm so sorry, Neddy." He looked both horrified by what had happened and embarrassed he'd misread the situation.

"I'm so glad you were there."

"I promise, it won't happen again."

I lay against the pillow and closed my eyes. I had never been so weary. Every word, every gesture required a huge effort. I was relieved Alex was no longer a threat to anyone, but I also knew we were responsible for his demented behavior. Would I ever be able to reconcile the two?

"You've been through a hell of a trauma." Charles's voice was firm. "And you'll never have to go through it again. I'll take care of you. Like I did this time."

My eyes remained closed. "I kept thinking you'd left the

room because I didn't hear you. Did you leave the room for a while?" My voice caught in my throat.

"No, no. I was behind you. Everything happened very fast. You remember me yelling at Alex, right?"

"Not really. I remember hearing some awful howl and then he had my hair." I ran my hand along my tender scalp and winced.

"He was crazed. I pulled him off, but he kept trying to get to you."

"I can't remember."

"Don't try to. Don't worry about anything except healing."

"What's going to happen to Erin?"

"I've been in touch with her. And HR has, of course. And all the engineers. They've been very supportive. She wanted to come visit you, but I told her it's better if she didn't."

"Oh my God. Charles—"

He stepped closer, held my hand, and held my gaze. "Neddy, none of this is your fault. It's my fault."

"Then you'll stop. You promise?"

He nodded. He turned to Dad. "She'll be okay."

"I know, but it's going to take a while. Honey, I'm so sorry you had to go through this."

Mom came in, looked from Charles to Dad, then pushed past them to sit on the edge of my bed. She took my face in her hands.

"Oh, my Neddy."

I tried to stifle the tears.

"You let it all out. Cry as long as you want."

"Myra," Dad said. "Don't upset her."

The men in my family had always been uncomfortable when the women cried. My dad claimed letting us sob got us "too worked up."

"Nonsense." My mother shooed them away. "Go get coffee or something. Neddy and I are going to have a good cry."

And we did.

"You should take Dad home," I choked out, after I'd blown my nose for the last time. "He's exhausted."

"We'll be here for a while. Daniel was admitted last night."

"Oh God. I didn't even ask. How is he, Mom?"

"He's on the ventilator again. That's getting to be a semi-regular occurrence now."

"Mom." I swallowed hard. "I told Dad, but I need to tell you. Charles is…not going to be able to continue the dream program. The guy—Alex—who grabbed me. He was one of our engineers—"

"I know all about it, Neddy."

"You do?"

"Dad told me. All of it. Your theory of the team and their ailments…" She glanced toward the door and lowered her voice. "Those are serious accusations."

"Mom—"

"Shush. You're mistaken, don't you think, Neddy? Charles would never do such a thing."

"It doesn't matter anymore, I guess."

"No worries, honey." Her voice animated as Dad and Charles returned to the room. She stepped back, never taking her eyes off me.

I'll be forever grateful to my mother for allowing me a much-needed meltdown that morning. Unfortunately, as soon as she left, I was sobbing all over again. The prospect of Daniel deteriorating while we pulled the plug on the dream lab was too much for me.

The police came an hour after my family had gone to visit Daniel two floors down. I pulled myself together enough to take them through the events leading to the attack, recalling a few more details as I went—Charles's attempt to help Alex meditate, Erin trying to calm him—but I left out the horrible argument Charles and I had had about Lutense.

"After Alex let you go, what happened next?" Detective Brooks, the younger of the two officers, asked.

"I don't remember, I…focused on trying to breathe. Big, deep breaths. At some point I heard a commotion behind me, and I guess I turned around because then I saw my brother fighting with Alex. Broken glass was everywhere. Charles saved me."

I started to sob again, shaking. I pulled the blanket up.

"Take your time." Lt. Chin spoke softly. "Sometimes the smaller details emerge slowly."

"It all happened so fast—I mean, the part where Alex grabbed me. But it seemed like hours before he let me go."

"When you observed the fighting, did you see the deceased, Mr. Ruindes, strike your brother, either with his arm or fist?"

"I saw Alex on top of Charles."

"You mean Charles was on the floor?"

"Yes, Alex sat on his chest, holding Charles's arms and screaming at him to 'calm down' or 'stop'."

"And at any point did Alex hit Charles?"

"If he did, I didn't see it."

"What happened next?"

"Charles hoisted himself up, kind of raised his hips very suddenly and managed to get out from under Alex. Alex sort of somersaulted over Charles's head and then stood up. Sorry, I can't describe it any other way."

"It's okay, continue."

"Then, like I said, there was glass everywhere. The coffee table had been smashed. I saw them on the floor, thrashing around in all this glass. Like you see in those ridiculous wrestling things on TV, rolling and grunting. Then I think Charles bumped into something and Alex stood up and—" I stopped talking. The tears were relentless.

After a few moments Detective Brooks touched my arm. "Ms. Emory. We know Alex stumbled and hit his head on another table. We went to the scene and saw the steps he tripped on. Your brother tried to protect you, and himself. He said Alex moved toward you again, threatening you, shouting, and he lunged toward Alex to intercept. Can you confirm his statement?"

I was confused, recalling part of the scene and conflating what I did remember—Charles lunging and Alex's fall—with what Charles had described to me after the fact. All I wanted was to move on.

"Yeah, that's what happened."

Later, I woke to find Mindy and Carollyn whispering in the corner.

"Hey, Neddy." Mindy stood and walked toward me, Carollyn following close. My mother had reached out to them.

"Oh, you guys. You didn't have to come." I propped myself up.

"My God." Carollyn moved nearer to the bed. "What happened?"

"It's a nightmare," was all I managed.

"It was that crazy employee, right?" Carollyn prompted. "That nut who beat up his wife."

"Alex. Yes. I really don't want to talk about it."

They looked at each other.

"Okay." Mindy stroked my arm. "We get it. What can we do for you? Who's taking care of Waldo?"

"My parents, I guess. I should be out of here in a day or so."

"You need your iPad or anything? I hope you're not going

back to work right away." Carollyn stared at my bruised neck and arm. "You're gonna need therapy."

"I have to."

"Don't be ridiculous, Neddy," Carollyn insisted. "No one, not even Charles, can ask that of you. Get out of town for a while."

"I can't."

"Baloney. You need to decompress, big time."

Mindy gave Carollyn a look that said *slow down*. "Neddy, wasn't there someone you were seeing? A new guy?"

"Yeah." I smiled despite my fatigue. "His name is Adam. I met him during the merger talks. He works for Salton-Winstrom."

"You still seeing him?" she asked.

"Yeah, we're taking it slow. But yes. He's...a really good guy, I think."

"We'll be the judges of that," Carollyn joked.

"Has he been by to see you?"

"I...haven't told Adam about this."

"Why?" Carollyn demanded. "Maybe he'll take you away for a few days. It'd do you good."

"Look, my parents don't know about him."

"What's he like?" Mindy smiled at me.

I knew she was trying to cheer me up, get my mind off the pain and fear I felt. Since I didn't dare tell the truth about what had prompted Alex's behavior, I followed her lead.

"Adam is really smart, a PhD in Pharmacology. He's funny and he knows what's important. He's balanced. It's the only way I can describe him."

"'Balanced.'" Carollyn raised an eyebrow. "That's an improvement."

"We hit it off right away, you know? Every once in a great while you meet someone who you just get along with and it's... not like you've been friends forever, exactly, 'cause you don't know each other's history. But somehow, you like the same movies, the same food, the same comedians, you have the same values, and you click right away."

"So why take it slowly?" Carollyn asked.

"Neither of us wants to make a mistake."

"Fair enough. You done the dirty deed yet?"

"Carollyn!" Mindy scolded.

"You want to know as bad as I do, hypocrite." She turned to Mindy, hands on her hips.

"What, are we sixteen again?" I laughed, forgetting my pain for a moment.

The two of them smiled inquisitively.

"Oh, all right, yes. Are you satisfied now?"

"No details?"

"No details, Carollyn! I don't kiss and tell."

"I only mean are you…compatible?"

I laughed out loud as a nurse entered the room.

"Visiting hours are over," she admonished.

"Oh God, Carollyn," Mindy shoved her toward the door. "Neddy's capable of determining *that* without reporting to you. Good night, dear friend, we'll talk tomorrow."

I waved and laughed again.

"Looks like someone's feeling better," the nurse said as she checked my chart.

Alone again, my thoughts seesawed between hopefulness and worry, finally settling in darkness. I thought about all the people who would learn about the attack. All the questions I didn't want to answer, all the pitying glances from those too reticent to speak, and the dramatic exclamations from those who talk incessantly.

And Adam. I needed to contact him, but I didn't trust myself to hold it together once I heard his voice.

> Guess where I am?

A ridiculous, breezy opening text, given my situation.

> You first. Hint: I'm not in California at the moment

> Really? What's going on?

> I had to fly out to a clinical site in Toronto. Some issues with a safety trial

> How long?

Was it possible I could delay telling him?

> At least another 4 days. I miss you

> I miss you too. A lot

> So where are you? Anyplace fun?

> No, I'm a little under the weather. Just resting

> Good, rest up. I'll try to call you later but things are a bit off kilter here

If only he knew.

> No worries. Let me know when you're coming back

I closed my phone and heaved a sigh of relief, hoping once Adam learned of my assault, he would not be angry that I had not told him immediately. With Charles no longer using Lutense on the engineers, I would never have to burden Adam with the full story.

But one thing nagged at me. Everyone believed Alex had been negligent: he'd stopped taking his medications, leading to his psychotic break, the assault on Erin, and all the resulting chaos culminating in his accidental death. I didn't want Erin and her family to forever suffer that lie, but as I turned it over in my mind again and again, I couldn't figure out how to set the record straight without exposing the company and my family, especially Daniel, to great peril.

TWENTY-ONE

"A PRESS CONFERENCE TODAY?" I was settled at my desk on the first day back at the office. Charles, after greeting me at the front door and escorting me upstairs, was seated across from me. "You didn't say anything about scheduling a press conference."

"I wanted you to focus on your recuperation."

"Thanks. I'm not looking forward to answering a bunch of nosy questions from the press."

"They'll be focused on the merger details. As far as Alex goes, all the information the press has is that he suffered an unfortunate accident here last week."

"What about the employees?"

"Still a bit rattled. We brought in grief counselors last week. I think that helped a little. The engineers started a fundraising effort for Alex's family, but otherwise they don't seem to want to talk about what happened. They will be glad to see you back."

How could I face the engineers after what had happened to Alex?

I waited until the press conference was well underway before I stepped in, to avoid the reporters, yes, but also to buy time before I had to interact with our staff. Charles and Marie headlined the event. I stood at the rear and scanned the crowd. In addition to the press, board members, executives, and rank-and-file employees from both companies sat in rows facing the lectern. Marie was radiant as she spoke about the "upcoming marriage" of the two firms, the expectations for greater research outcomes, faster product development, and greater shareholder value.

"One of the reasons I'm particularly excited," Marie said, smiling toward Charles, "is because of the innovative approaches Angiras has taken in product development. As you are all aware, the lucid dreaming methodology has produced tremendous results. It has expedited product testing and provided science a new tool for technical problem-solving. And Charles and I are thrilled to announce today, under the new merged entity, we'll be expanding—doubling—the size of the sleep lab and employing more innovation engineers to participate."

The two exchanged smiles as the cameras clicked and videos rolled. I stood stunned, as if I'd stepped on an electrical wire. The leadership of our company stood, applauded, and smiled. My dad was in the front row, enjoying accolades and congratulations. Max and Phil were jubilant.

I shuddered, closed my eyes, and turned to leave. Heading for the door, I locked eyes with Adam. I gave him a lackluster wave. He motioned for me to meet in the corridor. My gut wrenched. He'd finished in Toronto earlier than expected, but I'd barely responded to his texts and calls since then. I walked into the corridor and found him leaning against the wall.

"Adam, I'm sorry I've been so out of touch. I was sick." My hand went to the turtleneck hiding my bruised neck.

"Look, Neddy. I don't know what's going on. But I assume you're not ready to see me again."

"Oh, it's not that. I'm so sorry—"

He held up his hand. "You know what? I thought we were on a good path there for a while. But yesterday I realized we aren't. You are always apologizing for being unavailable, distracted, or tired. You're stretched too thin, and I hope it's no more than that because the only other thing I figured out is you're hiding something from me. And that's something I've experienced before. So let's part as friends for the time being. Soon enough, we'll be coworkers, and I don't want us to feel awkward, or like we need to explain ourselves to each other."

Kimberly walked by and smiled at us.

"Or to anyone else."

My heart ached for this man, who had been nothing but caring toward me. In all the madness of the last few weeks, I had not spent time with him, making excuse after excuse and figuring I'd make up for it when I finally came clean. Too late, I realized the absurdity of assuming he would wait indefinitely, like an inanimate object—a box of cereal with a shelf life, tucked into the cupboard—until I deemed myself ready. His sister had been right. I'd kept so much from Adam already, and I still couldn't share the complete truth.

So instead of loving this dear man, I let him go. I nodded.

He turned and went out the front door.

The press conference began to break up. I headed for the stairwell to avoid the crowds in the lobby. Once the door closed behind me, my eyes filled, my chest constricted, as if a band tightened over my ribs. I grabbed the banister with both hands to stay upright, taking the treads sideways in an awkward ascension. "One step at a time," I urged my quivering legs. "Just get to the office." When I reached the first landing, I heard the door below bang open.

"I wonder which office we'll end up at." I didn't recognize the female voice.

"Theirs, for sure. They have a lot more people," a male responded.

"Crap. My commute will double. On top of everything else." The third voice belonged to Jeff.

The three approached quickly, talking over each other about the extra work sure to be in front of them. Once they turned the corner onto the landing, they spotted me, facing the wall, still gripping the banister.

"Neddy!" Jeff said. "Are you okay?"

I had no choice but to turn and look at them, unable to hide the anguish on my face.

"What the hell?" Jeff said. The others stared.

"It's a leg cramp." I managed a pathetic smile. "I get them sometimes."

"It must be a doozy." Jeff stepped closer. "Can we help you? Do you want to sit down?"

"Nothing to worry about," I choked out. "It'll pass. You guys go on ahead."

"You sure?"

"Yeah, I need a minute until it passes. Go ahead."

When I finally pulled myself together and exited the stairwell, I walked quickly toward my office, shaky and desperate for privacy.

"Neddy?" Erin walked toward me accompanied by another woman.

I froze.

"Neddy." She came very close. Thinner than ever, pain and exhaustion had overtaken her delicate features. "This is my sister, Wanda."

I murmured a hello. Wanda nodded without smiling.

"I'm sorry to just stop by." Erin spoke quickly. "But I wanted to see you, to tell you—"

"How-how did you get up here?" I managed to stammer. Since the attack, I'd become hyperaware of security in the office.

"We checked in at the front, like we're supposed to," Wanda said. Her voice held a hint of aggression. Not loud, but austere. She was at least four inches taller than Erin, sturdily built with a face squeezed into what looked like a permanent scowl. "We told them we wanted to see you because—"

Erin interrupted her sister. "I'm sorry, Neddy. I wanted to talk to you. The receptionist called you, and when you didn't pick up after the big meeting, Ryan brought us up to the second floor. I hope that's okay?"

I eyed the engineering office.

"I wanted to tell you how sorry I am," she continued. "And how much I misjudged Alex's—"

"What Erin means," Wanda cut in, "is Alex hid the fact that he wasn't taking his medications. Erin was totally unaware of that fact." She shook her finger at me. "Totally. Not. Aware."

"I know." I sounded impatient, but Wanda seemed satisfied. I guessed she was either an attorney herself or acting under an attorney's advice: Erin must distance herself from Alex's actions.

"We—the family—had his funeral last week." Erin bit her lip. "His parents are devastated."

The tightness in my chest merged with nausea in my belly. I searched for something to fix my gaze on, finding the thermostat on the wall over Wanda's shoulder.

Deep breaths.

"And the funeral gave me a certain closure, I guess…"

I stopped listening, concentrating on not throwing up. Erin kept talking, until Wanda, watching me closely, nudged her.

"What I wanted to ask… Can I hug you?"

"Hu-hug me?"

"I feel so awful about what you've gone through, and I so appreciate you and Charles trying to help Alex. It means a lot to me. I come from a very affectionate family and—"

"Okay. Yes, it's okay," I blurted, desperate to end the conversation and get her out of the building. She stepped forward and put her arms around me. I patted her back half-heartedly and tried to extricate myself, but Erin held on. My initial mortification melted away as I realized how good it felt being embraced by this frail woman, whose fate was forever intertwined with mine. How strangely calming was her warmth and simple humanity.

"I hope you'll be okay," she finally whispered, pulling away. "I'm praying for both of us." The aroma of lavender floated off her skin, and the memory of Erin trying to calm Alex on the day he died broke my heart. I nodded, turned, and walked away, unable to look her in the eye.

———

Once in my office with the door locked, tears of rage and despair overtook me. I curled up in my chair and didn't move for more than an hour, when the incessant ringing of my phone forced me to my feet.

Unknown Caller. I ignored it, sat down at my desk, and stared at the wall. The phone rang again.

"The world's most persistent telemarketer," I mumbled, blowing my nose. "Maybe that'll be my next career move." The phone went silent, then lit up once more. This time I accepted the call, primed to first charm the fool into believing he'd reached a gullible warm prospect and then, once on the hook, unload my pent-up rage and frustration onto his unsuspecting shoulders.

"Hello," I cooed into the phone.

"Neddy? It's Melody."

My heart skipped a beat. "Oh," I managed to squeak out. "I've-I've been trying to reach you." I swallowed hard.

"Yeah, I'm aware."

I waited, but she didn't offer any further explanation. "Melody, I have so many questions—"

"I can't talk long. I shouldn't be talking to you at all."

"Why? I don't understand."

A long pause. "Look, Charles has made things difficult for me." Another pause. "Did you get the stuff I sent you?"

"Yes, yes. The, uh, Post-it pad, the breath freshener—"

"And the flash drive?"

"Yes, the flash drive with the video."

The video. I remembered grabbing the flash drive right before Alex attacked me. Had I lost it in the aftermath?

"Yes, yes, I watched it." My mind scrambled. "Can you help me out, Melody? Because although I watched it, I didn't see anything unusual. What am I looking for? Where is the Lutense?"

"The film. It's in the film," she said.

The call ended.

I sat down, cursing. Why had she bothered to call? She'd offered no new information, only talked in circles about everything being "in the film." Why now?

Then it dawned on me. The press conference announcing the expansion of the dream program—she'd seen it. Melody wasn't yanking my chain. She was giving me a call to action.

***

I raced down the freeway toward my condo, alternately cursing and beseeching. "Please, dear God, let it be there." I pulled into my parking spot and ran for the front door. Waldo jumped off the sofa and stretched, then yapped at my heels as I took the stairs two at a time to my bedroom on the second floor. I pulled dirty laundry out of the hamper until I saw the plastic bag the hospital had provided that held the clothes I'd worn the day of the attack. Upon returning home nearly a week ago I'd dropped the bundle into the hamper, unable to face unloading it. Had the small flash drive survived the struggle or been dislodged somewhere in Charles's office? Or in the ambulance en route to the hospital? I eased the cardigan, wrinkled and twisted, out of the bag, then held it for a moment.

"*Please* be here." I closed my eyes, held my breath, and slowly slipped my hand into the right pocket. *Please.*

My fingers grazed something small but solid.

As much as I'd wanted to locate that little orange plastic and metal device, when I held it in my hand, I was terrified. Once I watched the video stowed in its tiny circuitry and found whatever Melody assured me was there, I would have only one more chance to convince Charles to stop. And I wasn't at all sure he would.

I grabbed my laptop and inserted the drive. As it whirred and loaded, Waldo whined and turned in circles, needing to go out. I took the laptop with me downstairs to the coffee table. Waldo ran to the door.

"Waldo! Can you just wait?" I turned toward the screen. The video hadn't appeared yet.

He pawed at the door.

"Okay, while it loads up, we'll go out for a quick one."

I grabbed the leash and took him out.

A few minutes later, back in the living room, the video still hadn't appeared. I pulled the flash drive out, reinserted it, and opened the directory.

No Files Found.

TWENTY-TWO

"CAN I HELP?" Kimberly entered the IT office, where I'd been waiting while our help desk technician, Bailey, struggled to restore the flash drive contents.

I'd come in early, hoping to avoid her scrutiny.

"Kimberly, good morning. I'm having trouble with a flash drive and asked Bailey for help. And, full disclosure, I didn't fill out the help desk ticket. It's a bit of an urgent matter. I seem to have erased a file by mistake."

Kimberly stepped into the inner office, removed her coat, and sat at an immaculate desk. She pulled her laptop from its case. "Bailey, where are we on yesterday's tickets?"

"We had one outstanding and it resolved itself. Just a mouse needing a new battery." Bailey frowned at the screen. "I thought I could get this file restored, but I'm having trouble."

"You used FileDig?"

"Yeah, I thought for sure it would do the trick."

"Let me try—"

"Sure."

Bailey passed the flash drive to Kimberly, who sat, straight-backed, inserted the drive, and typed rapidly. Frowning, she pulled the flash drive from the port, examined it, then reinserted it.

"Let me try something else." She rose from the desk a minute later and began rummaging through a file cabinet. "I have some older software I took off my laptop. I'll reload it and try to restore the files. No promises."

"Will it take long?"

Kimberly looked at me, lips twisting. "Bailey and I have a couple of things we need to do this morning for Charles, related to the merger. Things he asked for yesterday."

I heard the annoyance in her voice—I was asking yet another favor after I'd repeatedly ignored IT protocols.

"How urgent is this erased file? Because I can always check with Charles—"

"No, no, go ahead with his stuff first. I didn't mean to jump the line." I backed out of the office. "Let me know if you get lucky."

Alone in my office, I considered my options. If Kimberly was unable to restore the file, which I was certain Charles had intentionally erased, I'd need to get another copy from Melody. But she proved impossible to track down. I wracked my brain, trying to think of who in our organization I could reach out to for better contact information. Stevie had spoken to Melody recently—dare I call and ask?

Then I remembered: Someone else who was mixed up in all this had worked with Melody and Charles at Paramount Pharmaceuticals. Someone I was overdue to speak with. I picked up the landline and punched in my voicemail password.

I relistened to Ron Dorsey's voicemail from so many weeks ago, jotting down his phone number. Then I replayed the message several times to transcribe it, first using my laptop and then, thinking better of it after typing a few words, I pulled out a legal pad and wrote out the whole message in longhand. If Charles was erasing files, this one was not going to be lost.

Then I called Dorsey. I minced no words, demanding he stop shipping Lutense to Charles and threatening to turn him in. At first, he denied supplying the drug, but when I asked what all the payments from Angiras had been for, he sputtered, blurting out his discomfort with the arrangement.

"Please, I have a family. I can't get messed up."

"Maybe you should have thought of that before. What did you think Charles wanted with it anyway?"

"He said he used it in some animal studies."

"And you chose to believe him? Angiras isn't doing any animal research."

"Look, I had no reason not to believe him." His breath came hard. "I don't work for the guy anymore. I don't know what his operation is all about. Listen…" His voice lowered. "I'll stop. And I won't take his calls anymore. I'm done. Okay? Miss, are you okay with that? Don't turn me in, please."

I had him where I wanted him. "Okay. No more shipments of Lutense. One more thing. I've been trying to contact Melody Wilson. Her old phone numbers don't work. Give me one she'll answer."

I phoned Melody, knowing I'd need to be far more diplomatic than I'd been with Dorsey. I had jotted down a few points I wanted to make and kept my pen and notepad handy in case she continued to speak in riddles.

This time my call went to voicemail.

I left a message, urging her to call me. "I promise, this will be the last time I ask anything of you, Melody. But I'm stuck, and you're the one person who can fill in the blanks."

I busied myself with emails until I heard a knock.

"May I sit?" Kimberly asked.

"Please do. Any luck?"

"I restored the file, and it seems intact. I didn't watch to the end, but I don't think it's corrupted."

"Oh, I'm so relieved."

"The thing is, Neddy, the file properties indicate Charles erased it, not you."

"Oh gosh, really? That explains why I have no memory of erasing it."

"Right. But it also implies the drive belongs to Charles. How did you get a hold of it?"

My face burned. She was never going to turn it back over to me without first clearing it with him.

"Well, technically, it was Melody's drive. You can tell because it's orange. Kimberly, you've seen the video. It's a recording of a sleep session—the one I observed. Charles asked me to consolidate all the notes and observations from the audit, and the video is part of that record."

She was silent. I hadn't answered her question.

"I asked Charles for it," I began, though I had no idea how to spin the rest of the explanation.

"That's all I need to know," she said immediately, reaching into her pocket and handing me the drive.

The video ended. I slammed my laptop closed and swore.

"What next?" I screamed. I'd been *so* sure I would find something, some evidence of Lutense I'd missed the first two times I'd watched that cursed video. Perhaps a vial of it had been sitting on a table in the lab, or on the shelf of the cabinet Melody had straightened. I'd pored over the images with painstaking determination, slowing, rewinding, forwarding, rewinding repeatedly. I was stuck.

Again.

I grabbed the papers and other items strewn over my desk

and Melody's first cryptic note, the invoice from Dorsey, the package of breath freshener she'd scribbled on. Then my eyes fell on my handwritten transcript of Dorsey's voicemail, and I noticed something I'd overlooked. *I also purchased a bunch of that film you said to get. BioGrad doesn't sell it in less than a case.*

Film. I jerked my laptop open and searched the internet for BioGrad.com. The company was a medical device and technology supplier. I clicked on Products, scanning through several items, and found that BioGrad manufactured a product called oral thin films or OTFs, described as "an extremely thin film that can be loaded with medicine, then dissolves immediately when administered orally to a patient who is unable to swallow medication, perhaps because of paralysis, age (the extremely young or the extremely old), or unconsciousness.

"Or because they're asleep," I gasped.

The message on the Pocketpaks finally made sense:

It's in the film.

All along, I'd thought Melody was talking about the video when she referred to "the film," assuming she simply used the two terms interchangeably. But "the film" was what Ron had ordered from BioGrad at Charles's request.

I'd searched the video until I was bleary-eyed. Repeatedly. But I'd not known what I was looking for: a tiny translucent square of oral film, thinner than a piece of adhesive tape, being slipped to each engineer.

My hands shook as I watched the video again, fast-forwarding to the moment Charles left the lab after the engineers drifted off, then forwarding again to two additional sections when Charles reentered. During the second of these, I finally saw it. He approached each sleeping engineer, adjusting their masks. I slowed the image, reversed, and hit play once more. With the practiced hand of someone who has performed the same task over and over, I watched my brother loosen the mask of each engineer in turn, ever so slightly, and slip something onto their lips.

Melody had sent me the Pocketpaks so I'd understand how the dosing had been done. Because of her severance agreement, she couldn't tell me anything.

But she showed me everything.

Charles and I had not spoken since the press conference. He had been sequestered in meetings with attorneys and patent lawyers, hashing out the remaining details of the merger agreement. As for me, my task was clear: Force Charles to modify the innovation program, even though doing so put the merger at risk. I left several messages for him, but by six p.m. had not heard back.

I waited until most of the employees had left for the day and then made my way upstairs to the sleep lab. I entered without switching on the lights. Though the lab was normally warm, I shivered. A muted, creepy sensation crawled over me, as if something malevolent watched. I opened cabinets and drawers, looking for more physical evidence with which to confront Charles. I jiggled the door handle of the locked cabinet behind the sleeping area. Then Charles came in, switched on the lights and sat at one of the workstations, booting up the computer. I walked toward him.

"Charles, we need to talk."

No response.

"I know everything, Charles. I know about Ron. I know how Lutense is put onto the thin films." He paused for a brief second before resuming his typing. I trembled as I carefully formed the words I needed to say next. "You administered

Lutense while the engineers were sleeping. I know how you've been doing it."

Still no response.

"Charles!" I stepped closer. "You have to stop! Lutense interferes with their medications. That's why they all have different symptoms. Think about what happened to Stevie! You have to stop. It's our last chance to do the right thing."

I reached for his arm, but he pulled away from me, standing up and moving deeper into the lab.

"Talk to me! We can figure out a way to salvage this and keep the merger moving forward. I know how much it means to —"

"Don't say any more, Neddy." His voice was low, but the threat resounded. "Now you listen to me. This time you listen to me! We're not stopping anything. We're almost there."

"No, Charles." I stepped closer again, struggling to keep my voice even. "I have the video."

"What are you talking about?"

"I have a video recording of you in the lab, dosing the team. I know how you've been doing it." I paused to lower my voice. "You have to stop."

"What are you going to do, Neddy? You going to show your little video to the board? They won't believe you, they don't even like you. Besides, they'd never let you stop the merger." He walked in a circle, jabbing his finger in the air as if my ideas were balloons he meant to puncture. "Dad? He'll do anything to help Daniel."

I kept my eyes on him, not wanting to expose the dread, confusion, and isolation within me.

"You always did have a distorted sense of reality. Even when we were kids you thought if you were more like me, Mom and Dad would love you more." He shook his head. His lips tightened first into a thin line, then an odd tortured smile. "When you couldn't make that work you went the other way. Yes, your rebellious teenage years. You cut school, snuck out at night, and hung out with the worst possible people. And I gotta hand it to you, you struck gold with Jeremy. Off you went."

I knew I'd never be able to make up to my family the hurt I'd caused when I left after college with Jeremy, barely staying in touch, not even telling them which town I lived in. But since I'd divorced him and reunited with my parents, no one had ever thrown this sad episode in my face.

Until now.

"But you came crawling back."

A flash of pain, then resolve. No more second-class citizenship. "I wasn't crawling then. And I'm not now."

"I picked you up when you were down," he went on, ignoring me. "I paved the way with Mom and Dad, I gave you a job, I taught you about a business you knew nothing about—a very lucrative business, I might add. And this? This is how you repay me?" He turned and walked toward me, anger and determination on a face I didn't recognize, its features distorted and manic. "And Daniel? Do you want to sign his death warrant?"

I stood still and met his eyes. "Don't make me do something that can't be undone, Charles. You can still change the program and save face. No one needs to know! Just you and me."

He glared at me. "It's too late."

"Charles, we can't continue. How many more of our employees do you want to put at risk? For God's sake." I grabbed his arms, pulling him closer, looking into his eyes, hoping I might still find my kind, smart brother somewhere in their depths. His pupils were large, dilated despite the brightness of the room. Lutense? Some other drug?

But I forgot all about his eyes the next instant when I smelled it: a fragrance, essential oil or men's cologne, earthy, mossy, evocative of winter. Sandalwood. Where had I encountered it before? A memory rose up, muddled and foggy at first, then suddenly sharp and horrifying.

I let go and ran.

TWENTY-THREE

THE NEXT DAY I took Waldo and went to see Daniel, who'd been released from the hospital and was at home once again. I'd called ahead and convinced my mother to get Dad out of the house for lunch and to take their time about it. I needed to speak to my younger brother in private to share some heartbreaking realities.

Robert, the health aide, let me in, and I went straight to Daniel's bedside, Waldo padding at my heels.

"Why so serious, Sis?"

"Daniel, I need to bring you up to speed on…a lot of things. Alvee isn't finished, and…we'll either run out of money or ideas before we solve it." His gaze never left me. "We're not going to solve it…in time to help you," I choked out.

He smiled. "We all knew a cure wasn't a sure thing. You did your best." He squeezed my hand. "Come up here Wald-man." He patted the bed and Waldo leaped into his arms. "Anyway, I don't want anyone being hurt on my behalf anymore."

"What-what are you talking about?"

"Charles. He's gone too far."

I stared at him.

"Mom told me what he did."

"Mom? Our mother?"

He laughed, then coughed violently. I grabbed his oxygen mask and placed it over his mouth and nose. He took several jagged breaths, then nodded at me to remove it.

"You underestimate her." He wiped his mouth.

"I guess I do." I hadn't thought my mother believed me. She'd always relied on Charles for the definitive truth. "But why did she tell you?"

"She's a realist. She figured out a long time ago I'm not going to make it."

"Daniel, don't—"

"Oh, it's okay. I've been okay with it for a while now. And so has Mom. We've kept up a good front for Dad, but…" He sighed. I heard the phlegm deep in his chest. "I've already lived seven years longer than anyone predicted. And I've done things no one else gets to do."

Now it was my turn to smile. "What a great attitude. You're amazing."

"It's true, it's not some Pollyanna bullshit. I watched a hundred movies, I read forty books, just in the last year. Travel, adventure, fantasy, poetry, science, science fiction. I mean, I was in a hundred and forty different worlds last year, in my mind. I didn't have to go to work, cook, clean up, or anything else. I went into my imagination whenever and for however long I wanted. How many people get to spend their days like that?"

"I thought you were just passing time."

"You need to read more." Then he took my hand again. "Look, I'm not saying I would have chosen this life over a so-called normal one. But these are the cards I was dealt. So I made the most of my hand. Every day, *every day* has been a gift. But I don't want that gift at someone else's expense. That's not fair."

"How much did Mom tell you?"

"Enough. Other people's health being put at risk for me? I don't want that, Neddy. Not okay."

"And Dad?"

"He's hanging on to the hope Charles will save me. 'Any day, Danny.' That's what he tells me all the time." He coughed again. "But I keep telling him, I want *you* all to have a normal life. I don't want to be the reason everyone in the family is constantly scrambling, always worried and sad. Or the reason Charles twists himself up to help me. It's not fair to any of you."

"It's not fair to you either," I whispered. "Why did you, of all people, get this horrible disease? You're too young!"

He nodded. His eyes started to close as sleep came on.

"You're the most real person I know, Daniel. You are exactly what you appear to be." I kissed his forehead, then tiptoed out of the room.

I sat on the patio with my parents and showed them the video, pointing out where Charles had dosed the engineers, then let them see the invoice for Lutense.

And then we talked about what needed to happen next.

"Dad, we have to convince Charles to stop. *Before* the merger. Otherwise, he'll be able to expand the sleep program. That's his plan."

"You'll ruin him. Not to mention Danny. Let it be. I'm begging you."

"I *can't*. It's illegal. And dangerous."

"Look what happened with Alex, Ed." Mom took his hand.

I shuddered. There was something they didn't know about what had happened the afternoon Alex died. Something I was not ready to tell anyone.

"What happened to Alex… That wasn't Charles's fault."

"Dad, even Charles said it was his fault. You were there in the hospital with me when he said it."

My father began to tremble. "He didn't mean what you're suggesting. He didn't mean he'd been *doping* the engineers."

"Ed, Neddy's trying to do the right thing, before something even worse happens," Mom said. "We should listen to her."

Instead, my father unleashed his anguish on me.

"Do you not see, Neddy? Do you not see how your stubbornness is ruining things? We asked you to be the CFO, not to play detective, not to find fault with every step in the research process. Just count the money."

I listened, reminding myself how much pain he was in and trying not to get dragged into his narrative, with me as the villain. I wondered, was it possible he'd been complicit with Charles all along? Or was he simply crazy with desperation to save Daniel?

"But no," he continued. "You had to keep at it. Seeing things that weren't there, pushing and pushing. Demanding a perfect scenario, where no one gets hurt but Alvee miraculously develops itself."

"There *are* other research methods, Dad. We could have switched gears and kept going."

"Bullshit. Nothing gets results like that dream program. It will save Danny and it will be Charles's crowning achievement. A legacy for him and this family."

"The ends justify the means, no matter what? Dad, it's too late to fix any of that. But we can still—"

He stood up and glared at me. "Where were you when Danny got sick?"

"Ed," my mother cautioned.

"You were off with your asshole husband. We didn't even know how to reach you."

"Ed!"

"You might as well go back to Jeremy, for all the good you're doing this family."

"That's *enough*!" my mother cried, grabbing his arm and pulling him toward the house. "I'll not allow you to talk to our daughter like that."

"I won't betray my sons," he turned to shout at me.

I stayed on the patio until my mother came out again, nearly an hour later.

"He's calm now. But I don't think he'll be of much help to you, Neddy. He can't— You heard him. He sees it as a betrayal."

I made a painful decision.

"Mom let's order in for dinner. We can all use a break. Then there's one more thing I need to tell you."

After an awkward meal, my parents sat opposite me on the sofa. Robert had left for the night and Daniel was asleep.

"I need to tell you something. I wasn't going to share this, but it may be the only way you are able to understand that Charles has become irrational and we *must* intervene. Please listen to me. Please believe me."

They looked at each other.

"The day I was attacked in the office… I realized yesterday it was Charles who grabbed me, not Alex."

My mother gasped.

"No, no." Dad shook his head. "Don't say those things about your brother."

Then my father, who abhorred weeping, lost control.

"You said Alex grabbed you. *Alex*." His voice snagged.

"Neddy, what are you saying?" Mom was crying now too.

"I was grabbed from behind. I never faced the attacker. Of course, I assumed it was Alex, because he had been so distraught. But I remembered something: a smell, aftershave, coming from the attacker. I'd forgotten about it after the assault, but yesterday—"

"No! Neddy. You're wrong. Charles would never ever, try to hurt you." My mother doubled over.

"Mom, Dad, listen to me! Right before the attack, Alex's wife had rubbed lavender on his wrists and his temples to calm him. If Alex had grabbed me, I would have smelled lavender.

That stuff was all over him." My hands were shaking. Any pain I'd caused my parents in the past paled in comparison to what I was revealing.

"During the attack, I didn't smell lavender. I smelled sandalwood. And yesterday, I smelled it on Charles again."

My voice cracked. I heard ragged breathing and saw Dad fighting to pull himself together. I waited and prayed the truth had gotten through.

"Why would he do such a thing?" My mother's voice shook.

"We'd had a huge argument," I choked out. "I'd started to put the pieces together—the symptoms of all the engineers, why they were different. I knew their medications were misfiring, but I couldn't figure out how he was giving Lutense to them. He must have known it was only a matter of time before I worked it out."

"Why the hell attack you, Neddy? He could have just fired you," my father challenged.

"I don't think he meant to really hurt me. Only slow me down, derail me from what I was discovering."

"*Why didn't he fire you?*" he yelled.

"Ed! You'll wake Daniel."

"Dad, firing your CFO in the middle of a merger negotiation would be a disaster. And in our situation, as a family-run company, a feeding frenzy for the press."

My mother sat back against the sofa and closed her eyes. "We put too much pressure on him. It's our fault, all of it."

"No, Mom. Charles lost his perspective. We have to help him see reason."

"I can't do this." My father looked away.

"Dad, we have to stop him. He *needs* us to stop him. Can't we work together as a family to salvage this?"

"I'll not turn on my own son. Not after what he's done for this family, what he's tried to do for Danny."

I should have experienced nothing but dread as I left and drove toward home. But in a strange way, my heart-to-heart with Daniel had reinforced my resolve. If he could turn away from denial and look fate in the eye, so would I.

"Siri, call Marie Becksall."

TWENTY-FOUR

THE NEXT MORNING, as I turned into the Angiras parking lot, my phone rang. I took the first available spot and accepted the call.

"Neddy, it's Melody."

My hand flew to my mouth.

"Can we meet for coffee? I want to speak to you, but not on the phone."

"Of course." I gulped. We agreed on a restaurant about five miles east. I turned the car back to the main road.

When I arrived at the café, I barely recognized Melody sitting at a corner table. She'd cut her hair, and her nails were trimmed and lightly polished. The spotless white blouse she wore was embellished with lace and embroidery.

"Thanks for coming. Do you want to order something?"

"Just coffee." I signaled the waiter, who came over and poured. Melody sat, sipping coffee and looking at me, apparently wanting me to direct the conversation.

"Melody, I feel like I've never really known you. I confess I've had several different impressions of you—not all flattering—but I have no idea which is most accurate. If any."

"I'm a pretty private person."

"I had that part right."

She laughed but grew serious immediately, looking down into her coffee. "Being private isn't always good. It can keep you from being understood, keep you from connecting with people." She twisted her mouth to the side and looked across the room, perhaps debating how much to tell me. I fought the urge to fill the silence. "And sometimes"—her eyebrows arched as her gaze moved toward the front of the restaurant—"other people can take advantage."

"People in power?"

"Yes. Just because a person doesn't always speak up or take action, doesn't mean they don't care about what happens."

I let out my breath quietly. The waiter came back, and Melody paused while our coffee was refreshed. Then, she cleared her throat and told me everything.

Initially, Charles had directed her to give tea to the engineers, which "smelled and tasted nasty." Later, after they'd stopped drinking the tea, he had her administer oral strips while they slept.

"He said essential oil was on the strips, and the scent helped the engineers stay asleep. But the oil had no smell, so I asked why. He said it activated from heat and moisture, which was why I had to put the strip just inside their lips." Melody took a big breath and exhaled slowly. "At the beginning, I didn't think too much of it, but one day—I guess I was bored or nosey—I wanted to know what the oil smelled like. So, after I'd given them the strips, I waited about ten minutes. Then I lifted Ryan's mask really carefully. And what I smelled wasn't essential oil. It was the same awful odor of that tea. Fainter, but definitely the tea smell."

"And this happened in early March."

"Yes. The team stopped drinking the tea after your audit. So I figured Charles had found a way to give it to them after all—by placing a few drops on the film. And I thought it was odd.

They didn't know, and they didn't want it..." Her voice trailed off.

"What did you do, Melody?" Jittery, I perspired and shivered simultaneously.

"Nothing at first. I thought it was just the damned tea. I figured, what the heck. They didn't have to drink the awful stuff, but they'd still benefit from it. The tea *had* seemed to help them stay asleep. But I thought we should tell them. Charles didn't want to. He got mad every time I brought it up." Her phone rang and she glanced at it, frowning.

I waited, silently imploring her: *Don't take the call.*

She put the phone away. "Then one day, when Charles was in Atlanta doing that consulting thing, a delivery arrived. And the label on the box said Keep Refrigerated, or something like that. The box wouldn't fit in the kitchen fridge, so I unpacked it." She stopped.

"Lutense," I whispered.

Melody nodded. "I recognized the vials from my time at Paramount. And a carton of those strips. I felt so stupid! Thinking all that time we'd just been giving them tea. But once I opened the box, I knew for sure."

I nodded.

"I need to use the restroom."

The color was gone from her face. I prayed she wasn't getting sick or losing her nerve. As she stood to go to the washroom, I saw she was wearing dark orange jeans. I smiled. Not everything had changed.

While Melody was away from the table, my mind raced. I needed to piece together the chronology. When had I visited the lab? Before or after her discovery? Why hadn't she come forward before now? When did the first symptoms appear? I reached for my briefcase and pulled out my laptop, then put it away. I didn't want to scare her off if she saw me taking notes or recording our conversation.

When she returned to the table, I noticed she'd applied lipstick while in the ladies' room. For some reason, the utter normalcy of this made me relax a little. But I fought the impulse to give her recognition or gratitude for what she'd shared. I didn't trust her completely.

"When Charles came back from the trip," Melody continued without missing a beat, "I told him I wouldn't do it anymore, which caused a big fight, a huge scene. He was crazy by then, said the program was the most important thing, a breakthrough 'is around the corner.'" Her fingers made air quotes. "I was worried the team was getting sick from Lutense. But Charles kept telling me, 'I'm the doctor, I'm the doctor.' And he is. They all had different illnesses. He kept saying, 'No common symptoms.' I didn't know why, but after a while it didn't matter anymore. I had to stop doing it."

"Then Charles started dosing them himself. I didn't know how to stop him. When you came to the lab to observe, I prayed you'd see him do it. Each time he went in and out of the lab that day, I watched to see when he'd dose them. And hoped you'd notice."

"Oh my God. I didn't realize."

The horrible irony became clear: that day, I'd misinterpreted Melody's actions. Her apparent nervousness was born from desperation to get me to pay attention. Worse, my own infatuation with Adam and the flirty texts I'd been so busy sending him meant I'd missed exactly what I'd been there to witness. "Oh my God. My God!"

"No, it's okay. I knew it was a long shot, which is why I decided to record it. He never knew I did that." She smiled at her own cleverness, but then tears spilled onto her cheeks. "Not too long after, he came unglued."

"What happened?"

"I told him again to stop doing it, stop the Lutense. He hit me. Then he fired me. Told me to get out right away. I had to leave all my things in the office."

"He hit you." I kept my voice even, careful to make it a

statement, not a question. That explained the severance payment.

She leaned forward. "Did you know about us?"

"I suspected, but he denied it. Until after you left."

"He told me you knew and you didn't approve."

No wonder she'd been so standoffish.

"He didn't want me talking to you." She nodded, seeming to piece things together. "He probably worried you might figure it out."

I watched her sadness turn to bitter anger.

"And I was too embarrassed to— Yeah, all to keep us from talking."

"But you *are* talking to me now. I wondered—"

"Yeah, I'm done being the private person who hides. I'm giving the money back. Voiding the severance agreement."

"What?"

"It's what I've been working on for the past several weeks. I hired an attorney to help me fix it."

"Fix it?"

"Come clean. I couldn't live with myself any longer. The money—I admit, I wanted it at first. Really bad. I never had much growing up. My parents were poor. So I talked myself into believing everything was okay. But after Charles and I split, I saw things more clearly. I realized what a fool I was. And then when Stevie lost the baby..." Her eyes filled. "That's when I decided to get an attorney. And I finally told Tim what was going on."

"I think Stevie's miscarriage was a turning point for me too. But if you're planning on coming clean, as you put it, why all the cryptic messages to me? The video, the breath strips?"

Melody took a deep breath. "I started sending you stuff before I made that decision. I had to make sure someone on the inside paid attention too. Someone at the top. Tim thought you were investigating, but—"

"Wait," I interrupted. "How did Tim know I was investigating? He kept making references to it, and I wondered if he was just guessing."

"He got confirmation from— Look, I don't want to get anyone in trouble."

"I think we're way past that, Melody. No one could be in more trouble than me. Except perhaps Charles."

"Tim had help from another person inside." She watched me closely. "Someone who tracked your online searches, the research, the FDA documents, all that time you spent reading about the drug and the side effects."

I thought for a moment before I understood. Only someone in IT had that kind of access.

"Kimberly."

"Yeah, after Alex's first meltdown, she became really suspicious."

"And that's why Charles promoted her. To get her out of direct management of the team." And why he'd had such "difficulty" finding a replacement for her and for Melody.

"So Kimberly was aware of what I was doing?"

"She was aware of what you were reading, so we hoped you weren't finished. What we didn't know was what you were going to do with the information. And because of the severance agreement, I didn't feel safe talking to you."

"But you talked to Tim."

"Yeah, but he and I are good friends. I wasn't worried he'd rat on me."

"Of course, makes sense. But you couldn't possibly have been sure about what I might do, yet you *did* contact me."

"Yes, to return company property. The severance agreement required me to do that." She smiled.

"Oh my God. Everything you sent me was company property! You found a way to get a message to me without risking a conversation."

"Yeah. My attorney thought that was a really good idea too." For the first time, Melody seemed proud of herself.

I shook my head in amazement.

My phone pinged. Max.

Ignoring him, I pressed her. "Melody, Tim was quite concerned about the sleep program. Do you know why the team didn't just decline to participate? We gave them the option."

She shook her head at me. "*You* gave them the option. Charles never did."

"What?"

"He threatened Tim. Said he'd replace them all with new, young guys. With degrees," she snorted.

"So Tim took a leave of absence to avoid going into the lab without actually refusing to do so. And the others? Why didn't they find a way to stay out of the lab too? How could Alex, of all people, have agreed to continue?"

"I know." She shrugged. "I've thought about that a lot in the last couple of weeks. Alex, Ryan, and Jeff never believed the sleep program was dangerous. They trusted Charles because he's a doctor. They told Tim I was just angry, vindictive after the breakup and being fired."

We were both silent for a long time.

Had Alex also been threatened with termination? The financial repercussions would have been a disaster for him and Erin. Or had his own denial, abetted by Ryan's and Jeff's views, doomed him? I'd never know for sure.

I thought about how naïve I'd been. No, not naïve. Arrogant. I'd misread Melody the same way I'd misjudged Erin; both believed in me, rooted for me even, while I discounted them, so certain they'd had ulterior motives. And Tim. He'd been counting on me to find the truth, all the while his hands were tied as he remained terrified for his colleagues, his friends. And all I'd offered was the one thing he couldn't do—stay out of the lab.

"You were all so sure I'd follow through?"

"You're a real strong person. 'Tenacious' is what Charles called you. I watched you, the others did too. And we all saw a good person. You were a little uptight, but I had faith in you. And today I heard the merger is off. I figured you were behind that, and I could help you with the rest of it."

"Melody, I want to ask you an important question. But first, I'm going to share something with you I almost never talk about, even with my family."

She frowned, confused.

"I was in an abusive marriage. For more than fifteen years. I know about the embarrassment, the cover-ups, the excuses, the promises of doing better. I blamed myself at first, believing I was somehow at fault. But after a while, I figured it out. And it still took me years to get out of the marriage."

"You? You seem so strong, confident."

"I finally divorced him. And my life is better now, yes, but it took me a long time to realize what kind of messed-up relationship I'd been in."

"Wow."

"The reason I shared this is because I want you to know when you hear my next question, I'm not asking for purposes of judging you or your choices—because I made those same choices. Charles became more and more distant and agitated as I kept asking questions. It was like he was a different person. But was he ever violent before, in the past? Did he overreact to things in a way that was out of proportion to the situation? It's important for me to know."

"He was never violent before. You know, Charles loved feeling calm and loved making other people feel that way too. I used to call it his superpower, that serenity vibe."

"Yes," I said. "He has a gift."

"The thing is, once the engineers starting getting sick and you began investigating the dream program, that became harder and harder for him. He couldn't calm everyone like before. You were asking questions, I was asking questions, Tim couldn't be persuaded—"

"You're really talking about control. His serenity gift was a way to control people?"

"I never thought of it that way before, but yes."

"All we needed was to continue with different research methods. If only I'd been able to convince him."

"But *he* needed his dream program to succeed so he could launch the next thing."

"You mean bring Lutense to FDA approval?"

"No. Too much of an uphill battle. And probably not glamorous enough. No, he had all kinds of other plans. Like starting a health organization that was half medical training center, half ashram."

"I never knew that."

"Yeah, his plan was to train doctors how to integrate wellness, meditation, yoga, and dream therapy into their patient care. He was going to revolutionize the medical profession. That was going to be his legacy."

Melody never asked me why the engineers' symptoms were all different, and I decided against sharing what I'd learned about drug interference. Lutense had never gone the distance in testing, so while I was convinced drug interference was the answer, that remained to be proven. Or would perhaps remain unprovable. It didn't matter. I'd secured evidence, and corroboration, that Charles had administered an unlicensed drug to the engineers without their consent. That was horrible enough.

After she left the restaurant, I sat for a long time. I knew from my experience with Jeremy that it would be months, perhaps years, before I fully understood everything Charles had done. At that moment I was sure of only one thing: My brother wasn't who I thought he was.

TWENTY-FIVE

WHEN I FINALLY STEPPED INTO the parking lot my phone rang again.

"Yes, Max?"

"Neddy, your services will no longer be required at Angiras." His voice was steely. "The board voted an hour ago. There will be no severance compensation, under the circumstances, and we will ship your personal items to your home tomorrow."

"I see."

He paused. "I'm not going to spell it out for you. You single-handedly destroyed the company when you talked, without authorization, to Marie Becksall and told her the lies you've—"

"You're spelling it out, Max."

"What the fuck were you thinking?"

"I was thinking about how sorry I was that the rest of the executive team refused to ensure our employees were safe. And what a waste it all is since you were too blind, arrogant, or perhaps greedy—"

"Now you listen to me, you little—"

I ended the call and went straight to the office, relieved to see Charles's car was not in his parking spot. The lobby was empty, save for the security guard who surprised me by waving me through. Apparently, neither Max nor Charles had yet informed the staff I was no longer an employee. Knowing I was on borrowed time, I hurried upstairs.

In the engineers' office, their beloved Hovel, I was surprised to see Tim along with Ryan and Jeff at their workstations, music blaring from unseen speakers.

I waved, and Jeff switched off the volume. "Hey, Neddy."

Ryan stood and stretched as Tim leaned back in his chair.

"How ya doing today, Neddy?" Ryan asked.

"I'm doing…okay. Tim, I wasn't expecting to see you. I hope you're well?"

"Thanks, Neddy. Charles called me last night and asked me to meet with him this morning, but he hasn't come in yet. So I thought I'd hang with the guys until he shows."

"Well, it's great that you're here, because I wanted to see you all before I leave."

"You takin' a trip?"

"No, Ryan. I'm leaving Angiras."

"What?" Tim stood.

"I wanted to let you know personally. And I'm guessing you haven't yet heard the merger is off."

"It's off?" Tim repeated. Three sets of eyes bore into me.

"Wait, that's bad, right? Real bad." Ryan looked at the other two.

"What's going to happen, Neddy?" Tim asked. "We can't keep the doors open without the merger. Is the company being sold?"

"I can't say any more, except one thing, the most important thing. I want you all to know, you're safe. I give you my word."

"Safe from *what*?" Tim demanded. "From getting sick? Or safe from being let go? And why isn't Charles telling us all this?"

"You idiot, Tim," Jeff scoffed. "Of course she's talking about no layoffs. We're the friggin' research team. They can't let us go."

"Neddy, answer my question." Tim's eyes narrowed.

"You're safe." I held his gaze for a long moment so he would understand. Then I turned toward the door.

"Okay," I heard Jeff behind me. "Back to work, guys."

I drove home, dreading the future. Charles and my father would never forgive me for what they considered an inexcusable betrayal. Mom was caught between us. And Daniel, he'd go to his grave knowing his family was torn apart.

Again.

I needed to make sure Daniel understood it was not his fault.

I parked and trudged up my front walk, lugging one of the boxes I'd hurriedly packed up from my office. Whatever else happened, I wasn't going to let Charles or anyone else rifle through my things, or worse, get their hands on the materials I'd collected in the last few weeks.

Fumbling with the keys, I pushed open the door and took the box down the hall to my den.

"Waldo," I called.

From the balcony, I heard yapping. "How'd you get out there?" I slid open the door, but still he didn't appear. Then I stepped out. Charles sat in my rocker, holding the squirming dog in his lap.

"Charles! You startled me. How did you get in here?"

"Mrs. Gladstone. She's as nice as ever. We had a lovely chat. She's so concerned about Daniel. It's good to know someone is." He tipped a beer bottle toward me and then took a sip.

A chill went up my spine. Despite his calm voice, I knew he was seething. And drunk.

"Waldo, come here, sweetie."

Waldo whined, but Charles held tight to his collar. "He's fine. But you, Neddy, not so much."

"Charles, I tried to reason with you."

"Do you have *any* comprehension of what you've done?"

"Let the dog go, Charles." I began to fear for Waldo.

"You've condemned Daniel. Do you know how a person dies from pulmonary fibrosis? Shall I tell you, Neddy?"

"It's over, Charles. We'll never agree on who's to blame, so let's agree to just leave it."

He jumped up, eyes bulging. "Oh, it's *not* over. *Not.*" He shifted Waldo under one arm, like a football.

"Give me the dog!"

"How does it feel, Neddy? To see someone else taking charge of something you care about. Something you've nurtured, loved, sacrificed for? Deciding its very fate."

"Charles! What's done is done. I'm sorry it ended this way, no one is sorrier than I."

"Oh please."

"Do you think I wanted Angiras to fail? After all the work we did. And Daniel? He's *my* brother too."

"Which makes this all so much more…twisted, Neddy." He looped his finger through Waldo's collar, putting more pressure on the dog's throat.

I lowered my voice, feigning calmness, though inside I was panicking.

"Okay, Charles, I want you to leave. Right now."

"Not so fast." He stumbled toward me, and I took a step back. Waldo whined.

"He's choking. Go! *Now.*"

"I told you to leave things alone. To let the research move forward. And you let me think you'd finished your snooping. But you weren't finished, you just stopped talking about it." He jabbed his finger at me and yelled, "You stopped coming to me and went on your own little fishing expedition."

I thought about the box I'd left in my den with the evidence of his deceit. I would offer it to him as leverage to save Waldo, if all else failed.

"I *begged you* to stop using Lutense on the engineers. You really expected me to let you keep hurting them?"

"Fuck them," he screamed. "You know what? Fuck you too, Neddy. You and your pathetic dog."

I turned and ran inside, Charles close on my heels. I pulled my phone out of my handbag, and he lunged for it, almost dropping Waldo, who twisted and yelped.

"Let him go, Charles!" I grabbed his arm and tried to free the dog. Charles turned away, blocking my access. Then he took a step back and slapped me across the face.

I ran for the stairs, screaming, "I'm calling the cops. Get out of here!"

Waldo erupted in high-pitched barking.

"Shut up," Charles snarled.

"*Let him go!*" I closed and locked my bedroom door, panicked for myself and my poor dog. "Let him go or I'm calling the cops."

"If I hear you talking to the cops, it's all over for this dog. Do you hear me?"

"Please, Charles, he hasn't done anything to you. He's an innocent—"

"Then come out. And no phone calls."

"I can't!"

"Come out!"

"So you can finish the job you started? The one you blamed on Alex? I know you were the one who attacked me. I know it was *you.*" My mind raced. I had no doubt he would hurt Waldo in order to punish me. Should I trade the box for the dog? If I did, I'd never stop Charles's madness. If I didn't, I might lose my sweet dog. How would I live with that? How would I explain to Daniel what had happened to Waldo?

Daniel.

As Charles continued to bellow on the other side of the door, I tapped Daniel's name on my phone, then hung up the moment he answered. As I hoped, seconds later Daniel rang me back and I let the phone ring repeatedly, ensuring Charles heard it.

"It's Daniel," I called to him on the other side of the door. "I'm answering."

As the words left my mouth, Charles simultaneously demanded, "Don't answer!"

"Daniel, how are you?" I nearly shouted into the phone.

"Sis, I saw you called, but we were disconnected."

"No worries. I'm here with Charles. I'll put you on speaker-phone." I said a little prayer, opened the door, and turned the phone toward Charles. My hand shook, but I held on.

He glared at the display, then at me.

"Hey buddy." He managed a faux cheerful voice.

The charade of normalcy bought me precious time, so I kept it going.

"So, Daniel, Charles stopped by to discuss the next steps for Angiras, and we were wondering if you wanted to weigh in on something. You see, Charles and I have a bit of a disagreement— well, more like a difference of opinion—about whether to invest what's left of the company's assets in another start-up or fund a more established entity."

I paused as long as I dared before I went on. "Maybe the Pulmonary Fibrosis Society? And we were wondering what you think. Or even if there is something else you'd rather see done with the money?"

Charles blinked at me. Waldo whined, desperate to be let go.

"There is something else I want, but it's not about the left-over money," Daniel said. "It's something I need to talk about with both of you."

"Go ahead."

If I kept him talking long enough, Charles might calm down.

"After I'm gone, you gotta…help Mom and Dad…figure out what to do."

"Oh, Daniel." I choked up.

Charles stared at the phone. The flush drained from his cheeks and his chin quivered.

"They've taken care of me so long, they don't do anything else. You gotta step in."

"I…we will. But please don't talk like this."

"No, you don't have to hold it all together for me. It's not about me anymore. I'm at peace."

My eyes never left Charles. He stared at the phone.

"Listen to me," Daniel continued. "Make sure they're okay. Make sure they do stuff—travel, get involved in volunteer work…something. They can't just mourn me."

And watch Charles go to jail, I thought.

"It's gonna kill 'em." He was more right than he knew—my parents were going to lose both of their sons, one way or another.

"You two have to be their rock now. It's up to you."

Charles slumped against the wall and slid to the floor, still gripping the dog. His eyelids grew heavy. The exhaustion and the booze were catching up with him.

I cried, no longer even attempting to hold myself together. "I'll try."

"No, Neddy, you can do it. You're stronger than you think." He erupted in a coughing fit.

As if on cue, Waldo started yelping again.

When Daniel's cough quieted, he trilled at the dog, "How's my boy? Last time you were here, you didn't tell me goodbye. You have a girlfriend now?"

The barking escalated, high and desperate.

"You gotta run off quick to see her?"

I held my arms out, beseeching Charles to let the dog go.

"Neddy, what's up with him?" Daniel finally asked. "Is there a cat on the balcony?"

I cocked my head at Charles. He shook his head and let the dog go, just as someone started pounding on my front door.

Waldo switched from high-pitched anxiety barking to

watchdog mode, flying down the stairs and skidding over the entry hall tile. I inched past Charles and followed.

"Daniel, I'll call you back."

"Police! Open up, now!"

The police separated us, the male officer keeping Charles upstairs while the female sergeant interviewed me on the front walk.

"One of your neighbors called 911. She reported hearing a lot of loud yelling and was concerned about your safety. Is the guy upstairs your boyfriend?"

"N-no," I stammered. "He's my older brother, Charles."

"He doesn't live here, I gather?"

"No. Look, he's angry at me. We work together, and he's—"

"What's he angry about."

"Work. Something I did that made him…crazy mad. Some decisions I made."

"Were you two drinking this afternoon?"

"No. I got home about a half hour ago. He's drunk."

"Did you let him into the apartment?"

"No, Mrs. Gladstone—probably the neighbor who phoned you—she has a spare key."

"She knows him?"

"They've met a few times."

"Were you expecting him?"

"No. I thought he might call me at some point. But he was here when I got home."

"Did he strike you in any way? Push you, pull your hair?"

"No." My answer was automatic and followed immediately by the same pit in my stomach I'd endured each time I'd lied to the police for Jeremy, denying he'd hurt me. My legs wobbled.

"No matter what the argument is about, he doesn't have the right to lay a hand on you. Do you understand that?"

"I just want him to leave."

"We take domestic battery very seriously. There's no shame in—"

"Look, I get it. I was in an abusive marriage. For years."

She paused. "You have a friend or a family member who can come stay with you?"

"Yeah."

"Okay, give them a call. Go stay with them or have them come here. If you change your mind, here's my card. And if at any time you don't feel safe, call 911 immediately."

"Thank you."

"And tomorrow, first thing, get a restraining order. Many times, restraining orders cool things off. But again, don't hesitate to call us."

I nodded.

"Okay, I'm gonna check with my partner now. When we're ready to bring Charles down, I'll let you know and you can stand over by our squad car or go to a neighbor's house. You don't have to speak to him."

"What's going to happen to him?"

"If he's not impaired, we'll send him on his way. If he is, we'll drop him at his home. That's what you want, right?"

"Yes."

Twenty minutes later, the two officers escorted Charles out my front door. I stood mute on the sidewalk, watching in shock and embarrassment.

"Neddy, I'm sorry. I didn't mean it." Charles twisted to make eye contact.

"Don't speak to her," warned the male officer.

"Neddy! It'll never happen again! It won't happen again."

"I *said*, shut up," the cop growled.

I remembered the day three years before when Jeremy, also in the escort of the police, had shouted the same thing to me— the day he'd broken my jaw and I'd finally had enough. He'd made the same empty promise dozens of times before.

I looked at Charles. "That's what you said last time," I screamed, then burst into angry tears.

"*Last time?*" The sergeant looked from me to Charles. "Okay, asshole, you're coming with us."

TWENTY-SIX

I SPENT several hours at the police precinct, sharing the complicated story, giving dates and employee names, and providing a copy of the video. I held back about the two assaults Charles had committed upon me, despite the police pressuring me for additional details. But that was not because of any misguided lingering allegiance to my older brother. There was little to be done for Daniel, but at least I could let him die believing Charles had simply done the wrong thing for the right, valiant reasons in trying to complete Alvee. I would amend my statement to the police once Daniel passed. I owed that to Erin and her family.

A team of detectives was assigned to investigate the Angiras research program. They would eventually interview everyone involved and asked me not to talk with anyone while the investigation proceeded. They needn't have—I was done talking, wanting only to curl up in a tight ball and pull a blanket over my head for the next decade.

The sky was dark by the time I left the precinct. I checked my phone and saw a text from Carollyn:

M and I are with your parents and Daniel. We'll stay here till you get back xox

And there was a voicemail from my mother. My heart lifted as I listened to both Daniel and her on the recording.

"Honey, we're all okay. Dad told us what happened with the business and that Charles is"—her voice caught—"at the police station. We're talking to your father." Mom inhaled deeply. "Things will be hard for a while, but you aren't to worry, okay? You did the right thing, and we'll *all* get through this."

"Neddy, we love you. Hang in there," Daniel breathed into the phone, struggling to get the words out. "Call when you can. And bring Waldo by, I have a score to settle with him."

I waited until I reached my car to let the tears flow. I still had Mom. And Daniel, for now. And my dear, faithful friends. As for my dad, I'd figured out that he had shared with Charles everything I'd said during our talk at Starbucks that painful day. Whether that betrayal had contributed to Charles's desperation, I'd never know. Either way, it would be a very long time before my father and I were okay with each other.

I drove home, packed Waldo up, and headed to my parents' home. When I arrived, Carollyn's car was in the driveway. Dad let me in, mumbled something about going to clean up my mess, and walked past me out the front door.

Mindy and Carollyn stood as I entered the living room.

"We're gonna get out of here now, unless you need us to stay?" Carollyn asked.

I hugged my two friends, knowing I would need them more than ever in the coming weeks and months.

"Go," I said. "Have dinner on me tonight."

"Temp's a little high, but not as bad as last night." Mom

removed the thermometer from Daniel's ear and went down the hall to the bathroom.

He was pale but brightened when he saw Waldo. "Hey, puppy, come up here." He patted the side of the recliner.

Waldo peered into Daniel' eyes, unfazed by the plastic mask and the constant drone of the oxygen machine.

"What the heck were you barking at today?" Daniel looked up at me.

"Oh, a commotion today at the condo complex—some family having a gathering outside. Lots of…people." I sat down on the side of the bed and took his hand, which felt hot. "How are you feeling tonight?"

"Not so great." His voice sounded weaker than ever.

Mom came in and placed a wet washcloth on his face. "He's been running a fever." She wore her oldest sweatshirt, faded and stained with coffee.

"There's going to be a lot of fallout from today." I fought to keep my voice steady. "A lot of legal crap. And some of it will get ugly."

"It's not your fault," Mom said. I had never seen her so sad.

"It's not your fault either, Mom."

"Isn't it? We put so much on Charles, such high expectations. Maybe he couldn't bear to let us down. Why else would he act so horribly?"

I didn't have the heart to tell her what Melody had said. While it was true there had been a great deal of pressure from our family placed on Charles, his ambition to revolutionize medical research ultimately got the better of him.

"I'm not sure how we'll get through this." Her voice cracked as she hurried from the room.

Daniel gestured toward me to remove the oxygen mask.

"Hey, buddy, you don't need to say anything," I whispered to him. "I came by to be with you and bring you some puppy love. I swear, this dog should be living with you guys."

"Ssshh," he managed. "I need…you."

"Okay." I took his hand.

"What I talked to you and Charles about on the phone today—getting Mom and Dad to live a little. It's gonna be on you, Neddy. I know Charles is in trouble. But don't let him become their next project."

"Oh, Daniel—"

"*You* have to be their rock now. They won't have Charles to lift them up. It's up to you."

I wiped the tears away. "But I don't know how I'll be enough. You boys have always been their whole world."

He frowned, looking at me, his eyes glazed from the fever. "You have no idea how wrong you are. Mom and Dad went crazy when you disappeared with Jeremy. And when anyone criticized your choice, they shut it down. No one dared to—" He erupted in a coughing fit.

When he recovered, Daniel went on, surprising me with details of how my parents had mourned my estrangement.

"Sometimes they wouldn't leave the house for days. Mom talked to a therapist, but Dad wouldn't go. Their friends stopped calling. Finally, Charles suggested hiring a private investigator to find you."

"You're kidding."

"The guy found your house and we had it watched for a while."

"My God. That must have cost a fortune. Why didn't they ever tell me?"

He shook his head.

"I never knew any of that," I said. "I thought they were so mad, so hurt they'd never have me back."

"Where'd you get that idea?"

I didn't have the heart to tell him.

He made a huge effort to take in a ragged breath. "They were scared they'd lose you. It only came out as anger. The fear was too much."

We were both quiet for a moment, Daniel catching his

breath while I thought about all the time I'd lived with false assumptions propped up by Charles's lies.

"The mind can't accommodate anger and fear at the same time," Daniel said. "I read it somewhere in all that." He gestured toward his psychology books.

"So the anger masked the terror I'd never be back?"

He nodded, his eyes growing heavy.

I thought again about the afternoon at Starbucks with Dad, how he'd been so angry with me. Had he simply been masking his terror at the prospect of losing Daniel?

"How did *you* cope with all that?" I was afraid of the answer.

"I focused on them. Made sure they were eating at least one decent meal a day. I kept bringing my buddies over to the house to break up the monotony." He held the mask to his face and inhaled. "Once we knew where you were living, it was easier. Mom made me drive Dad by your place once or twice a week. Knowing where you were living helped a lot. At least they knew we could get to you if need be."

"And then you got sick."

"Yeah, that was lucky."

"*Lucky?*"

"Yeah. Gave them something else to focus on."

"Oh God. I'm so sorry I put you all through that." I cried again. "And now this. Can you forgive me, Daniel?"

He waved the apology away, his thin arm barely clearing the mattress. His eyes closed, and I thought he'd gone into a deep sleep. I heard Mom wrestling pots and pans in the kitchen. He opened his eyes, yawned, and resumed the conversation, as if no time at all had passed.

"You think you put us through hell, and in some ways, you did. But I think it was good for us. For me, anyway. I stopped taking you for granted."

"But you never took me for granted. Mom and Dad, yes. Charles, to some extent. But not you."

"Yeah, I did." Daniel reached for my hand and gave it a weak squeeze. His skin burned with fever.

"Daniel, you're burning up. I think we should call an ambulance."

"No. No more hospitals. I'm done."

I opened my mouth to object, but then stopped.

"Okay, if you're sure. You scared?"

"Yeah, but I'm doing it anyway." He gestured for the oxygen. Before I repositioned the mask over his nose and mouth, he turned to me. "Just like you, Neddy. You did a scary hard thing. Never forget."

I stayed all night by Daniels bedside, dozing off and on. Near dawn, Mom came in and told me to go get some sleep.

"Check his fever—it went up again during the night."

"I know, honey. He wants to stay home now."

I nodded, bleary-eyed and weepy, and went to bed. At ten I awoke, checked on Daniel, who was still asleep but even paler than last night. I found Mom in the kitchen.

"What's going to happen to him?"

"He's not taking any more meds. He wants to let nature take its course."

"Does Dad know?"

"Yes, that's why he's so scarce around here, running to emergency board meetings, spending hours and hours with Charles—he can't deal with it. As usual, it's the women who have the tough work left to them."

I thought about what Daniel had said last night about fear and anger. I reached for her and hugged her for a long time.

"I think Dad's got his work cut out too," I sighed.

"You're right."

"Mom, tell me what help you need. I'm not working anymore, so load me up."

"For now, just stay here. Having you with us is a big help."

"It's the least I can do. How is Charles? What's Dad telling you?"

"He has a lawyer, a good one. Someone on the board recommended him. And he'll be evaluated by a psychologist, psychiatrist—whatever. It's all we can offer at this point."

"Have you seen him?"

"For a few minutes. He's not very talkative. I tried to assure him we all love him and are rooting for him. But I have to say, he has an awful lot of things to account for."

My phone rang.

"Mom, do you mind if I take this?"

She shook her head, and I tiptoed into my room.

"Adam?"

"Neddy. I'm so glad I caught you. Can you talk? I mean, do you have a few minutes?"

"Yes, I'm at my parents'."

"I'm so sorry," we both blurted at the same moment.

"Let me go first," Adam said. "I want to thank you for telling Marie what was really going on at Angiras. A merger would have been disastrous for us. She asked me to tell you she'll be calling you personally. You saved our company."

"Well, I sunk ours. So I guess it's a wash." I laughed at the irony. "Look, I'm sorry. I don't mean to sound so flip."

"You've had a terrible time of it. How's Daniel?"

"He's in control now. He's home and making his own decisions." I understood Daniel's choices once I'd realized how little power the dying have, and the importance of granting as much say-so over their final days as possible.

"Is there anything I can do?"

"I don't think so. I'm going to be staying here for a while unless my dad kicks me out. He's still pissed at me."

"Do you think you can get away for dinner or lunch in the next day or so?"

I was stunned.

"Adam, are you sure? I'm a hot mess. I'll probably be sued by half our employees, the police may not be finished with me yet, I've no job, one brother who's dying and another who's a criminal…and who I happened to turn in."

A fit of uncontrollable laughter hit me. The impossibility of my current life and the big, unknown void that lay ahead suddenly seemed absurd. A moment later I was crying again, overcome by big, gulping sobs that went on and on. I'd never felt so sad, but at the same time so relieved.

"I've lost everything," I murmured to no one, certain Adam had hung up, as I'd been incoherent for so long.

"No."

Surprised, I took in a huge breath. "Oh boy. You see what I mean? Laughing one second and melting down the next? What a prize."

"It's a fine line between laughing and crying."

I grabbed a tissue and blew my nose.

"You deserve more, Adam. Find someone normal."

"Oh no. I don't want 'normal.' I want extraordinary."

"That's not me."

"Oh yeah? You did something extraordinarily difficult, and at extraordinary personal cost, because it was the right thing to do. I'll take that over normal any day."

How could he still want to be with me, after all my obfuscation and neglect?

"You're still—you still want me?" I swallowed. "Are you sure?"

"I am."

"But I treated you so badly for so long."

"Not out of malice or lack of caring. Or blind neglect. You deserve to be happy, Neddy, don't you believe that?"

I stared at the wallpaper of my childhood room, recalling all the time throughout my life I'd spent thinking I wasn't good enough—not a good enough sister, not a good enough daughter, wife, friend, CFO. I was done with that.

Adam was right. And so was Carollyn. I deserved to be happy.

I'd let Charles promote the narrative about my place in the family my entire life, not realizing how beautifully it served him rather than me. I *had* been a good daughter and sister, a good wife to Jeremy. And I was deserving of happiness, despite how far away happiness seemed to be at that moment.

Charles was going away. It was time to start writing my own story.

THE END

ACKNOWLEDGMENTS

I want to thank all the incredible people who helped me develop and write this book, and the ones who supported and encouraged me to keep going. Each made an important contribution, perhaps some of them without even realizing it.

Sarah Richards, a very early mentor and the first person to tell me I could write dialogue.

Allison K Williams for her developmental editing. This book would not exist without your guidance in how to craft a story.

Aviva Layton, whose manuscript review was key in giving me the confidence to know I was (almost) done!

Rhiannon Navin—though you may not remember me, you inspired me by writing and publishing a novel without having any previous work published. Thank you again for connecting me to Allison Williams.

Weike Wang, whose course at Gotham Writers Workshop was fascinating, instructive, and inspiring. I love your books!

The late Blake Snyder, whose book on screenwriting, *Save the Cat*, helped me understand the critical reasons why readers must care about the main character.

Dr. Clare R. Johnson, PhD, whose book, *Complete Book of Lucid Dreaming*, answered so many of my questions about this fascinating science.

Diane Salvatore, whose knowledge and connections in the "old" publishing industry helped me determine my publication journey.

John Searles, who I met many years ago and described writing two of his novels in completely different ways. I never forgot that "one size does not fit all."

Tracey Guth Spangler for spending an hour with me over lunch explaining copyediting vs. every other type of editing, and whose Goodreads selections never fail to give me great books to pick up.

Eva Natiello for your marketing expertise and sage counsel on self-publishing.

Bradlee Frazer for your generosity in answering my questions about use of brand names.

Christie Santos, of Proof Positive for your final proofreading and editorial suggestions.

Jane Friedman, whose incredible FREE blog is a one-stop wonder of information.

Beat Barblan for your generosity with your time, perspective, and extensive resources.

My beta readers, Tina Cifelli, Lauren Wiesenthal, and Jennifer Bruno. Thank you again for reading the manuscript and for your honest, timely feedback.

My incredible book group who never forgot that I was writing this, and never failed to support and encourage me. Thank you, Suzanne, Susan, Noreen, Missy, Martha, Kate, Jane, Diane, and Phyllis.

The Sweet Dreams book group, which reignited my love of reading.

Maria Aguirre for Spanish translation.

My dear friends who encouraged, cajoled, and kept me going, even when *I* lost interest in the book! Charlotte Durnin, Linda Watt, Donna Roper, Betsy Sobo, Debbie Taffett, Diane Pohl, Bob Robinson, Joanne Mortimer, Heather Asfour, Linda Kafafian, Chris Hepburn, Ken Martin, Amy Raditz, Fran Kelley, Cheryl Swingle, Leslie D'Ascoli, Elese Tonelli, and Claire Whitcomb.

Special love and thanks to Kathy Shoaf, one of the finest human beings I have had the privilege to know and call a friend.

My yoga teachers, Cindy Pitcher, Emma Magenta, Julie Margolis, Radikha Truffa, Deanna Sidoti, Sarah Ehnert, Tami Frankel Rogan, and the incomparable Dana Cilento. For over twenty years, these amazing and dedicated teachers have kept me loving the asanas and the dharma of this ancient practice, which somehow manages never to feel old.

And finally, to my family who were (mostly) patient with me during this long journey—first wanting to write, then learning to write, and finally actually writing. Barry, Lesley, Josh, Terry, Lynn, Scott, Cath. You gave me space and support to figure it all out in my own time. And that is saying something.

Finally, to my sweet dog, Woody, who spent many hours curled up next to me while I stared at a computer screen, and was the perfect inspiration for Waldo.

ABOUT THE AUTHOR

Judy Kroll worked for over twenty years in large and small corporations, including four years in the pharmaceutical industry, as a human resources professional and later as a career counselor. She provided job search assistance to hundreds of individuals, including physicians, pharmacists, medical device developers, chemists, and other scientists impacted by mergers and downsizings. She has practiced yoga for twenty-three years. Both corporate experiences as well as many years 'on the mat' inspired this book. In both of these very disparate worlds, Judy observed the same phenomenon: the devastation wrought when a much-respected boss or mentor turns out to be unethical, and one must choose to continue to follow that leader, or forge a new path forward. Judy lives in northern New Jersey, and in addition to writing, gardening, and practicing yoga, she co-chairs a not-for-profit conservation organization.

A NOTE FROM THE AUTHOR

Thank you for reading BREAKTHROUGH. If you enjoyed it, I hope you'll leave a review on Amazon and Goodreads. Even a few words will be helpful to me and readers looking for books like this. As a book group veteran, I know how much fun it can be to have an author attend and discuss their book. If you select BREAKTHROUGH for your book club, let me know and perhaps I can join you remotely.

Drop me a line at judykrollauthor@gmail.com.

BOOK GROUP DISCUSSION TOPICS

1. For much of her life, Neddy labors under the assumption that her family would have preferred she'd been born a male. Near the end of the book, she discovers this may not be a truth but rather a narrative perpetuated by Charles. Did you see evidence of manipulation or other intentional misdirecting on Charles's part? Are there ways in which Neddy actually benefitted from this narrative?

2. Neddy clearly loves and needs Adam's support, yet she continually avoids sharing her most difficult struggles with him, and keeps her relationship with him secret, until it's too late. Do you agree that Neddy was in an impossible situation, given the pending merger, and could not share *any* of her fears about what was going on at Angiras? Or did she let her lack of confidence in restarting a relationship cloud her judgment?

3. Melody sends obscure clues to Neddy, hoping to keep her on the trail. Neddy confuses some of these clues, interpreting "film" and "video" to mean the same thing. This delays her ability to put the final puzzle piece into place. As a reader, did you interpret these clues the same way Neddy did?

4. Much of the story centers around the attempts by the engineering team (Tim, Alex, Jeff, Ryan, and Stevie) to solve technical problems with the scope by

relying on ideas generated by lucid dreaming.
Though it becomes more and more clear to Tim that
something is amiss with the dreaming program,
others remain unconvinced. Even after the
tampering with Lutense is revealed to them, Jeff,
Alex, and Ryan willingly use the sleep lab. Was this
solely dedication? Or fear of reprisal? What would
make a person continue to run such a risk with their
health?

5. Neddy decides to withhold information from the
   police about the assault she suffered at Charles's
   hands, in part to spare Daniel from learning his
   older brother is violent. Do you agree with her
   decision?

6. Neddy desperately seeks help from numerous
   insiders at Angiras—her father, two board members,
   Charles himself—to reverse course and salvage the
   merger. But she is ignored, rebuffed, and dismissed
   as "imagining things," despite the evidence she has
   amassed. Was her decision to stop the merger by
   herself justified? Are there other courses of action she
   might have considered?

7. Charles threatens to hurt Neddy's dog, Waldo, in
   retaliation for what he perceives as betrayal. He backs
   down only after hearing Daniel's affectionate
   expressions to the dog over the phone. What does
   this tell us about Charles and his motivations?

8. Who are the heroes of the novel and why?

9. Sometimes a strength overdone becomes a liability.
   How did Neddy's perseverance both help and
   hinder her?

10. Neddy is initially dismissive of both Erin and
    Melody, perhaps seeing too much of herself in them.
    How does her relationship with and opinion of these
    two women change by the end of the story?